REQUIEM FOR A SOLDIER

THE LAST ETERNAL
Book Two

By

JACOB PEPPERS

This book is a work of fiction. Names, characters, places and incidents are either the product of the author's imagination or are used fictitiously. Any resemblance to actual persons, living or dead, or to actual events or locales is entirely coincidental.

Requiem for a Soldier: The Last Eternal Book 2
This ebook is licensed for your personal enjoyment only. This ebook may not be re-sold or given away to other people. If you would like to share this book with another person, please purchase an additional copy for each person you share it with. If you're reading this book and did not purchase it, or it was not purchased for your use only, then you should return to the retailer and purchase your own copy. Thank you for respecting the hard work of the author.

Copyright © 2022 Jacob Nathaniel Peppers. All rights reserved, including the right to reproduce this book, or portions thereof, in any form. No part of this text may be reproduced, transmitted, downloaded, decompiled, reverse engineered, or stored in or introduced into any information storage and retrieval system, in any form or by any means, whether electronic or mechanical without the express written permission of the author. The scanning, uploading, and distribution of this book via the Internet or via any other means without the permission of the publisher is illegal and punishable by law. Please purchase only authorized electronic editions, and do not participate in or encourage electronic piracy of copyrighted materials.

The publisher does not have any control over and does not assume any responsibility for author or third-party websites or their content.

Visit the author website:
www.JacobPeppersAuthor.com

For you, dear reader
There are millions of worlds out there,
A thousand, thousand lands to which you might journey
Yet you have chosen this one, have chosen to travel here, with me
Here, then, is my thanks, and my sincere hope that you find the journey worthwhile

Sign up for my VIP New Releases mailing list and get a free copy of *The Silent Blade: A Seven Virtues novella* as well as receive exclusive promotions and other bonuses!
Go to JacobPeppersAuthor.com to claim your free book!

CHAPTER ONE

The wanderer stared at the dead man and the dead man stared back.

One hundred years, he thought. *One hundred years spent running and hiding, an exile, a refugee. One hundred years that the people of the world would not have had, if he hadn't fled with the cursed blade. And now it might all be over.*

"*I see you*," the Revenant had told him. Only, Revenants could not speak, were not really "living" at all, at least not in the sense that most men thought of it. They were merely puppets, automatons given tasks by their masters. Not even like dogs or other favored pets, for a dog might balk at its master's wishes, and the Revenants, like those other monstrosities, like the Unseen, did not consider or question—they only obeyed.

It had not been the Revenant then, who had spoken, at least not truly. It had been used by another, and who else used a puppet save the puppet master? Which meant that the words had been spoken by none other than Soldier himself. Or, at least, the creature who had spent the last one hundred years posing as the dead Eternal.

The end was close now. The end of everything, of every mortal man, woman, and child. Closer than it had ever been save perhaps on that fateful day when the Eternals did battle with the forces of the enemy...the day they lost.

That end was so close that the wanderer thought he could almost taste it, like ash on his tongue.

"I've...I've never seen anything like that."

The wanderer turned to regard Dekker, the big man gazing at the corpses scattered about the ground with eyes as big as dinner plates.

"It is a Revenant," the wanderer said, "a monstrosity much like the Unseen. And if we stick around much longer you will likely see worse."

"No, not that," the big man said, slowly raising his gaze to meet the wanderer's eyes. "I mean, the way you fought. I...it was too quick for me to follow."

"Still," a third voice said, and the wanderer and Dekker turned to see Clint, the leader of the Perishables, walking up to them. "Those things are...I cannot believe they exist."

"You had best come to believe it and quickly," the wanderer said. "These are just the beginning. He knows where we are now, knows where *I* am, and he will send the full weight of his power against us." He turned to Dekker. "Sarah and Ella. Get them. Now."

To his credit, the big man didn't hesitate or argue, only gave a nod and sprinted toward the house. The wanderer watched him go then turned and started toward the stables.

"Hold on a second," Clint said, "where are you going?"

The wanderer turned to regard the leader of the Perishables. "To get my horse."

"And then?" Clint pressed.

"Then we're leaving," he said.

"And going where?" Clint asked. "Listen, Ungr, just hang on, alright? Let's come up with a plan, figure out the best course of a—"

"There is no *time,* Clint," the wanderer snapped. "Don't you understand that? They will be here soon, and you and your men stand no chance against what is coming."

"And what are you suggestin' we do then?" Clint asked.

"Run," the wanderer said immediately. "Get out of the city. Get as far away as you can as fast as you can."

"And if these things really are as dangerous as you say, what good will that do?"

"Probably none," the wanderer admitted. "But what choice do you have?"

Clint watched him for a few seconds then nodded, turning to the nearest Perishable. "Tell everybody to gather their belongings—we leave in five minutes."

He walked off then, shouting orders as the Perishables hurriedly set about preparing to leave. The wanderer left them to it, shuffling toward the stables and cupping one arm against his bruised ribs. Inside, he made his way past carriages that Will the nobleman's parents no doubt made use of when they went into the city, or for longer travels where they might have their staff and house guards accompanying them. The wanderer paid them little mind, though, moving past them to where his horse, his friend, waited.

Veikr was walking nervous circles in his stall as the wanderer approached, but he let out an excited whinny when he noticed him.

The wanderer moved to the stall door and threw it open. He grabbed his saddle, slinging it onto the horse's muscular back, then he grabbed the saddlebags and secured them before running a hand over the horse's muzzle. "I'm glad to see you too, old friend. And don't worry, I'm not dead—not yet anyway. But we've got to go. Now."

He leapt into Veikr's saddle, and the horse, needing no more urging than that, trotted out into the yard. The wanderer glanced at the guest house where Dekker had gone to retrieve his family, feeling the minutes adding up as if they were a physical weight, one that would crush them, in time. As he waited impatiently for the man to return with his wife and daughter, he looked around the grounds of the noble's estate.

Men and women rushed to and fro, hastily retrieving anything they deemed too important to leave behind while some others helped themselves to the horses in the noble's stables. There was an air of panic as they hurried about their tasks, yet for all their efforts, the wanderer knew that most, if not all of them would be dead before the sun rose again on the world.

For what they faced was not some angry leader that might be assuaged by an apology or by making an example of a few of their number, nor were those troops that would be sent against them normal men. Men that might grow tired or bored, that might question their orders, that got hungry or sick. For those troops which would be sent against them—that had no doubt been sent already—were not men, not anymore. They were something more, something less, and they cared for nothing at all except completing the task given them. They would not hesitate to sacrifice anyone or anything, including but certainly not limited to themselves, in order to achieve the will of the being who had created them.

They were fast, strong, and without remorse.

And they were coming.

No, the Perishables would prove their name before the night was out, of that the wanderer was grimly certain just as he was certain that there was nothing, he could do for them. The fact was that, with what was coming, he and Dekker's family stood little chance of getting away. Should he try to help the other Perishables, that small chance would quickly become no chance at all.

So, he would leave them, just as he had left the others over a hundred years ago. He would do it because he had to, because there was no choice. Or, at least, because the only other choice was to die and, in so doing, deliver the cursed blade to the hands of the enemy, an enemy who would immediately set about using its potent magic to rid the world of its mortal enemies once and for all.

The wanderer was still thinking of the Perishables' plight when Dekker rushed up to him, his wife, Ella, looking harried and scared beside him, their daughter riding on his shoulders.

"Ready?" the wanderer asked.

Dekker gave a nod. "Ready," he said grimly.

"Do we really have to go, Mama?" Sarah asked. "I'm hungry."

"We'll eat later, sweetie, I promise," Ella said, clearly struggling to keep her tone light. "But remember, I told you, we have to leave."

"Because the bad men are coming?" Sarah asked softly.

"That's right, Sarah girl," Dekker said. "Bad, mean men, and we don't want to be around when they get here, do we?"

"I guess not, Daddy," the girl said with obvious reluctance. "But...can Uncle Clint come? I like him—he told me stories."

Dekker glanced at the wanderer who shook his head. He liked Clint as well, but he knew that even with just the four of them, they were unlikely to make it away. Adding another would make it that much harder to escape. More than that, though, he thought he had a good idea about Clint, about the type of man he was, and he was confident that the Perishables' leader would not accept any possible escape plan that did not include those men and women who followed him.

"I'm afraid not, little one," Dekker said, watching the wanderer for another moment before finally turning back to his daughter. "You see, Uncle Clint has his own way of getting out of here…that is, I mean—"

"We have to go," the wanderer said. "Now."

The big man winced, then handed his daughter to his wife before moving toward the wanderer. "Don't seem right, leavin' 'em," he said quietly.

"No," the wanderer agreed, "it doesn't." And that was true. He knew that in the days to come, he would think of the Perishables often, would replay this moment over and over again, trying to find something he might have done, some way he might not have failed them. He would be haunted by the certainty that there had been another choice, that he had missed something. But just as he knew that, he knew also, that in time the guilt would lessen. Not much, but a little more with each year that passed. The ghosts of the dead, their recriminating faces, would slowly fade farther and farther back into his mind. Never all the way, but enough.

Or so he told himself.

"There's got to be somethin' we can do," Dekker said, an almost childlike desperation in his voice.

"There isn't," the wanderer said simply. Then, looking back at the men and women milling about the yard, rushing this way and that, an idea struck him. A desperate idea. But then, he was a desperate man. "Unless…"

"Unless what?" Dekker said.

"Follow me," the wanderer said. Then he set off toward the Perishable leader, Clint, who was currently helping a woman who'd fallen to her feet.

Fifteen minutes later, the wanderer stood, Clint on one side, Dekker on the other, examining the product of their efforts.

"Think it'll work?" Dekker asked.

The wanderer frowned, looking over the carriages carefully. Four in all, each with two horses harnessed at their front. Inside the wagon rode those too old or too young to fight. Gathered around the wagons were other Perishables, all dressed in uniforms they'd appropriated from the servants' quarters and guardhouse. But uniforms were one thing—the men pretending to be guards looked nothing *like* guards, were possessed of none of their common, inherent arrogance, born from the knowledge that they could, at their word, see a man or woman, guilty or innocent, thrown in the dungeons.

Instead, those in the guard uniforms looked exactly like what they were—impostors. Men who wore stolen, ill-fitting clothes and whom for the most part had not the slightest idea of how to use the swords sheathed at their waists. The wanderer glanced at Dekker and was not yet prepared to destroy the hope in the man's eyes. "There's only one way to find out," he said.

The big man grunted at that, his gaze traveling to the first of the carriages, the one in which his wife and daughter had taken shelter. The wanderer saw the man's worry, understood it, for he felt it too. In a very short amount of time, Sarah, Ella, and Dekker himself, had come to mean a lot to him, and he promised himself that, if things went badly, he would do everything in his power to make sure that those three, at least, made it out. To sacrifice himself, if need be, to ensure it, for what the three had was beautiful, and he had learned long ago that beautiful things were often fragile and must be protected. In the same way that a flower, in a field of ash, might be protected, else the world be ugly and that only.

And so he would protect them...until he no longer could.

"I just want to tell you, Ungr," Clint said from his other side, drawing his attention, "however this turns out...thank you."

The wanderer turned to regard him, and the man gave him a tight smile, one that seemed to cost him. "I know what you're doing," he said, "by helping us." His gaze traveled to Dekker, then to the carriage where his family sheltered. "I know what you risk, and I just wanted to say thanks. That's all."

The wanderer was moved by that, and looking at the man's face, listening to the genuine sound of his voice, he felt something that he had not felt in a very long time. Something that he had thought he would never feel again.

Pride.

He felt that now, at least, if no other time in his life, he had done not just the right thing but the *good* thing. Often, it seemed to him that those were rarely the same. Sometimes, it seemed that they never were. "You're welcome," he said. "And good luck," he finished, turning to Dekker to make the words include both of them.

"To you as well, Ungr," Clint said, giving him another smile.

Dekker grunted. "See you on the other side."

Then the two men walked away, Dekker to see to his family, and Clint, the wanderer thought, to see to his own. Which left him to do the same. He turned to regard Veikr. "If anything should happen to me—" He cut off as the horse gave an angry shake of its head, snorting. "*Listen,*" he said, "I do not mean that I will risk myself unnecessarily. And no, I have not forgotten what I carry, have not forgotten my task. How could I? For the last one hundred years I have thought of nothing, have *done* nothing else. But I need you, my friend, to listen to me now. Should something happen to me, I ask that you see the family safe, if you can. And then...then you will be free. Free of the cursed blade, free of duty...free of me."

He realized that he was looking at the ground, and the next thing he knew Veikr was pressing his muzzle against his chest. The wanderer gave it a soft pat. "I know," he said. "Me too. Now come—there is work to be done, and hours yet before the sun comes again."

He grabbed hold of the horse's saddle and swung himself onto Veikr's back. That done, he checked his back, ensuring that his regular sword, as well as the cursed blade, were secure. Next, he checked his neck for the locket. It was a ritual of sorts, one he had performed thousands of times over the years and in it he found some degree of comfort. Veikr was beneath him, his sword in its sheath ready to be drawn, and within the amulet at his neck waited the accumulated wisdom of men and women once thought gods. Things were not good, perhaps...but they were as good as they were likely to get.

"S-sir?"

The wanderer looked to his left to see that the nobleman, Will, had walked up and was now offering up a dark blue tunic similar to those worn by most of the Perishables, one which would mark the wanderer as a member of the nobleman's household guard.

"Thanks," the wanderer said, taking it and slipping it over his head. It was a little tight around the neck, but he thought that if the day ended with the worst part being that his collar had been a little uncomfortable then he could mark the whole thing down as a win.

"Y-you're welcome," the young man said. The wanderer noted the nobleman hesitating, clearly having something else on his mind.

"What is it?"

"I..." The young man winced. "That is, I don't mean to give offense, sir, but I think...you see, my father and mother were very particular about me being educated. They hired tutors, lots of them, and—"

"If you have a point, lad," the wanderer said, "you had best make it quickly. We'll be ready to go soon, and we dare not waste any time."

Will cleared his throat. "Right, it's only...well, I know your name, what it means. Youngest. And I heard that somewhere before. I couldn't place it, at first, but then I remembered it, from a really old text, one which one of my tutors made me read. It told of the Battle of the Gods..."

He trailed off, and the wanderer did his best to keep the wince from his face. Battle of the Gods. It was the name the peoples of the world had chosen to give to that night, the night when the Eternals, in force, stood against the power of the enemy.

The night when they lost.

The wanderer said nothing, though, only waiting and finally the young nobleman swallowed hard. "I...that is, the book, it told of the newest Eternal, the one called the Youngest. About how he betrayed the other Eternals, how he sided with the enemy and was slain."

"I have seen such books," the wanderer said.

"But that is..." The man paused, licking his lips. "You're him...aren't you?"

"Who?"

"Th-the last Eternal? The...the traitor?"

"I am no traitor," the wanderer said. "I am now what I have always been."

"What is that?"

"The Youngest. Now, you had better find a mount—we leave in moments."

"O-of course, yes, sir," the man said, starting to turn.

"Will?"

He turned back, a frightened look on his face as if he supposed that by pointing out that he knew the wanderer's identity, he would be killed. The wanderer did not blame him for the thought—after all, the enemy had made of his name a by-word for cruelty. It was not the truth, but then the wanderer had found over the course of his life that often people were far better at swallowing lies than the truth. No doubt owing to all the practice.

"What about him?" he asked, nodding his head at the gate to the nobleman's estate where a single guardsman stood.

The young man followed his gaze. "Captain Ferilax is the head of our household guard," he explained. "I asked him to come but..." He shook his head. "He said that he will not leave his post."

Then he will die, the wanderer thought, but he did not bother saying as much. One look at the man's face where he stood showed that he did not mean to be swayed, and the wanderer did not mean to sway him. Much of a man's life, he'd discovered, much of what happened to him, was beyond his control. If the guard captain had decided that he would control his death in such a way that he could not control his life, then the wanderer would not try to take that from him. A man does not choose his life, after all, but perhaps, if he's lucky, he might yet choose the manner of his death.

"Go," the wanderer told the young nobleman, his eyes still trained on the guard captain. He knew that time was short, so he did not waste it. Instead, he walked to where the guard captain stood at the gate. The man watched him come, a stubborn set to his jaw as if he already knew what the wanderer might say and was busily preparing his counter arguments.

The wanderer dismounted, leading Veikr forward. "Hello," he said. "It's Captain Ferilax, isn't it?"

"That's right," the man said, his tone not overtly rude but not far from it either. "And you're the man they call Ungr."

Requiem for a Soldier

"They've called me worse."

The captain's mouth twitched at that, as if he wanted to smile. "You and me both."

"So, you mean to stay then?" the wanderer asked.

"It is my duty," the captain answered quickly, as if he'd been searching for a reason to say it.

The wanderer nodded. "You have seen them," he said, glancing back at the courtyard. "What they are?"

The man swallowed hard, paling slightly. "Yes," he said.

"And yet you wish to remain?"

The man took a deep breath, squaring his shoulders. "It is my duty," he said again.

The wanderer watched the man for a moment then, seeing that he would not be swayed, nodded again. "Very well. I won't try to talk you out of it. A man has to make his stand some time or other, and only he can say when that will be. But I will tell you this much, if you will listen. Do not let them take you alive."

The captain frowned. "And why is that?"

"Your duty," the wanderer said, "it is to protect this place, this family, is that right?"

"Of course it is."

"And you take pride in that duty. In doing it and doing it well."

"As any man should," the captain said, sounding suspicious, as if he were being led into a trap but could not see how.

The wanderer inclined his head in agreement. "Then please, do not let them take you alive. For if you do, they will ensure that you have forsworn that duty, before the end."

"Nothing could make me do such a thing," the man snapped.

"I have seen it," the wanderer said. "But...perhaps you are right. Now, we must be off."

"Where will you go?" the man blurted.

The wanderer paused from where he'd been turning away, looking at the guardsman. "We will go to the southern gate by way of Discipline Lane and Courage Boulevard." It felt strange, the names for the streets, even now, so many years later. When he had first come to stay in Celes with the other trainees, Soldier had explained the names, saying that each street was named after a different virtue a good soldier—a good *person*—should exemplify, to serve as a reminder to the city's citizens.

The guard captain frowned. "It would be faster to take Mercy Avenue all the way."

"Nevertheless, our course remains the sa—"

"Ungr."

He turned to see Dekker walking up. "Everything's ready."

The wanderer nodded. "Very well." He turned back to the guard captain. "Good luck, Captain."

"And to you all," the man returned.

Dekker and the wanderer walked off then. "You told him we're goin' by Discipline, then Courage," the big man said.

"That's right."

"But...we're not, are we?"

"No," the wanderer said. "We're not. You'd best get ready—it's time."

The wanderer walked to Veikr and mounted. Meanwhile, Dekker moved to the lead wagon, climbing into the front.

The wanderer took a moment, looking over the four carriages and the men and women wearing the colors of the nobleman's house. An honor guard, or so they were meant to appear, but looking at them he did not see how anyone might be fooled, for they looked, to him, like what they were. The terrified men and women of a secret organization that was secret no longer. Shadows which had operated in darkness, suddenly thrust into the light.

And even a child knew what happened to the shadows when the light came.

But what choice did he have but to try? What choice did any of them have? "Come, Veikr," he said quietly. "It begins."

CHAPTER TWO

They moved through the streets of Celes with the wanderer at the lead. Behind him, Dekker rode at the front of a carriage, flanked on one side by Clint on a horse. The wanderer examined the streets as they rode. He saw no soldiers appearing out of the alleyways rushing toward them, but that was little comfort. Often times—most times, in fact—he found that a man rarely saw his doom coming. After all, if he did, he would not stand and wait for it.

Still, there was nothing to be done but to continue down on...so they did. He was aware of men and women pausing to watch them as they passed. Were they wondering where such ruffians and commoners had found the clothes of noblemen and a nobleman's staff perhaps, or only curious as to the identity of those traveling within the carriages?

They did not head directly south into the city. Instead, the wanderer led the procession east, hoping that if Soldier had set a trap, he would have done so somewhere along the most direct route from the nobleman's estate to the southern gate.

They continued on that way until, after half an hour of slow travel, they reached Discipline Lane. Another half hour later, they reached the intersection of Courage, and they cut onto it, then continued farther east until they hit the next road, one that ran, at least for a time, parallel to Courage. Courage was one of the main thoroughfares through the city as, according to Soldier, it was one of the most important virtues a man might possess. That meant that it was crowded with far more people than the lesser-used Patience. Which, he supposed, was fair, for while Soldier had been a powerful man, menacing and awe-inspiring, a terror on the battlefield and as steadfast a companion as anyone could wish, he had not been known for his patience.

The wanderer traveled on, marking each alley entrance as a site of potential ambush, noting every man and woman they passed, wishing he could know some of their mind. But while Oracle's gift had allowed her to catch glimpses into the hearts of men from time to time, the wanderer had never shared the talent. His gift, if gift it was, was simply to linger. To survive where others did not, to watch as all those he loved and for whom he cared went back to the dust, leaving him alone, him and Veikr. To linger, not to live, for what he had done over the last hundred years and more could not be called living, not by any man or woman who knew it. It could be called only what it was—surviving. Putting one foot in front of the other, breathing in and out over and over and over again.

They traveled on and despite all the many fears crowding the wanderer's mind, they continued through the city unmolested. Time passed, and as they drew closer to the southern gate the wanderer began to think that they might actually manage to slip out undetected after all. At least, that was, until Veikr let out a soft whinny beneath him, tossing his head in agitation before turning to regard a nearby building.

The wanderer frowned, his hand going for the sword sheathed at his back as Veikr came to a stop in the road. A few moments later, Dekker rode up beside him in the carriage, pulling the horses to a stop. "What is it, Ungr?" he asked, his voice betraying his anxiety.

"I don't—" the wanderer began, then cut off at the sound of a woman's scream. He drew his sword in one smooth motion, watching the building and expecting someone to charge out of it, blood on their mind. But then another scream rose, and another, and he realized that they were not screams of attack but screams of terror, of pain and horror. And he realized something else, too, listening to those screams. They were not coming from the building, as he had first thought. Instead, they were coming from the next street over.

"That's...that's coming from Courage, isn't it?" Dekker asked beside him.

"Yes," the wanderer said.

"But...but we're not on Courage," he said. "And the only person who thought we would be was the captain of the guard for Will's estate, wasn't it? So that means..."

"He let them take him alive," the wanderer said grimly. And he spared a moment then, in pity for the man. A man who had only meant to do his duty and do it well, who had been willing to sacrifice himself in the pursuit of that duty. But he'd had no idea, at the time, the true manner in which the enemy might make a man suffer. Even now, though, the wanderer suspected he was learning it. If, that was, the enemy had not been so kind as to kill him quickly, but as much as he would have liked to think so, he did not. The enemy enjoyed his cruelty too much for that, would savor it in the same way that a child, given a treat, might savor its taste.

"We have to go," the wanderer said. "Now. The guardsman told them what he thought was the truth, but if the enemy hasn't discovered that we're not there yet he will soon enough." He turned to Clint who had ridden up beside them. "Tell your men to run—as fast as they can."

"Run?" Clint asked. "But won't that give us away? And what about those people, those innocent people? They're being killed."

"The time for subtlety has passed," the wanderer said. "Now, it's time for speed. This is our chance—likely our only one. As for the people, there is nothing you can do for them except to die with them, and that will serve no purpose. Now go—quickly. I do not know what the enemy has sent, but whatever it is it will not take it long to finish with some townsfolk."

Clint gritted his teeth, his jaw muscles flexing as he thought it over. In the end he gave a nod. "You heard the man," he yelled, turning back to the convoy of Perishables, all of which were pale and terrified as they listened to the screams from one street over. "We go—now!"

Then they were moving again, not studying the people in the street not now, and there were few enough for them to have looked at even if they had been, for the screams had made those few travelers taking the street decide it would be best to make themselves scarce for a while.

The wanderer wished them the best, but he paid them little attention besides that. Instead, he was only focused on the road in front of him, only focused on moving as fast as he could while keeping an eye on Dekker and his family.

They continued on down the street until they came to an intersection where the road split going east and west. East would continue further into the city, away from the screams and their source, yes, but also away from the southern gate. They had to go west then, had to have the courage to revisit Courage Street, the one which would lead them to the gate. The others came up beside him, panting not so much from exertion, for it was, for the most part, the horses who were doing all the work. Instead, their chests heaved with fear and adrenaline and that he understood well.

"What do we do now?" Clint asked.

The wanderer glanced over the Perishables, all of them looking at him, waiting for an answer, for him to tell them some way out of this. "We head for the gate as quickly as we can. Do not wait for anyone else—many will not make it. If you stop to help, none of you will, do you understand?"

They nodded at that, several of them with grim expressions on their faces, some of them, like the nobleman Will, looking close to tears. "Then we go," the wanderer said. He turned to Dekker, speaking in a quiet voice so that only the big man could hear. "Whatever happens," he said, "stay close to me, do you understand?"

"I understand," Dekker said.

And then there was nothing left but to do it. The wanderer took a deep breath, gave Veikr a pat. "It's time," he said.

Veikr took the right street, heading west, and the Perishable convoy followed, the screams growing louder and louder as they approached, terrible, heart-wrenching screams.

The wanderer closed his ears to them, for he could do nothing for those people. He could not save everyone, after all, could not save the world—he could only hope to save one single family.

They came upon Courage Boulevard, and he looked behind them to see dozens of men and women lying bloody in the street, dead or dying. A dozen or so still stood, their features twisted with terror as they spun left and right as if searching for something. Even as the wanderer watched, one of them staggered, blood fountaining out of a cut across his chest that seemed to appear out of nowhere before he screamed and fell, and the wanderer felt his heart slamming against his chest.

The Unseen. They were here. "Go," he told Dekker and the others. "Go, damnit. As fast as you can."

Dekker did, turning the carriage toward the southern gate. The wanderer watched the distant massacre until Dekker was moving then he followed on Veikr, riding beside the carriage carrying the big man and his family.

They were no more than a hundred feet from the southern gate, when the wanderer noted something strange—namely that there were no guards stationed at the gate. Perhaps they had heard the screams amid the pandemonium and had gone to see what was amiss, but he had not seen any of them among the dead and even if they had gone, they would have at least left one of their number to man the gate.

So where were they?

But then the door to the gatehouse creaked open, and he *did* see them. Or, at least, what was left of them. It was only a glimpse, no more, before the door swung closed again, but it was enough to reveal at least three, perhaps four men—with the amount of damage that had been done it was hard to tell for sure—lying sprawled on the floor of the gatehouse in pieces.

But the wanderer paid this only a moment's attention. Instead, what drew his gaze—and held it—was an almost invisible form which moved almost leisurely out of the gatehouse. A form that *would* have been invisible had it not been for the blood spattering it.

"Shit," he said quietly as Veikr snorted beneath him. Different sounds, perhaps, but originating from the same sentiment. An Unseen ahead and at least one, likely more, behind them.

"What...what is it?" Clint asked, staring at the distant figure who had stopped and was currently standing perfectly still in the street as if regarding them.

"It's one of the things killed my father-in-law," Dekker growled from his place atop the wagon. "Isn't it?"

"Yes," the wanderer said.

He turned to regard Dekker. "When I've got its attention, get you and your family out of here as quick as you can. Don't look back, do you understand?"

"I understand," the big man said, "but…" He paused, glancing back at the bloody form standing still in the road. "Do you think you can take it?"

"I don't know," the wanderer answered honestly.

"Can we help?"

The wanderer turned to regard Clint. The man looked terrified—as any sane man would—but he also looked determined. As the wanderer had thought upon first meeting him, the leader of the Perishables was made of sterner stuff than most. "No," he said. "If you try, you and your men will only get in my way."

"What should we do then?"

The wanderer glanced at the nearest Perishables, watching him with wide, frightened eyes, many of them looking as if they were seconds away from bolting. "Get through the gate," he told them. "If you can." He didn't bother telling them what would happen if they should fail, for he saw by the looks on their faces that there was no need. The screams from behind them were proof enough that the Unseen had not stopped their assault, and the wanderer knew, as Clint must, that it would not take them long to finish their work. And once they did…well, it was enough to know that if the Perishables did not make it through the gate quickly, they would not make it through at all.

The wanderer turned back to look at the Unseen and although the majority of the creature was invisible save those parts of its flesh which had been stained with the guardsmen's' blood, he thought that he could feel the weight of its regard.

"Are you ready, boy?" he asked softly.

Veikr gave a snort and a toss of his mane, and a small smile came to the wanderer's mouth. "Me neither. Now come on—show me just how fast you are, Weakest."

Veikr rose on his back legs, kicking his forelegs in the air and letting out a cry. Then his front legs struck the ground, and they were racing forward, the world flying past them on either side. As they barreled toward the creature, the wanderer focused on clearing his mind, of forgetting all those worries plaguing him. He could not afford to worry about the Perishables, could not consider the safety of Dekker and his family, not now. Now, there was nothing but the creature in front of him, could *be* nothing else. He whipped his sword from its scabbard, and then they were passing the creature on one side. The wanderer gave a shout, bringing his blade down. But the creature had already moved, and his shout turned into a grunt of pain as something struck him in the side.

The next thing he knew, he was lying on his back, the breath wheezing out of his chest, his side—already bruised from his battle at the nobleman's manse—aching terribly. His sword, he was glad to see, was at least still in his hand. He started to rise when there was a blur above him.

No more than that, certainly not enough for him to get any detail, but he spun to the side, rolling over, and a moment later there was a loud *crack* as something struck the cobbles where he'd been a second earlier, breaking them. He rolled to his feet in time to see the creature flying toward him, its body a blood-covered blur. He brought up his sword, more by instinct than any conscious thought, and the creature cried out, a terrible, inhuman cry as the blade cut deep. Severed from the rest of the creature's body and thereby separated from its magic, a taloned hand and wrist suddenly appeared in the air before falling to the ground.

A good strike, but the wanderer didn't take any time to celebrate it, for he knew that to do so would be to invite death. Instead, the moment his blade finished its course, he ducked just in time to feel the wind of the creature's strike as it passed over his head. The wanderer spun, lashing out with his sword. There was a brief resistance but in another moment the creature pulled away, and he was rewarded with only a small cut along its arm.

The wanderer rose, watching the creature as it stopped a short distance away, and they slowly began to circle each other. Then suddenly the creature spun, regarding something behind it, and the wanderer, who had allowed himself no distractions during the fight, looked past to see that Dekker, and the wagon carrying the big man's wife and daughter, were currently hurtling past.

The wanderer frowned as the creature turned back, cocking its blood-spattered head to one side. *"Friends of yours?"* it asked in a voice that was a dry, croaking rasp, barely recognizable as anything human at all.

The wanderer had a wild moment of panic as he realized that the creature was the creature no longer but was instead possessed by the creature posing as Soldier. "No," the wanderer growled, rushing toward the creature, but it spun, taking advantage of its incredible speed, to outdistance him as it raced toward the wagon.

The wanderer hissed, taking off after it in a sprint. He'd barely managed a step when one of the horses pulling the wagon screamed in pain as three bloody furrows appeared down its side as if by magic. Blood fountained out, coating the Unseen as it continued past, dragging its claws down the poor beast's flank. The galloping horse continued to scream, a terrible, heart-wrenching sound, then collapsed to the ground, bringing the wagon and the other horse pulling it to a terrible, crashing halt, and sending Dekker flying from the carriage seat.

There was a woman's scream from inside the carriage, and the wanderer gritted his teeth as he pushed himself harder, sprinting toward where the big man was looking dazedly up at the blurred, blood-covered form of the Unseen. The wanderer called on every ounce of strength, of speed he had, but knew even as he did that he would not be fast enough, that he *could not* be fast enough.

And so, he did something he had been taught never to do voluntarily—he relinquished his weapon. Only, he relinquished it by grabbing it and hurling it through the air. The move of a desperate fool, but then in that moment that was exactly what he was.

The creature seemed to sense the blade flying toward it or, perhaps, it had been watching him all along—there was no way to tell for sure with so much of it invisible to the naked eye. All that he *could* be certain of was that the sword stopped in mid-air as the Unseen caught it with apparent ease. "*A mistake,*" it rasped, "*to give up your weapon. Now I will kill you and they will die anyway.*"

The wanderer didn't offer any argument—mostly because he had none. He was just preparing to draw the cursed blade from where it, too, was sheathed at his back, but the creature chose that moment, as if divining his intention, to rush toward him in an incredible burst of speed.

He had enough time for his fingers to wrap around the handle of his sword, but not enough time to draw it before the creature barreled into him, shoulder first, and he was sent hurtling through the air. He spun end over end until finally striking the ground.

His forehead struck the cobbles of the street hard, and he grunted in pain as he continued to roll. Finally, he came to stop on his side, groaning in pain. He knew he needed to get up, *had* to get up, but despite his entreaties to his body, it responded slowly, sluggishly. He was still trying to turn back in the direction of the creature when something struck him in the stomach, sending him onto his back.

He groaned, staring up at the form above him.

"Finally, we have you," the creature hissed. *"And now the Shard will be returned to us, to its rightful place. You have failed, Youngest, have allowed your mortality to prove a weakness and so you and all those you love and care about will suffer. But we will not stop there. They will all die. Every. Single. One of them."*

You have failed. Those words hit him with the power of a lightning strike. Mostly because in the end, he knew they were true.

How long had he traveled the world? How much had he endured, how much of the suffering in the world had he ignored only to fail? He had known, of course, that it was only a matter of time. That sooner or later, they would catch him or, if not, eventually even his magically-extended life would come to its natural end. And with him no longer alive to act as its caretaker, it would not have taken long for the cursed blade to find its way back to those who had created it. He had known that his was only a bid for time, a bid to keep the world and the mortals living upon it going for a little while longer, like a man seeing the sun setting, seeing the shadows lengthening across the ground and backing up to stay within the sliver of light as it shrank. Not because he was fooling himself into thinking it would last forever but simply because men stayed in the light for as long as they could. It was what they did.

He had known that the time would come when he would fail, sooner or later, had thought he had made his peace with it. But now, facing that end, he realized that he had been wrong.

"*Have you no words?*" the creature asked, and in its rasping tone, he heard its pleasure. "*No entreaty to make?*"

He said nothing, for there was nothing to be said. It was over, that was all, and some small part of him...perhaps, a part that was not so very small...was glad of that.

"*Leave him alone, you fucking bastard!*"

It was a voice he knew, and the wanderer had time enough to feel a wave of despair wash over him before something struck the creature. He would think of it later and wonder how it was that Dekker had managed to hit a creature whose speed could be measured several factors above his own. Perhaps it was because the creature had underestimated him or that it had not expected him to remain—certainly the wanderer had not. Whatever the reason, though, the blow *did* land, and the Unseen went sailing through the air as if struck by the hand of some all-powerful god.

Then Dekker was standing over him, offering his hand.

"Dekker," the wanderer said. "What are you doing here?"

"Savin' your ass, it seems to me," the big man said. "Now, you gonna lie there all day or get up?"

The wanderer took the man's hand, allowing himself to be pulled to his feet and doing his best to ignore the wave of dizziness that swept over him. He brought a hand to his forehead and the fingers came away stained bloody.

"They don't seem so tough," the big man observed.

"You don't understand," the wanderer said quietly as he turned to look in the direction the Unseen had flown. "You have not killed it. You have only made it angry."

The big man frowned at that. "Are you su—"

"Go back to the carriage, Dekker," the wanderer said. "You have one good horse left—it should do to pull the carriage, at least for a little while. Leave the city as quick as you can. Now. There might yet be time."

"*Oh, but there is no time, not for him and not for you, Youngest. Not for anyone.*"

The wanderer turned back to regard the blood-stained creature as it rose to its feet. He reached behind his back, meaning to draw the cursed blade, but a jolt of panic ran through him as he realized it was no longer there. He looked around and finally saw the blade lying on the ground at least ten feet distant where it must have come loose when he'd been thrown. Only ten feet, but it might as well have been a mile for all the good it would do him.

The creature let out a rasping, hissing laugh. "*No, I am afraid the Shard cannot help you. But then, it was not made for you, was it? You are not its rightful owner—only the thief who spirited it away in the night. Now, you will di—*" The creature suddenly cut off, its head seeming to slide off its neck to fall onto the ground. The wanderer stared in confusion as the body followed, revealing a familiar figure standing behind it, gripping a sword in two white-knuckled hands.

The leader of the Perishables' face was parchment white as he stared at the ground in front of him. "That thing is…horrifying," Clint breathed.

The wanderer followed the man's gaze to see that, now that it was dead, whatever magic had made the creature invisible had departed, revealing it in all its hideousness.

"Damn nice strike, Clint," Dekker said, clapping a hand to the man's shoulder and making him jump. "Good thing the bastard didn't see you comin'."

"Yeah," the leader of the Perishables said, licking his lips nervously. "Good thing."

"A clean strike," the wanderer observed, staring at the beast's severed neck.

Clint cleared his throat. "Was aimin' for its back, you want to know the truth."

"Still," the wanderer said, "thank you."

Clint gave him a sickly smile. "You're welcome."

The wanderer nodded, inclining his head, then he turned back to the street to see how many of the people who'd been crowding it were left. He didn't like the answer. For even as he looked, the final man fell, and a second blood-spattered Unseen turned to regard him from where it stood over the man's corpse.

"*Sir!*"

The three of them turned to see Will, the young nobleman who had allowed the Perishables to make use of his family manse, rushing forward.

"What is it, Will?" Clint asked. "What's the matter, lad?"

The wanderer thought that there was plenty that might be the matter, but as the young nobleman spoke, he was reminded, yet again, that no matter how bad things were, they could always get worse. "There are more of the beasts on their way, sir," the nobleman blurted. "Ones that appear the same as those which Ungr fought at my family's manse."

"*Revenants,*" the wanderer hissed, and as if their name was a cue, suddenly dozens, what might have even been hundreds of the creatures began to pour into the street from every alleyway. Soldier, it seemed, had chosen to bring the full weight of his power against them, and the only thing for which the wanderer was grateful was that there were no side streets between them and the gate.

The wanderer turned to Dekker. "Go—now. I'll hold them for as long as I can. Get you and your family out of here."

"No chance I'm going to leave y—"

"Damnit, Dekker, *listen* to me," the wanderer snapped. "We cannot win this—no one could. If you stay, you will die. And not *just* you. Sarah and Ella will *also* die, do you understand? Now go. Perhaps there might be time enough for the three of you to get away."

Dekker turned to Clint as if looking for support, but the Perishable's leader only shook his head. "He's right, Dek. You saw what these damned things can do. Get Ella and that sweet little girl of yours out of here, while there's still time."

Dekker hissed. "You two bastards stay alive, if you can," he growled. "That way I can kick your asses later on."

The wanderer gave him a small smile. "Good luck."

The big man nodded, meeting both of their eyes. "To you as well," he said, then he was turned and running toward the carriage.

The two of them watched him go for several seconds, watched him right the carriage and cut loose the poor horse that the Unseen had wounded so horribly. "So, what's the plan?"

The wanderer turned to regard Clint then glanced back at the road where the Revenants were continuing to pour in. Then he checked on the other Perishables. Some tried to force their way into the buildings and houses crowding the street, but he was impressed to see that these were only a small minority. Most were, instead, moving toward where he and Clint stood, wielding weapons of varying quality ranging from swords appropriated from the nobleman's armory, to fire pokers and candlesticks to one gray-haired man carrying a brick. They all looked terrified, as well they should, but they came anyway, lining up on either side of him and the Perishable leader. The wanderer watched them, impressed, nodding to the noble youth, Will, who stood gripping a broken chair leg in two hands. Then he turned to Clint. "We hold them for as long as we can," he said.

The Revenants lined up behind the Unseen, visible because of the blood staining it from the slaughter it had wrought on men and women whose only crime was from being at the wrong place at the wrong time.

The wanderer waited, tense, expecting the creature to burst forward with its incredible, characteristic speed. It didn't, though. Instead, it cocked its head, much the way the other had done, as if puzzling over a particularly difficult question, then it turned, regarding the carriage, driven by Dekker, as it traveled through the gate as fast as the lone horse could pull it.

"It means to go after them, doesn't it?" Clint asked.

The wanderer looked back at the creature, watched as it bared bloody teeth in what might have been a grin. "Yes," he said quietly, his voice coming out in little more than a croak.

Clint grunted. "Well. Best you go on then," he said, his eyes tracking the carriage as it disappeared beyond sight.

The wanderer turned to him, frowning. "What?"

"You heard me," the other man said. "Go on—save them, if you can."

"What about you?"

The leader of the Perishables gave a shrug. "We'll hold 'em as long as we can. But you get Dekker and his wife and daughter away from here, keep them safe. You manage that much, I'd say I can go to the afterlife with a smile on my face."

"You sure?" the wanderer asked.

"Would your stayin' mean we could win against that?" Clint countered, nodding his head to the nearly hundred Revenants crowding the street in front of them.

"No."

"Then I'm sure."

The wanderer knew he should go—not only would going give him a better chance of saving Dekker and his family, it would also give him another opportunity to keep the cursed blade from the hands of the enemy.

Yet his feet did not want to move.

"Go on then," Clint said, giving him a smile. "Who knows? Might be we'll see each other again."

The wanderer winced, glancing back at the Revenants. *I do not think we will,* he thought. *I really don't.* He was considering staying anyway, but suddenly the Unseen exploded into action, racing forward, and several of the Perishables cried out as it hurled at them. The wanderer tensed, expecting to see several of their number scythed down, but nothing happened. Instead, the bloody, nearly invisible form hurtled past them and then toward the open gate, and the wanderer did not have to wonder where it might be going, for he knew well enough.

"Good luck, Clint," he said. Then he was leaping into Veikr's saddle. He grabbed hold of the horse's reins. *"Ride, Weakest!"* Propelled by Veikr's incredible power, they barely seemed to touch the ground, cutting through the air like a bird. They reached the gate in moments. The wanderer glanced back once over his shoulder to see the Perishables facing off against the Revenants who had now started forward. He said a silent prayer for them before turning back and scanning the fields beyond the gate. At first, he saw nothing, then he caught sight of a red blur, up ahead and moving fast. And beyond it, approaching the distant tree line, rattled the carriage holding Dekker and his family.

"Come, Weakest," the wanderer roared, *"let us show this creature your true strength!"*

Veikr tossed his head as if in response and then they were moving faster still, the horse's great legs pumping forward again and again, his hooves lashing against the ground with each galloping stride. Impossibly, the wanderer realized that they were gaining on the Unseen, but he realized, also, that the creature was closing the distance between it and the carriage far more quickly than they were the distance from them to it.

In a minute, perhaps less, the creature would be on them. Dekker must have realized this, for he veered off the road at an angle that would put him into the trees much quicker. Likely, the big man was thinking that with so many trees to negotiate, the creature's speed would prove far more of a liability than it did on the open fields. It was a smart move. The problem of course was that however much it might increase the difficulty of the Unseen's maneuvering, the cramped confines of the forest and its trees would make it that much more difficult for the carriage to maneuver within it.

But even as the wanderer noticed all of this, he noticed another thing—the carriage wasn't going to make the tree line, even with the more direct approach Dekker had taken. The Unseen was moving too fast, and the wanderer and Veikr were still too far behind to help. There was nothing he could do, though, so the wanderer gritted his teeth, praying for a miracle.

"*Ride, Veikr!*" he roared, but he knew that already the horse was pushing himself to his limits, putting every ounce of energy and strength he could muster into catching up with the Unseen.

They rode on, the Unseen chasing the carriage, the wanderer chasing the Unseen, until the creature caught up to it. It ran alongside the horse, a horse to which the wanderer was now close enough to see was panicked with fear, foam frothing out of its mouth, its eyes wide and wild. And then there was a blur, and the horse cried out as several deep lacerations appeared in its side as the unseen scraped its talons across it. The horse veered, trying to get away from the terrible source of its pain, but in so doing it fumbled its run, tripping. There was an audible *crack,* and the tortured beast screamed as its leg broke. Its other legs couldn't accommodate the abrupt extra weight, and they went out from under it. The horse struck the ground hard, the carriage, tipping on its side from the horse's momentum, following a moment later.

Horse and carriage struck the ground with a crash and a cloud of dust billowed up as their momentum sent them sliding across it. The wander did not hesitate, riding into that cloud of dust, knowing that to waste any time would be to doom Dekker and his family to certain death. He held his arm up in front of him, blocking as much of the dust from his eyes as he could as he charged into the thick cloud.

He saw the Unseen standing over Dekker who was lying on his back from where he'd been thrown from the wagon. The wanderer and Veikr charged directly toward it.

The creature seemed to turn to regard them at the last moment. It moved, quick enough to dodge the wanderer's blade but Veikr pivoted, striking it hard with his flank, and the Unseen was flung through the air to land twenty feet away, rolling.

He leapt from the saddle. "Dekker," he yelled, running toward the man and dropping to his knees, "are you okay?"

"*My...family,*" Dekker groaned, blinking, blood leaking from a shallow cut on his forehead. "Are they...okay?"

The wanderer looked back at the carriage in time to see Sarah and Ella climbing out of it. They both looked terrified, shaken up, but unhurt. At least for the moment. The wanderer turned back to the big man. "They're fine—come on, let's get you up."

Dekker took his hand, and the wanderer hissed with the effort of pulling him to his feet. The big man wobbled uncertainly for a few seconds, then gave his head a shake. "Damned thing is fast."

"Yes, yes, it is," the wanderer said, glancing back at it. The Unseen was beginning to stir now, working its way to its feet. "Dekker, listen to me," he said, "get on Veikr, you and your family—get out of here."

The big man blinked. "What? What about you?"

"I'll catch up to you."

"But...how will you know where to find us?"

I won't, but it will not matter, the wanderer thought, for he did not like his chances alone against the Unseen, not at all. Still, he knew that if he said the wrong thing the big man wouldn't go, and it would all be for nothing. He bit back a sigh of frustration. "Head east, stay along the road. I'll catch up to you before nightfall. But if I don't," he went on, meeting the big man's eyes, "you keep going. Do you understand?"

Dekker gave a wince. "I don't like this, Ungr."

"You don't have to." Veikr gave a snort, and the wanderer patted the horse's muzzle as he glanced at the creature to see it coming to its feet. "There's no choice, my friend," he said softly. "You know what happens if I don't do this—it would catch them. Sooner or later, it would catch them, would catch us. You know this."

Veikr studied him with eyes that seemed to say so much, then slowly lowered himself to the ground as Ella approached, holding her frightened daughter.

"You both okay?" Dekker asked.

"Just a bit shaken up is all," Ella said, giving a smile that obviously cost her.

"Well thank the Eternals for that," Dekker said. "Come on then, Sarah girl," he went on, kneeling and stretching out his hands, "how would you like to go for a ride on your friend here?"

Despite her confusion and fear, the girl's eyes widened in delighted surprise. "You mean it, Daddy?"

"I mean it," he said.

The wanderer turned and regarded the creature as it finished making its way to its feet and drew his sword. "Better hurry," he said, watching the creature as it turned toward him and the others.

"I-is Mister Ungr coming with us, Daddy?"

Dekker turned and met the wanderer's eyes. "He'll...he'll be along directly, sweetling. Now, let's head on out."

They were moving then. The wanderer watched them, watched Veikr, his only friend for the last hundred years. He felt his emotions beginning to stir within him, but he forced them down as he turned back to the creature. They would not serve him here. The creature started toward him slowly, circling around him.

"*It matters not,*" it said in a voice which matched that used by the other Unseen, as well as the Revenant back at the nobleman's manse. "*After I am finished with you, I will hunt them down and kill each of them. Slowly. They will suffer for the trouble you have caused.*"

"I've heard this before."

"*Perhaps,*" the creature said, still circling him, "*but you will not have the big man here to save you, nor the other.*"

The wanderer said nothing to that, for the time for talking was past. He would either win or he would not and talking would do nothing to change that. So he stopped, holding his sword so that it hung down and at his side at an angle and regarded the creature.

"*I see,*" the creature said, a mocking sort of humor in its tone. "*Are you truly so eager to die, then?*"

The wanderer turned so that the shoulder of his free hand faced the creature, studying it through the dry dust floating up around them. "Say that I am."

"*Very well,*" the creature said. "*Then you will have your wish.*"

The wanderer watched the creature, knowing that he had gotten lucky a few times before over the years, but this was the first time that he had ever faced an Unseen without some advantage, whether that advantage be another person or the waters of the lake in which he had fought one before meeting Dekker and his family.

The creature was faster than him, stronger too, and there was no one around, not*hing* except the dust billowing between them in the slight breeze. That and that only, no advantage to be had, no tricks.

But that isn't true, is it? A part of his mind asked. *There is one trick left to you. One advantage.*

It was an advantage he'd held for the last hundred years, that he had, so far at least, managed to keep secret from the enemy. But as much as he hated the idea of betraying that secret, it would matter little if he was killed. And so the wanderer reached up to his neck, to the amulet hanging there.

He opened it.

And he let the ghosts speak.

Their voices poured over him, rushed over him in a wave, the sound like some great susurration, of water crashing against the shore. "*Quiet,*" he told the dead, and this time, at least, the dead listened.

"*What is that?*" the creature hissed. "*What did you do?*"

"*Soldier,*" the wanderer said, ignoring him and keeping his voice low yet noting the way the creature paused, cocking its head as it studied him. "*I need you.*"

I am here.

"Do you have anything that might help?"

It is faster than you. Stronger, too.

He winced. "Thanks."

Focus, lad, Soldier said in his mind. *It may be faster, stronger too, but whatever it once was, it is a man no longer and so does not possess a man's instincts, a warrior's instincts or his cleverness. Remember, lad, your speed and strength are not your greatest asset—your greatest asset is your mind.*

"Doubt I'll be able to stop its talons with my mind," the wanderer said quietly, "and if I do, I don't think I'll enjoy it overly much."

It's fast, Soldier said, ignoring him. *Its speed is its greatest asset and so like the big man who was once a big boy and learned to rely on his strength and that only, it will rely too heavily on it. In so doing it will turn its greatest advantage into its greatest disadvantage.*

"How does that help me?"

Speed, Youngest, Soldier said, *it cares about speed, that most of all. And what is the fastest path between two points but a—*

The voice cut off as suddenly the creature burst into speed, launching itself toward him. The wanderer did not think, for there was no time for that. He did not create a plan for he would be long dead before he'd finished devising a plan let alone had a chance to implement it. Instead, the moment the creature moved, he stepped to the side and with a roar of defiance brought his sword around, two-handed.

The creature and the blade met in a shocking impact that made both his arms go numb, knocking the sword from his hands. He had misjudged it, though only a little, and so the creature's shoulder clipped him and with the momentum it had accumulated, the blow was enough to spin him around and his legs went out from under him.

He hit the ground, grunting with the pain of the blow, then rolled to his feet, taking a fighting stance with his hands out to his sides only to see that the creature lay a short distance away, a massive gash out of its midsection where the blade had cleaved through it. It flickered in and out of visibility like a guttering candle flame, its taloned hands clawing at the ground, digging great furrows into the dry earth as it tried and failed to stand.

The wanderer rubbed idly at his shoulder as he watched it, feeling a fresh bruise coming on where the creature had struck him. Then he started forward, shuffling with pain, gritting his teeth against it. He retrieved his sword then shuffled toward the creature.

In another minute he was standing over it, staring down at the Unseen, seen at last, as it looked up at him, baring its teeth and letting out a furious hiss. *"Fool,"* it growled. *"Surely you must know that this makes no difference. This body is just a vessel."*

"A broken one," the wanderer observed.

"And what does that matter?" the creature demanded. *"It is but one of thousands, and you cannot hope to win. You cannot run far enough or fast enough. You and your new friends. I will find you, can only find you, and when I do, you will all die."*

The wanderer grunted. "Well. See you around then." And with that, he brought his blade down, severing the Unseen's head from its shoulders and stopping the dreaded flickering. Then he turned, looking past the cloud of dust slowly rising from the ground like fog in the early morning and stared off in the direction Veikr had taken the others. They were gone, carried beyond his sight by Veikr's speed, the only evidence that they had passed that way at all a trail of dust lingering in the air.

He turned back and regarded the distant city. They had traveled far away from the southern gate in the chase, and he was too distant to make out any details. He wondered if the Perishables still fought against the Revenants, the creations of the enemy, or if they had already fallen. It was possible—perhaps even likely—that the Revenants had already dealt with Clint and the others and were currently in pursuit. They would not move fast, the wanderer knew, creatures not built for speed as the Unseen but instead with an eye toward durability, endurance. But while they might not move quickly, they would not stop or falter, for unlike mortal men and women, the Revenants, the products of those cruel experiments of the enemy, did not require sleep or sustenance.

Which meant that the sooner the wanderer caught up with Dekker and his family, the better. His shoulder hurt, his head too, but a quick check showed that the wound in his head had, at least, stopped bleeding. The wanderer glanced once more at the corpse of the Unseen, thinking that there had been a time, not so very long ago, that he would have hidden the body, lest someone discover the truth of the creatures which roamed the world. Now, though, he did not. The cursed blade had left its sheath, and the enemy turned its gaze toward him. Likely, he would not survive the next few weeks, and if the people of the world were not yet aware of the monsters the enemy could produce with their experiments, they probably soon would be.

He turned and left the monstrosity behind, starting down the road at a jog.

CHAPTER THREE

On the sun-bleached road of the fields, it was easy enough to make out the imprints Veikr's hooves had left, not that he needed to as he knew well enough what direction Dekker and the others had gone.

The trip to the woods, which had taken Veikr only five minutes, took him nearly half an hour. He did not slow as he reached the tree line, knowing that it would be best if he could reach Veikr and the others before night fell. If he didn't it would prove far more difficult to find them in the darkness, and he knew that the Revenants, while slow, were also relentless and would catch up to them sooner or later.

He ran on for another few minutes when he heard something in the trees off to his right. He came to an abrupt halt, his hand moving to his back where his sword was sheathed only to pause, listening. After a moment, he let his hand fall back down to his side. "You may come out," he called. "It's safe."

Seconds later he heard several grunts and bitten-back curses then Dekker appeared pushing his way through the forest undergrowth and onto the road, followed by Ella who cradled Sarah against her, the young girl's legs wrapped tightly around her mother's waist. Veikr appeared last, looking sheepish and ashamed. Which, as far as the wanderer was concerned, was only right.

"I told you to keep going," he said abruptly to Dekker.

The big man winced. "Yeah, I know you did, only, it didn't feel right, leavin' you like that. Thought we'd wait a bit. If you won, well, we figured you'd be along directly, and if you didn't..." He paused, shrugging. "It's the reason we hid. In case it was that thing that come up behind us instead of you."

"Hiding would have done you no good," the wanderer said. "The Unseen, like some other of the enemy's creations, are designed to be hunters. If I discovered you, it would not have had the slightest difficulty in doing so." He met the man's eyes. "You should have kept going."

Dekker looked away from his gaze, the big man glancing at his feet and fidgeting like a child being called out. "Maybe. Anyway, where is that damned thing?"

"Dead."

"Well, see there? Everything worked out."

The wanderer glanced at Veikr, the horse meeting his eyes timidly then quickly looking away as if to say that the big man didn't speak for him. Then he turned back to Dekker. "Can I talk to you for a moment? In private?"

The big man regarded his wife and daughter, gave a brief nod, then allowed the wanderer to lead him a little way farther down the road. "Feel like I'm about to be sent to my room," Dekker observed in a voice that tried for light-hearted but didn't quite make it.

The wanderer met the big man's gaze. "I have been traveling for a long time, Dekker, have been hunted for a long time," he said. "A very long time. And I have seen these creatures, what they are capable of. I know their dangers better than any man living. So, when I tell you that the best way to protect your family, the *only* way, is to do what I say when I say it, I mean it. Do you understand?"

"I understand," the big man said. "Just didn't like leavin' you."

"Would you like your family dying?" the wanderer asked, his voice harsher than it needed to be, harsher than he'd *intended* for it to be—but he was angry. Angry at Dekker, at himself, at the world in general.

The big man recoiled as if slapped. "Ungr, there ain't no need to—"

"Yes, there is," the wanderer said. "You stayed when I told you to leave and, had the creature killed me, you, your wife, your *daughter* would have followed soon after."

Dekker frowned, his eyes narrowing. "That's enough, Ungr."

"Is it?" he challenged. "I told you before, Dekker, to leave, you and all those Perishables serving under Clint. You ignored me then and because of that dozens died at Will's manse. And those that survived are now being slaughtered in the city street outside the southern gate, if they aren't already dead. Will you continue to ignore me until you have no one left to lose?"

The big man said nothing, only watching him with anger dancing in his eyes, and the wanderer thought that was fine, perhaps better than fine. Better for the man to be angry at him than to underestimate what they faced. "The next time I tell you to leave me," the wanderer said, "do it."

The big man's upper lip peeled back from his teeth in a silent snarl. "No problem," he said. "We done?"

"We're done," the wanderer said.

Dekker gave an angry nod then turned and walked back to his wife and daughter. The wanderer watched him go, hating himself, hating that he had taken what might have been a friend and turned him into, if not an enemy, then at least someone who would not weep should he die. But he did not say anything, did not take the words back, for they were true ones. Brutal yes, perhaps even cruel, but words that might well save Dekker's life, that might save the life of his wife, his daughter, and so the wanderer let them remain. He left them the way a man might leave in an arrow stuck into his thigh, knowing it was the only thing keeping him alive and that to pull it out was to invite death.

The wanderer walked up to the family, the three of them turning to regard him, but it was Ella who spoke. "What do we do now, Ungr?" she asked, glancing at her husband, obviously curious what had been said between them but also obviously planning to leave it, at least for now.

Which was just as well. The wanderer did not doubt that Dekker would tell her soon enough, that soon enough she would hate him as Dekker did. He thought that he could accept that hate, if he had to, if it meant that they would be safe, but he did not want to see it come upon her, to see the transformation in the woman's eyes that that hatred would bring.

"We continue west. He will not stop looking for us. He will continue to send his creatures until we are found."

"Creatures like the ones back at the estate?" Ella asked.

Dekker grunted. "What do you know of it? I thought you were in the cellar."

"Eternals, Dekker, I'm not blind, am I? I could have seen enough, *more* than enough, when we were leaving. Anyway, I left the cellar for a moment—Sarah was still there, of course—to check on you. I saw them out of the window."

"Left the cellar?" Dekker sputtered as if he couldn't believe what he was hearing. "Damnit, Ella, I told you to stay there with Sarah."

"And I will tell you now, as I have many times before, Dekker, that I am willing to listen to you just as long as what you say is not foolish."

"Foolish?" Dekker said. "Foolish like risking leaving Sarah without a mother?"

"Or without a father?" Ella rejoined instantly. The big man winced at that, but she wasn't finished. "Do not think, given what you have been up to, Dekker, to shame me."

"Wasn't tryin' to shame you," the big man said, avoiding her gaze, then letting out a heavy sigh. "I was just tryin' to protect you, both of you."

"I know that," she said softly, putting a hand on his shoulder. "And I appreciate it. But as much as Sarah needs her mother, she needs her father too. Do you understand?"

Dekker glanced at the wanderer, as if somehow he was behind this, then sighed again. "I understand."

"Good," she said. "Because even though you're a pain, I'd prefer keeping you around for a while. Otherwise, who am I going to get to lift all the heavy things?"

Dekker sighed, shaking his head and glancing at the wanderer. "Wives, eh?"

"So I hear," the wanderer said, trying a smile past the pain the thought brought him, for he had never had a wife, only *her*, and he had left her alone. She was long dead now as were likely any children she might have had, living their lives, aging and dying while the wanderer continued to linger. She was dead, dead and gone and, with her, the man he had once been, the life he *could* have led.

Dekker nodded. "Anyway," he said. "Do you really think he'll send people after us?"

"I'm sure of it," the wanderer said instantly. "He would not allow me to escape so easily, for he has seen me now, has seen what I carry. He will be coming."

"What you carry," Dekker said, his eyes traveling to the wanderer's shoulder where the hilt of the cursed blade was sticking up. "You mean the sword."

"Yes."

"Why?" Dekker asked. "I mean, all this just for a sword?"

"It is not any normal sword," the wanderer explained.

"Never mind that," Ella said, exasperated. "This 'he' you speak of...you mean *Soldier,* don't you?"

"Yes."

"You're saying that Soldier is after us."

"I am saying that the creature who has, for the last one hundred years, claimed to be Soldier is after us."

"I...I don't understand," Ella said.

"I know," the wanderer said, "and I have no time to explain it to you, not now. We must leave, quickly. There is no knowing how many Unseen he has under his command which are near at hand. No doubt he has summoned all within his power by now and sent them against us. Even if there are no Unseen nearby, it will not take long to them long to catch us up. And there are the Revenants to think of as well, not to mention the hundreds of mortal troops under his command. The three of you, hop on Veikr."

"What about you?" Ella asked.

"I will run," he said, giving her a tired smile, "I have had a lot of practice."

CHAPTER FOUR

They traveled on for the next several hours, the wanderer constantly checking behind them. He did not like taking the main road where they could easily be spotted, but he knew that should they try to go into the forest they'd be forced to cut their way through undergrowth, slowing their progress considerably. And just then, all he could think about was putting as much distance between them and the city of Celes as possible, a city which, just now, likely looked like an anthill that had just been kicked with troops of all types spilling out of it in search of them.

He told himself that they still had a chance. After all, the road on which they traveled was deserted, a far cry from the busy avenues farther north. Here, this far south, few braved the roads and with good reason. The villages and cities which made up Soldier's territory were the last signs of civilization this side of the continent. Should one travel farther south beyond those towns and hamlets, they would enter the Untamed Lands.

A wilderness full of monsters and bandits and all other manner of danger, creatures and threats that the men and women of the civilized world had not seen in centuries and in the face of which they would be wholly unprepared. Such creatures, such dangers, had been everywhere centuries ago, but the Eternals had waged war against them, carving out a piece of the world in which their people might live and prosper. The border between Soldier's lands and those Untamed regions beyond, then, marked the place where the Eternals, exhausted from years of battle and grieving for several of their number lost in the fighting, chose to stop their advance, deciding that those lands they had won were sufficient.

The wanderer knew the stories, for the man he had been, long ago, had listened to them eagerly. First, he'd heard those told throughout the world, at his father's knee and in his bed when his mother sought to help him find sleep. Then, later, when he had joined their ranks, he had listened to accounts from the Eternals themselves, ones that were far grimmer than those the populace knew. For in the stories the people of the realm recounted, the Eternals stopped their holy crusade because they chose to. But in the stories of the Eternals themselves, in the *true* stories, they stopped fighting because they had no fight left within them. They stopped to mourn their dead, three men and women thought to be more like gods than normal men or women, who had given their lives in the effort. Scout, Archer, and Berserker. Each with tales of their exploits that were more incredible than the last, men and women of legendary strength and cunning and skill, yet all three of whom had been brought down by the dangers the Untamed Lands held.

Yes, the people of the world avoided this road, and they were right to do so, at least so far as the wanderer was concerned. After all, there was enough evil in the world already that a man had no need to go looking for more.

Thankfully, their path would not take them any closer to that wild place where life was said to be so very cheap. Instead, he would continue to lead them west and, in time, escape Soldier's territory, put enough distance between them and the city that the enemy's search area would simply be too large. That was his plan, to stay ahead of them as best they could.

And to hope...that most of all.

They continued on through the forest until the girl, Sarah, fell asleep against her mother's chest, until the sun was sunk low on the horizon, the shadows stretching across the land like the great questing fingers of some giant eager to grasp it all in one crushing grip. Then the wanderer clucked at Veikr, and the horse eased to a stop.

"What is it?" Dekker said, glancing around, blinking as if he, like his daughter, had been dozing or nearly so. "Have they found us?"

"Nothing like that," the wanderer said quickly when he saw the little girl's eyes flitter open. "We are safe. Only, I think it time we made camp."

Dekker frowned, glancing behind them in the gloom. "Are you sure that's a good idea, what with those things chasing us and all?"

"There is little choice," the wanderer said. "You are tired, all of you, and while Veikr is the greatest of all horses, he cannot keep you in the saddle simply by willing it. Anyway, we will be fine," he went on with far more confidence than he felt. "Even if the enemy's creatures do somehow catch us up—which I doubt—then the darkness will cover us." *Or so I hope.*

He led them off the road and into the woods. He would have liked to have found a cave or at the least a large rock, somewhere that might have allowed them to have their backs against something solid, but it was too much to hope for. Night was coming on quickly, and so he picked a spot far enough from the road that there was no chance of someone spotting them accidentally and close enough that they would have little difficulty finding it in the morning.

"This will do fine," he said, stopping.

Dekker frowned. "What's different about this spot than the others we passed?" he asked, seemingly genuinely curious.

The wanderer gave him a smile. "This one's here."

The big man, still angry, did not return the smile. Instead, he only grunted. "So it is," he said, dismounting. Ella was still holding their daughter, sleeping once more, against her chest, and Dekker lifted both of them off the horse gently, as if they weighed nothing, setting them down on the ground.

"There's a spare cloak," the wanderer told the big man. "In the saddlebags. It's no feathered bed, but perhaps it will be better than nothing."

Dekker nodded, opening the saddlebags. In moments, he'd retrieved the cloak and was spreading it out for his wife and daughter. The wanderer watched, watched the way the big man was so gentle with the two of them, as if they were precious glass that might be broken by any sudden movement. He understood that. After all, they were precious—on that much he agreed. And he knew well, better than most, just how easily men were broken.

Dekker bent and gave them both a kiss, and the wanderer, feeling as if he were intruding, turned away from them, looking back at the direction from which they'd come, trying to think about anything he might have missed or not thought of. Anything that would come back to haunt them. He could think of nothing, but that was little comfort.

Men missed things, that was all. You need only ask their wives that much, or so he had once been told. He could not speak to the veracity of it, for he had never had a wife, but he did know this much at the least—men missed things.

It was one of the most common mistakes they made. And he knew another thing, too. The world had a way of making men pay for their mistakes.

"Everything alright?"

He turned to see that Dekker had come upon him while he'd been lost in thought. "Fine," the wanderer said.

The big man grunted. "You sure about that? If I'd have had to guess how you were doin' from the lookin' while I was makin' my way over here, I wouldn't have come up with 'fine.'"

"I was just thinking," the wanderer said. "Trying to decide if there was anything else that might be done."

The big man nodded slowly. "And what did you come up with?"

"Nothing."

"I see. So, Ungr, I been thinkin'," Dekker said. "You've told us that Soldier ain't really Soldier."

"That's right."

"But you ain't told us who he is then. Nor nothin' else. Seems to me there's an explanation in order."

"Yes, and we will talk. But later."

The big man frowned. "And if I told you I wanted to know now? You know, considerin' as it's my wife and daughter's lives that are at stake?"

The wanderer glanced past him to see Ella watching them, her eyes shining in the darkness where she held Sarah. "I would say to you that the story you ask me to tell is no bedtime fairy tale. It is a tale best told in the light, with the sun warm against your skin. For in the darkness, Dekker," he went on, meeting the man's eyes, "a man's ghosts find their form, their substance. In the darkness, in the night, memories live."

The big man watched him for several seconds, an expression on his face that said he wanted to argue. "Fine," he said finally. "Your way, then. Always your way, is that it, Ungr?"

The wanderer said nothing to that, for there was nothing he could say, and after a moment the big man spat then turned and made his way back to his bedroll.

The wanderer watched him for a minute, wishing he could make the man understand that he tried to do him a service, that he did what he did not out of cruelty or some desire to be obtuse. It was only that the story the man wanted to hear was full of pain. The wanderer knew this for he had lived it, and the woman and girl had both suffered more than enough pain in the last days, some of it even thanks to him such as Felden Ruitt's death. He did not want to make the family suffer anymore on his account, not if he could help it.

The big man lay down beside his wife, and the two began to talk in hushed voices. The wanderer turned and moved to where Veikr cropped at the grass a short distance away. The horse looked up at him with his big brown eyes, eyes that seemed to see so much, to *know* so much.

"I'm alright," the wanderer said quietly. "He's right to be angry."

Veikr gave his head a toss at that, and the wanderer shook his own. "He's *right,*" he said again, more emphatically this time. "They did not ask for this, not any of it."

The horse cocked his head at him, as if to say that that wasn't altogether true. Of course, he was right. After all, Dekker had already been involved with the Perishables long before the wanderer had shown up at their door. But knowing that did nothing to make him feel better. "You had best get some rest," he told the horse, suddenly not wanting to talk, even to an animal could not talk back.

Veikr nuzzled him softly, and he gave his muzzle an absent pat. "Go on then," he said. "I'll keep watch."

The horse gave a soft snort, shaking his head again as if to argue. It turned and glanced at the family lying on the cloak then back at him, somehow communicating a world of meaning with the simple gesture.

"Leave it," the wanderer said, a rasp to his voice. "They are not for us, Weakest. They have their own lives, and we have our quest." *Always our quest. Our mission.* There was nothing else, could *be* nothing else.

Veikr gave another snort, another shake of his mane.

"*Leave it,*" the wanderer hissed, and the horse recoiled as if shocked, as well he should have been, for the wanderer himself was shocked at the anger in his voice. The horse watched him for a moment with his large, sorrowful eyes, then he turned and moved a short distance away.

The wanderer watched him, feeling of two minds then. Part of him wanted to call the horse back, to apologize. He had never raised his voice at him before. After all, Veikr deserved far better treatment than that, for he had saved his life countless times over the years, had been with him through all the pain and suffering he had endured, his silent—or at least *mostly* silent—companion. That part is what caused his hand to lift, as if to call the horse back, but it was the second part, the part that was angry, which kept him from speaking.

He knew, deep down, that he was not really angry at the horse. Neither was he angry at Dekker and his family or Clint and the other Perishables. He was not even angry at the Eternals, those ghosts who had left him to wander the world alone, always to wander. He was angry only with himself.

But anger would do him no good, not now, so he did his best to push it aside. It did not go far, though, and he did not call the horse back. Whatever had transpired between him and Dekker was, after all, none of the horse's business.

And what of saving your life? Part of him thought. *Had that been Veikr's business?*

The wanderer's upper lip pulled back from his teeth in a silent snarl, and he turned and stalked away into the trees. He set about the task of gathering up some deadwood, small branches and twigs mostly. When he judged that he had enough, he sat and withdrew the small knife from the sheath at his side and began to trim the branches back. He cut away the bark, working at it with a sort of absent-minded focus as he crafted a snare that would, he hoped, serve to find them breakfast. After all, they would need it. His own stores were nearly non-existent now, and the family would be hungry in the morning.

He took his time, some part of him enjoying the crafting of it, for there was joy to be had in doing a thing, even a simple thing, and doing it well. And the wanderer had learned long ago, in a life of torment and pain and things given only to be taken away once more, that a man had to find what joys he could where he could.

He was working on a second snare, nearly finished, when she came upon him. He looked past her and saw that Dekker was asleep, the big man's great arm draped protectively around his young daughter as night came on the world in full. She walked up almost shyly, a nervous smile on her face. "Hello, Ungr," she said.

"Hello," he said, resuming his work on the snare.

She was silent for several seconds then, "Will you not sleep?"

"I will keep watch," he said. "In case they come in the darkness."

She nodded, swallowing hard, her face looking pale in the moonlight. "Will they, do you think?"

"I don't know. We are some small distance from the road, perhaps enough that they will pass us by, but I think it better not to leave it to chance."

She nodded. "But...that is, aren't you tired?"

He considered lying to her, but he was sick of lies, sick of half-truths, so he only nodded. "Yes."

"But you won't sleep."

It wasn't a question, but he chose to answer it. "No."

"Why?"

He frowned, looking up at her again. He hesitated, unsure of how to answer her question, unsure of what the question actually was, for it seemed to him that she asked more than what it appeared on the surface.

"I mean, why do you help us?" she said, clarifying. "Why go through all this trouble? Understand that I am grateful, very grateful. I love my husband, my daughter, but I have to believe that you would be safer on your own...wouldn't you?"

"Yes."

"So what is it then? Is it guilt? About...about my father? Because you have nothing to be guilty for. If what Dekker tells me is true, you were only there because you came to help us, afraid that those...those *things* would come. You only came to protect us."

"But I did not protect you," the wanderer said. "At least...not all of you."

She sighed, shaking her head. "You believe you're responsible for his death."

"Someone must be."

"Is that it then?" she asked. "Why you help us? Is it because you feel guilty? About my da?"

He considered that for a moment then, finally, shook his head. "No. It was at first, but it isn't any longer."

"Then...why?"

He opened his mouth to give her an answer but then found that, at that moment, he did not have one to give. He found himself thinking of Felden Ruitt then, of the young man, Scofield. Of the Perishables, too, Clint and all the rest. "Because...because I'm a part of this world," he said, echoing Felden's words. "And people...people need people. Because there's enough evil in the world that a man, if he wishes to call himself a man, should protect what good he finds when he finds it."

She nodded, glancing back at her husband and daughter where they slept. "Not just men...women, too."

The wanderer found himself thinking of the Eternals and their final stand against the enemy. They had lost, yes, but they had fought bravely, men and women, side by side, fought not for themselves but for the world they protected, and though they had always been great, been reckoned gods, to him, at least, it was then that they had been at their greatest. When they sacrificed everything to protect the world, to protect men and women they did not know, who they would never meet. "Yes," he said. "And women, too."

She was silent for a few minutes but, in time, she spoke again. "I don't know the whole story, but I hope that you will tell me—tell *us*—soon. But I think...you've sacrificed a lot for us...for the world. Haven't you?"

He found his eyes drawn to Veikr, his companion these last hundred years, as the horse lay on the ground, sleeping soundly. "We both have."

"You love him."

"He is all that I have," he said simply.

"No," she said, giving him a small smile. "He isn't. Perhaps he was once, Ungr, but no longer. We're all…we're all grateful for what you've done. And I think I can speak for all of us when I say that we consider you—and Veikr—friends."

The wanderer thought of the conversation he and Dekker'd had earlier, and he found his gaze drawn to the big man where he lay with his daughter.

"My husband is a good man, Ungr," she said, noting the direction of his gaze. "I know that it's fashionable, now, for wives and husbands to speak ill of their spouses seemingly at every opportunity, but I will not. Dekker is a good man, and I would even say that he is, in truth, a perfect one. Only…sometimes it takes him a little time to find that perfection. He's angry, that's all."

"Angry because he thinks I'm wrong, that he thinks he was right to wait."

"No," she said instantly. "He's not angry because he thinks you're wrong, Ungr. He's angry because he knows you're right."

He frowned, turning to her. "I don't understand."

"As I said, Ungr, my husband is a good man, and despite his size and the look of him, he's a kind one. It does not sit well with him, leaving the Perishables, leaving you. He cannot reconcile himself to it, but neither can he reconcile himself to the idea of endangering his wife and daughter by trying to stay and help. Do you see?"

"I…begin to."

She nodded. "He is torn. For what is worse to a good man, Ungr, to a *truly* good man, than to be left with only bad choices? You ought to understand that, shouldn't you? After all, you're a good man, and I get the feeling that you've found yourself in similar situations."

"I would not speak so quickly, Ella," he said. "To call me a good man…you do not know my past, the things I've done."

"Everyone has a past, Ungr," she said. "How you were in the past, that doesn't mean anything except for how you were in the past. It's how you are in the present that determines what type of man you *are*. Trust me, for I was raised by one and married another—you're a good man."

That hurt him, wounded him in a way he might not have expected. But it was a good hurt. Not a wounding in truth, but the cleaning of it, like the scouring out of an infection. Painful, yes, but a good kind of pain.

And yet…he thought it was dangerous, too.

He had traveled the world for a hundred years and more, had witnessed one tragedy after another. And he had learned something during that time spent bent over his saddle, Veikr as his only company. He had learned that a man could not protect himself from heartache, could not shield away all the hurts and woundings that life would offer him, not so long, at least, as he *was* a man, a man who felt and hoped and dreamed.

The only choice, then, was to make himself something else, to *become* something else. Something, some*one* who did not feel the pain, who did not dream but instead closed his eyes only onto darkness. But most important of all, the wanderer had learned that a man without hope saved himself the agony of seeing that hope dashed before his eyes. The way his own hope had been dashed so long ago when he and his brothers and sisters, the other Eternals, had stood in defiance of evil, he, at least, confident that good would win, that it *had* to win. Confident that, in the end, good always prevailed. It had been his hope, his belief, and he had lived long enough to see that hope dashed, to see that belief proven the lie that it was.

"Ungr," Ella began in a soft voice, making it obvious that she had seen at least some of his thoughts on his face, "listen—"

"This is finished," he rasped, raising the snare, "I'd best go place it. Sleep well, Ella."

He stood, then turned and walked away from her, into the woods. *No,* part of him, the part that understood his cowardice thought, *call it what it is. You do not walk—you flee.*

"And you, Ungr," she said behind him, but he did not turn, did not dare turn, for he thought that, if he did, she might see the truth of him, of the terrible things he had done, leaving the other Eternals to die while he fled. She would know it soon enough, for he knew now that he would have to tell them the truth. He would tell them, and he would see their opinion of him change as they realized that he was not the man they thought he was. He did not want to tell them, but he would. Only…not tonight.

He set the two snares around the camp, then began searching for an ideal spot to keep watch. The problem, though, was that the whole area was flat, choked with trees and underbrush. That made it a good choice as far as places to hide and hope that they went unseen but a poor one when seeking to keep an eye on it in case someone tried to sneak up on them in the darkness.

There was no rise in the ground where he might sit, so he did the next best thing. He made sure the two swords, his own and the cursed blade, were secure along his back, then he found one of the largest trees that was nearby and began to climb.

He was glad for the chance of it, the opportunity to make his body work, for often the only answer to a mind that refused to stop working was to work the body instead. There was something peaceful about a methodical task, something almost cathartic, almost healing about the steady rhythm of placing one hand after the other, one foot after the other. The sweat which escaped his skin in the hot night carried with it some bit of his anxiety and, more than that, his shame. A shame he had known for a hundred years and more.

In time, though, the climbing was done, the healing done, and he happened upon a likely branch, hidden from the ground by enough leaves and other branches that the only chance of seeing him would be to look directly at him and even then he might yet pass unnoticed. From the high vantage, though, he would be able to see the camp and some distance around it, at least the parts of it not covered by the leafy canopy of the trees.

And so the wanderer propped his back against the tree's trunk, a leg hanging over either end of the large branch upon which he sat, and he waited. Waited for a sign or sound that he hoped would not come while the family and Veikr slumbered beneath him.

He wondered how many nights he had sat so, waiting. A thousand? Two? He did not know the exact number, knew only that, this time, his nerves were up far more than they normally were, for it was not only his life at risk, not only the world, should the cursed blade fall into the wrong hands, but also the lives of those three sleeping below.

It didn't make sense, perhaps, for the three to matter more than the world and yet, they did. After all, men had their talents, but making sense was rarely one of them.

As he sat there, cooling from the exertion, listening to the sounds of the crickets and the frogs and a lone whippoorwill singing its lonesome song, the memories began to return. Memories awakened by Ella's words, memories he had tried to bury for the last hundred years.

Memories of his friends, his family—certainly the closest thing to family he'd had—lying dead or dying on the ground, the only ones still standing Leader and Soldier, the strongest of the Eternals. And Youngest, of course. He had stood with them. But while their faces had been ones of defiance, of courage and righteous anger, his own had been nothing but terror. Fear. Fear of those creatures, terror that had grown within him as he watched one after the other of the Eternals cut down. He had been one of them, yes, but he was new, he was the Youngest, and even though he had been counted among their number, he had never felt as if he belonged to such a group. Mythic figures out of legends, whose exploits throughout the centuries were well known and documented, celebrated across the land.

He had watched these, these who he had considered so much stronger, so much wiser and cleverer than himself cut down one after the other, had watched Tactician curse as he was impaled by one of the enemy's swords. He had watched, in mounting horror, as Scholar's head was ripped from his shoulders, all of the centuries spent increasing his intelligence, his wisdom, amounting to nothing in that moment. He had watched as Charmer found her own talents lacking and was cut down, her once beautiful face—celebrated in the songs of thousands of bards—split at a diagonal, bloodied and bruised and lifeless as it fell to the ground.

And so one after the other they had fallen until only three remained. *"With me!"* Leader roared, and he had led them in a charge against the enemy commander. Leader had come in first, each of his blows precise and as targeted as the man himself. Soldier next, his sword in close right guard, favoring his left leg slightly from an old injury yet no less formidable for all that, his blade flashing this way and that as he protected Leader from counterattacks. And then the wanderer had come, only he had not been the wanderer then, he had been only Youngest.

He had always reckoned himself a great fighter, with a natural talent for it that none of those boys he'd grown up with in his village so long ago could have ever matched, a talent that meant that every game of knights and bandits always ended the same, with his side winning. He had gloried in that, when he was a child, enjoyed winning yes, but enjoyed also watching others lose, watching them be less than him, knowing that they could not stand against him.

That belief in himself, in his ability, had only grown more pronounced as he grew older, and even when he had gone to train under Soldier, he had been the best. Perhaps he had not shown a connection to the world around him like Oracle had hoped, or a charisma to match Charmer's expectations, but at least in his martial prowess he had told himself that he excelled. He had not just been good—he had been great. And he had grown to think he was better even than Soldier himself.

But when they attacked the enemy leader, he saw, within the first thirty seconds, just how wrong he had been. Beside the two men, he looked like nothing, looked once more like the child he had been, the child who had wielded a stick and shouted *"Yaah!"* and been so brave when fending off the evils of the world...just so long as that evil was not real, just so long as the fending off left him time to get home for supper.

They were gods in truth then, gods who fought with such speed and strength that it was difficult to believe. And yet, for all their speed, for all their strength, the enemy leader was faster, stronger. The wanderer nearly died several times in the space of that first minute, skewered or torn in half by a blow from the enemy that was too fast for even his trained senses to see, let alone follow. The only thing that kept him alive was Soldier and Leader interposing their own blades between him and death time and again.

But the enemy had noticed, and in its noticing, it revealed its cleverness. It baited Soldier by swinging its sword at the wanderer. The man took the bait, moving forward, blocking the blow, only for it to pivot and bring the blade back—easily done as it had never committed to the swing. And then Soldier was impaled, staring down in disbelief at the sword in his stomach before raising his head to regard the wanderer.

The wanderer had thought of that moment often, of Soldier, looking at him, of the way the man's mouth had moved, clearly trying to say something. He had thought of it and had wondered, over the decades, what he had meant to say. He'd decided that surely the man had meant to blame him, to tell him that it was his fault, and he would have been right to do so. But whatever it was Soldier had meant to say, he never got a chance, for another swing of the creature's sword sent his head flying from his shoulders and that was the end of him.

Then the sword had flashed out again, impossibly fast, and the wanderer stumbled away, just in time to avoid a fatal wound, instead taking a deep cut on his arm.

But Leader had not wasted the opportunity the creature's distraction had afforded him. Instead, he stepped forward, knocking the creature's blade out of its grasp. The cursed blade spun through the air, landing at the wanderer's feet. *"Take it!"* Leader had shouted. *"Run!"*

And the wanderer had done so. He had not even hesitated, thankful for the opportunity to be away from that terrible horror. He had been near the exit when something had grasped his ankle, and he had looked down at what he had thought had been the corpse of Oracle to see the woman craning her neck to look at him, not dead but dying. *"Take this, Youngest,"* she had told him, withdrawing the amulet from her neck and offering it to him with a bloody hand.

He now found his hand going up to the amulet he wore, the same amulet that Oracle had given him so many years ago.

"Wh...what is it?" he had asked her. And she had favored him with a pained smile.

"It's us," she had told him. *"It is hope. Now go."*

And he had. He had gone and leapt onto Veikr's back, had ridden away as quickly as he could, doing his best to block the sound of Leader's voice as he roared in defiance, doing his best to block the other voice, the one that was far louder, for it came from within his own mind. The voice that said he was a coward, that he had fled and left them to die when he should have died with them.

He had thought of that moment often over the years, for the shame of it had been his constant companion, always following him in his waking hours, snuggling tight against him when he slept.

He felt restless, the memories closer, hauntingly close, ghosts of his past looming around him in the dark heat of the night. They huddled tightly against him, so that it was difficult to remain on the branch, difficult even to breathe. He did his best to ignore them, those ghosts. Often, doing so would cause them to retreat into the shadowed corners of his mind. This time, though, they did not retreat. Instead, they loomed closer still, taking his silence, his lack of regard as permission or, perhaps, as a challenge. They were all around him, crushing him, and he found that he was gritting his teeth, his body tensed as if in preparation for a fight. But a man could not conquer his past, and the demons which lurked inside his mind were not ones that might be defeated, only endured, suffered until it passed.

He was still waiting for it to pass when he heard a quiet sound.

He became alert immediately, his gaze snapping up and roaming the forest, his hand drifting silently toward the handle of his sword. There might have been a thousand explanations for the sound. The rasp of a fallen leaf blown across the ground, the creak of a tree branch in a gentle breeze, or the warning groan of a limb threatening to give way beneath some squirrel or forest animal. Only, the wanderer knew, in an instant, that it had been none of these. The sound came from one thing and one thing only, could *only* come from one thing—it was the sound of a twig, like one of those which littered the forest floor, snapping underfoot.

The wanderer glanced back at the spare cloak where Dekker and his family had lain down. Ella had returned over an hour ago, perhaps two, and they all appeared to be in a deep sleep, peaceful expressions on their faces. He wondered, for a moment, when had been the last time that he had slept so peacefully. Wondered, in truth, if he ever had.

But it was a thought he quickly dismissed as he turned back to regard the forest. Some men, after all, some lives, were not made for peace. Some, like his, were fashioned for violence, for war, and that was just as well, for he knew little else.

The sound of his sword leaving its scabbard was as silent as death's whisper. He saw nothing, heard nothing, but while that might have reassured another, the wanderer had traveled long, had spent nearly his entire life being hunted, and so he knew well the signs in himself, the raising of his heart rate, the slight shallow quality to his breathing, that indicated that his subconscious had picked up on something even if he had yet to understand what that was. But in another moment, he realized what had alerted him.

Not a noise, but a lack of it. Beneath the boughs of great trees thousands of animals and insects, predators and prey, lived out their lives, and the only time such a place grew as silent as it was now, as silent as a graveyard, was when a predator approached. Death came then, stalking beneath the verdant green canopy, moving along the forest floor, laden with shadows in the moonlight. It came, and he did not need to see it to know of its approach.

After all, it had come before. Many times.

He rose silently so that his feet were beneath him, and he crouched on the balls of his feet, waiting, listening. From his vantage up in the tree, he could see much of the surrounding forest, though that only in brief snatches not covered by tree or bush. He rotated slowly, making no sound as he regarded the woods around him. In time, he heard another sound, the cracking of dry leaf underfoot, and he turned to regard the trees from whence it had come.

At first, he saw nothing, but even the lion stalking in its domain must show itself at the last moment as it rises out of the tall grass, preparing to strike. So, too, did the Revenant appear like some silent phantom out of the green. It was still some distance away from where Dekker and the others rested, too far away to see them, but in another minute, perhaps two, its methodical approach would bring it to a place to where it could not help but notice them.

The wanderer looked behind the creature but saw no more of its number. Unlike the Unseen, Revenants, from his experience, cared little for whether they hunted alone or in pairs or in great groups, and so it might well have been the only one to venture this way. There was a lot of forest to cover after all, even if the entire group that he had seen inside the city's walls had come, and he expected that they had. It was unlikely indeed that the Perishables had managed to fell one, but if they had, the wanderer expected that it would have been one and one only.

Still, he saw no more of the creatures, and while it was a risk to engage this one, he thought it a necessary one. It would not take the creature long to reach the sleeping family, and the wanderer did not need to guess what it would do when it came upon them. He knew, though, that if he meant to do it, then he had best do it silently, must be sure to end the creature before it even knew that its end had come upon it.

After all, he did not want it to alert any of its fellows that may be nearby to its whereabouts. More than that, though, the wanderer was all too aware of how the creature calling itself Soldier had taken control of the Revenant back at the nobleman's manse, when it had spoken to him, as well as the Unseen in the city. And as dangerous as the experiments of the enemy were, they were nothing when compared to the enemy themselves. It would not do for the one pretending to be Soldier to be made aware of his and the others location. They had escaped once—it was too much to hope that they might be so lucky again. Just as it was too much to hope that the creature might happen by the family without seeing them.

His course decided, the wanderer did not hesitate, for there was little time. He leapt to the next tree, to an outreaching branch, landing on it as softly as he could, using his free hand on the trunk of the tree to absorb most of the impact. Still, nearly silent was not silent, and he winced as the limb shook gently, its leaves rustling. Not much more than the sort of movement a squirrel might cause, but he tensed anyway, looking back to the Revenant. The creature, though, did not seem to have noticed and was only continuing forward on a course which would lead it if not directly to the family, close enough as to make little difference. It would be unlikely that it would see Veikr where he lay, still asleep, some distance away, but that did not matter.

The wanderer glanced over to the next tree, frowning as he saw that there was no limb within easy reach. There was one that appeared big enough to hold his weight, but it was on the side of the tree and would be difficult to reach. He considered climbing down but immediately dismissed the idea. Partly he did this because there was always a risk, however small, of losing track of the creature if he took his eyes off it. Mostly, though, it was because he thought that he would make too much sound walking across the forest floor and would inevitably alert the creature, much as it had him. Instead, he gritted his teeth, glanced back to the limb—which by some cruel magic seemed to have grown even farther away—and then did the only thing he could do.

He leapt.

At first, he was confident that he would not make it. In another moment, though, he grew sure that he would, continued to be sure until his left foot struck the very edge of the branch and immediately began to fall away. Which was bad. What was worse, though, was that his right foot missed the branch altogether, hitting the air in front of it instead. Then he wasn't jumping anymore but falling, and in silent desperation he lashed out with his free hand, grabbing hold of the limb.

He managed it just at the last moment, holding back the grunt of pain as his full weight came down on that single arm, his sword-wielding hand hanging below him. Straining with the effort of holding himself up, doing his best to ignore the small pains of the scratches along his body and his hand where he'd struck the branch, he looked around, sure that the creature must have heard.

He caught sight of it a moment later and to his shock saw that it seemed to not have been alerted to his presence. He felt a great sense of relief at that, one that lasted for another second—until he heard a rustling in the underbrush and looked over to see another of the creatures pushing its way through, oblivious to the thorns and twigs and outreaching branches which scratched it as it passed.

Another came, then another, and the wanderer frowned. Too many. It was clear, then, that somehow the creatures had marked that he and the others had come this way. He wondered for a brief instant how they had managed it before dismissing the question. The how did not matter. All that mattered was that if he and the family remained here, they would die.

He glanced back to Dekker and the others, still sleeping, unaware of the danger approaching them. The ground looked soft, covered in forest loam, and hanging closer to it as he was, there was a chance he would make little noise should he drop. The problem, of course, was that the forest floor was littered with vines and plants and leaves and there was no knowing if some twig waited beneath that loam to snap under his foot. Still, he was running out of time, the family was running out of time.

He let himself drop.

He landed softly, bending his knees to absorb the shock as well as he could, tensing in expectation of some betraying noise. But he was surprised to find that the loam held, and that the sound he'd feared did not come. He took a slow, steadying breath, and then started into the trees at a jog.

He would have liked to have moved faster, knowing that each moment squandered was one he would likely come to regret, but he dared not. He had seen several of the creatures, had a good idea of the path those at least meant to take, but that did not mean there weren't others that had escaped his notice. And should he wander into one of them, it would take but a moment for it to alert its fellows and then he, and the family he meant to protect, would be doomed.

He was treading a line then between speed and stealth, like a thief hurrying across a roof ledge, hoping that the guard roaming the street beneath him did not look up, hoping that his own balance did not give way in his haste.

But despite the many worries in his mind, he made it to the family in half a minute or less without bumping into any Revenants. He knelt, not daring to waste any time, and clamped a hand over the big man's mouth. It was enough to wake him, and Dekker struggled, only for a moment, before opening his eyes and seeing the wanderer kneeling there.

The wanderer pointed, and the big man followed his gaze where the Revenant could just be seen moving through the trees.

Dekker gave a single nod, and the wanderer let him go, motioning to the man's wife and child. While Dekker set about the task of waking his family, the wanderer rose, his gaze roaming the forest around them. The creatures were not in plain view yet, and he was confident that they had not seen him or the family, but he was also confident than they soon would.

Feeling the seconds slipping away, the wanderer turned back to check on the family in time to see Dekker standing, holding his daughter, Sarah, with her head cradled against his chest, still asleep or nearly so. Ella stood beside her husband, her face pale and scared in the moonlight.

They were all watching him, ready to follow him without complaint. The wanderer felt a mixture of contentment and unease at that, but he didn't dwell on it, just as he didn't worry about Veikr. The horse was a short distance off, perhaps still sleeping, but none of the Revenants the wanderer had seen had been moving in his direction. Anyway, the wanderer was confident that, if it came to it, Veikr could escape them easily enough.

No, Veikr could save himself—the family could not. So he gave them a nod then turned and began moving in the opposite direction from which the Revenants were coming.

He moved so that the trunks of several large trees would block them from the creatures' view and was just beginning to feel some small amount of relief, to think that they would escape without incident, when he caught a flash of movement up ahead. Some might have thought it a squirrel or the flitting wing of a bird, just some coincidence, perhaps, or an artifact of his paranoid, over-anxious mind. The problem, of course, was that the wanderer had traveled the face of the world for many years and had learned in that time that those things which men chalked up to coincidence spoke not of coincidence at all but a lack of understanding. And as for paranoia, he had never seen a man die from being too careful, but he'd seen plenty die for not being careful enough.

He hesitated then eased to a large nearby tree, motioning for the family to do the same. They did so without argument which was just as well for in another few seconds the source of the movement he'd seen revealed itself to be not a squirrel or a bird but another Revenant. This one in front of them and, worse yet, not alone, for looking closely the wanderer could see several others moving in their direction. The creatures did not seem to have caught sight of them yet, but if they remained where they were they would in less than a minute.

Gritting his teeth in frustration, the wanderer glanced behind them. He could not see the creatures which were coming from that direction, but he knew that they *were* coming just the same and soon he would be seeing far more of them than he would like.

"*Shit,*" Dekker murmured, and the wanderer could not help but nod his head in agreement. The creatures were all around them. They could not move forward without being seen, but neither could they back-track, for those behind them would surely catch sight of them if they did. Nor could they attempt to climb a tree and hide for, this close, the creatures could not help but notice. The only option then—and it was not a good one—was to try to escape between both, fleeing like a rat scurrying out from between the cat's two closing paws. Sometimes the rat escaped, it was true, but more often it got eaten.

And even if they *did* somehow make it past, there was no way of knowing if others waited up ahead. For all he knew, they might be surrounding them on all sides and in their haste—for if such an escape would have any chance of success they would have to move fast—they could stumble directly into them.

The wanderer glanced at the family then, but by the looks they gave him it was clear that they knew as well as he how much trouble they were in were counting on him and him alone to see them clear of it.

I will disappoint you, he thought as he gazed at those desperate, frightened faces. *I can only disappoint you. It is what I do. You need only ask the ghosts, and they will tell you as much.* The wanderer knew that even a lack of a decision, in such an instance as this, would be decision enough, knew that with the Revenants coming at them from both sides, any choice was better than no choice, and yet he could not see his way clear to make it.

The last hundred years of his life had been lonely, it was true, years spent alone save for Veikr, but as lonely as they had been, he had at least only been responsible for himself. The world, sure, should the enemy retrieve the cursed blade, but that had begun to matter less and less with each day that passed. In the short term, he had only needed to worry about himself and if he had failed, then he had only failed himself. Now, though, he stood to lose everything. That had always been true, of course, for a man who has little might lose little and yet still lose all that he possesses. But now, he felt that truth in a way he had not before. If he failed, they would die. And in their last moments perhaps they, likely as Soldier had done, would realize his lack of worth.

The decision needed to be made, *had* to be made, and yet he could not, no matter how hard he tried, no matter how much he felt his muscles tensing, his body trembling with the need of it. The creatures were coming, though, he could hear them now, moving through the underbrush, close enough that even their slow approach could be heard in the rustle of bushes, the crunching of grass underfoot.

Half a minute, or less, and they would be there. He decided to run for it then, along with the family, confident even as he made the decision that they would not be fast enough. It was too late, had been too late from the moment he had spotted the first Revenant from his vantage point in the tree. "With me—" he said, beginning forward then freezing as there was a great *crash* in the undergrowth, followed by a loud whinny.

The next thing he knew, a familiar white form shot in front of them, and he was left to stare in wide-eyed shock as Veikr exploded out of the undergrowth in which he'd slept, stopping twenty to thirty feet ahead. The horse turned and regarded the wanderer who realized, in an instant, what he meant to do.

The wanderer glanced to his right where the Revenants were now emerging from the wood, deviating from the path they had originally been taking to move toward the horse. A glance in the other direction showed much the same as those creatures which had been approaching from their front also started toward the horse, no doubt well aware that the beast belonged to him.

Veikr turned then, meeting the wanderer's eyes, and he felt his heart skip a beat, felt fear, *true* fear in a way that he never felt it when his own life was in danger. "*No,*" he breathed, but the horse only gave a shake of his head, as if he was saying that the wanderer could not tell him what to do.

The wanderer shook his head again, starting to rise from his crouch only to get caught as a hand clamped around his arm like a vice.

He turned to see Dekker regarding him, the big man's expression sad. Dekker said nothing, didn't move, but then he did not need to, for in looking at him the wanderer saw also his wife and his daughter, and understood well what was at risk.

And so he remained still, feeling more helpless than he had felt in a hundred years, as helpless as he had felt when Soldier had sacrificed his own life to save one of far less worth, as helpless as he had felt as he'd fled into the night with the enemy's sword, leaving his friends dead behind him.

The Revenants quickened their pace, breaking into a jog as they moved toward the horse. They often took their time, the creatures, but the wanderer knew, as Veikr did, that while they did not share the speed of the Unseen they were at least as fast as a man when they chose to be. However, the biggest difference between them and a man—or a horse, for that matter—was that the Revenants did not tire, did not stop or sleep. If anything could be said about them it was this and this only: they *continued.*

The wanderer watched, his body tense, Dekker's hand still on his arm, not meaning to stop him now but seeming to offer some comfort, as the creatures drew closer. The horse only stood, waiting until the closest were less than a dozen feet away, their swords in their hands, then Veikr turned and crashed through the undergrowth, heading back in the direction of the road.

The wanderer waited, tense, until the last of the Revenants vanished into the wall of green, then he waited some more, to be sure. Finally, he turned to meet Dekker's eyes. "Come," he said. "Veikr has risked himself to buy us time—we must take advantage of it, while we can."

"Not so great a risk though, is it?" Dekker asked, pausing when the wanderer turned back to look at him, a bit sharper than he'd meant. "What I mean," the big man said, wincing, "is that only, well, that horse of yours, he's the most capable horse I've ever seen, and I'd wager the fastest horse walkin' this world. Seems to me that it'll be an easy enough thing for him to outrun those bastards."

The wanderer nodded slowly. "And if there are more up ahead?" he asked. Dekker frowned, saying nothing to that, but the wanderer was not finished, not yet. "Or if the enemy has other Unseen, ones that he would doubtless find it worth sending after him? Veikr is fast, but in a forest with so many trees and his larger form, he could not hope to match their speed."

Dekker's face paled as he talked. "Sorry, Ungr, I...I wasn't thinking."

"Forget it," the wanderer said. "It is too late now—whatever will happen will. There is nothing to be done but to move forward." *Always to move forward.*

He started off at a jog then, the family following. They'd been going for less than a minute, though, when the night was split with Veikr screaming in what sounded like pain. The wanderer froze, his entire body going rigid. The scream cut off a moment later, and the wanderer's thoughts went wild. What had happened? Had the horse been frightened? Hurt...or worse? Had the scream ended too abruptly? The way it might if Veikr had been knocked unconscious or...no. No, he could not finish that thought, refused to finish it. Veikr was alright. He had to be. Because if he was not, neither would be the wanderer.

"Ungr?"

He spun at the sound of Dekker's voice and some part of the storm of emotions within him must have shown on his face, for the big man took an involuntary step back, raising a big arm in front of his wife and daughter as if the wanderer was a wild animal, one that might attack at any moment. It hurt, to see that, but he did his best to ignore it.

"Yes?" he asked, aware that his voice was a dry rasp.

"What...what do we do?"

The wanderer stared at the man, at his wife, watching him. Then he turned to look in the direction Veikr had gone. "There is nothing we can do but to continue," he said. "Veikr has bought us time, bought and paid for it, I think, and we will do neither him nor ourselves any favors by tarrying."

And with that, he turned and started into the woods at a jog again. Another man, in his place, might have prayed to the Eternals for Veikr's safety, but he knew enough not to. It was not that the gods had never existed—they had, the wanderer knew this as well as anyone. It was only that the gods were dead, and demons stood in their place.

And so he did not pray, nor did he dare to hope, for he knew that the world was the executioner of hope, knew from experience that it sought it out, hunted it, eager to destroy it. He only ran, and as he ran, he thought of Veikr, his friend.

They continued through the forest, running in a direction he believed parallel to the road, for he knew that the forests here, near the Untamed Lands, were deep and wild, and he dared not venture too far away from the road despite the dangers the Revenants presented. After all, as dangerous as the creatures of the enemy were, they were not the only dangers the world had to offer, far from it.

Each step he took away from Veikr, from his friend, was a special kind of torture all its own, a pain which he was forced to grit his teeth against. He did not think, only ran, for the entirety of his mind, of his *being,* was taken up replaying that scream in his head. Over and over and over again.

They had traveled for no more than fifteen minutes when the woods opened up into a small clearing. The ground in front of them went down a small hill. At the base of the hill was what appeared to be the opening to a small cave, the entrance no more than four feet high. "Remain," the wanderer said, drawing his sword.

Neither Dekker nor his wife said anything, as the wanderer walked down the hill sideways in order to keep his balance. He reached the cave and stepped inside warily, watching the shadows in case some beast had chosen to call it home. It was empty, though, and a brief search revealed that it went only half a dozen feet back. Enough to accommodate the family, then, but not much more than that.

An idea struck him. An idea that, in another moment, turned into an urge, and from an urge into a necessity. He stepped out of the cave, moving back to the family. "Come," he said.

They did, and in moments he, along with the family, were standing in front of the cave entrance. "It will be a tight fit," he said to Dekker, "but it will serve to keep you hidden well enough until I return. I will cover the front with branches."

"Return?" Dekker asked.

"Do...that is, you mean to leave us?" Ella asked.

"Only for a little while," the wanderer said.

"I'm coming with you," Dekker said.

"No, you're not," the wanderer said. "Your family needs you here." He noted the big man's troubled look at that, the woman's frightened one. "I do not believe they will find you—if I did, I would not go. You will be safe, from the Revenants, but of course you are as aware as I that there are other dangers in the forest."

Dekker grunted, giving a sour nod. "Doesn't seem right, lettin' you go off alone after all you done."

"There is no choice," the wanderer said simply.

"Go on, El," Dekker said to his wife, "go on in. I'd speak to Ungr for a moment."

The woman watched her husband for a moment then, finally nodded before turning back to the wanderer. "Good luck, Ungr. I...I hope Veikr is okay."

Hope. There was that word again. The sound of it made him scared and angry all at once. It was not just that the world sought out hope so that it might destroy it—though it did. It was also that it seemed so inadequate, so...weak. He *hoped*, when sleeping in the woods, his only roof the canopy of the trees, that it would not rain. He *hoped* that his saddle straps would hold until he made it into a new town, or that a snare he'd planted would have found a rabbit or a squirrel. He did not *hope* for Veikr to be safe. He *needed* him to be.

Still, she would not understand that, could not understand what it was like to face the possible loss of what had been your only friend for over a hundred years, and he did not have the time to try to make her, nor the inclination even if he had. So instead of answering, he simply nodded. "Thank you."

She gave him a fragile smile, glancing at Dekker once more before turning and heading into the cave with her daughter.

The big man watched them go for a moment before turning back to the wanderer. "You sure you want to do this?" he asked.

"I don't have a choice."

Dekker grunted, giving a nod. "I just wanted to say, Ungr. I appreciate everythin' you've done for us, and...I'm sorry. About Veikr, I mean."

A chill ran over his spine at that. "There's no reason to be sorry," he blurted, quicker than he'd have liked. *At least, not yet.*

"Of course," Dekker said, wincing. "Damnit. I'm not good at this sort of thing. Talkin' I mean. I just wanted to say I apologize, for treatin' you that way earlier, gettin' mad. I just...I ain't accustomed to bein' helpless, you know?"

"You get used to it," the wanderer said, giving him a small, humorless smile in order to show he meant no offense.

Dekker nodded. "Right. Well, good luck, Ungr. You'll be back soon?"

"Yes," the wanderer said. "I suspect so. But if the sun rises and I am still not here, take your family and go. Head west. Do not go south or—"

"You don't need to warn me about the Untamed Lands, Ungr," Dekker said. "I've lived in the south my whole life, been hearin' the stories since I was old enough to hear anythin' I reckon. I'm well aware of the dangers."

The wanderer nodded. "Good. That's good then." He knew that he needed to hurry, that each moment was another moment that Veikr might need his help only to find himself without it, yet the wanderer hesitated. He wanted to say something. The problem, though, was that he wasn't sure what. In the end, he only nodded again. "Good luck, Dekker."

"And to you, Ungr."

"If you would like to go into the cave with the others, I can cover it with some branches to camouflage it and—"

"Oh, I reckon I can manage that much," the big man said, giving him a small smile. "You just go on and find that horse of yours."

"Very well," he said.

Then he was running. The wanderer might have been the weakest of all the Eternals, but thanks to his training, thanks to the magics involved in him becoming one of their number, he was as different from a normal man or woman as Veikr was from a normal horse. And so, without the family to concern him, he made good time, sprinting through the trees, counting on his own instincts and quick reflexes to keep him from barreling headfirst into their trunks as he made his way toward the road.

He could not guarantee that Veikr would have continued in that direction, but he thought that likely he would have. After all, within the confines of the forest, crowded on all sides by trees and underbrush the horse would not have been able to take advantage of his great speed as much as traveling on the open road would allow. Yes. He would go to the road.

If, that is, he is still alive to go anywhere at a—

He strangled that thought quickly, cut it off and focused on moving faster, redoubling his efforts as the scream, *Veikr's* scream, replayed over and over in his mind. He was so focused on it, on it and nothing else, that he barely noticed a tell-tale feeling. A sort of tickling at his mind, his instincts telling him something was off, something was wrong. It was a feeling he'd had before, one that had saved his life and that more than once, and so, while he couldn't figure out what it was that had alerted him, he listened.

He immediately dropped into a roll and was rewarded a moment later by the *hiss* of an arrow or crossbow bolt as it flew through the air where he'd been moments before. He rolled to his feet and had time enough to get a brief glimpse of the man who'd taken a shot at him—to see that it was in fact a crossbow, the man wielding it no more than a few dozen feet away, standing so that he was mostly blocked from view by a tree. While the man bent to reload his weapon, the wanderer rolled to the side, putting his back against a tree trunk as he drew his sword. He shot a quick glance around the tree and saw the man finishing reloading. *"Over here!"* his attacker called, and the wanderer frowned.

There were others, then.

The wanderer became aware of footsteps in the trees, the snapping and cracking of twigs as the man's companions approached. He couldn't be sure, but he thought, by the sound, that there were at least three.

"Now then," the same voice, which the wanderer ascribed to the crossbowman called, "that's better. Got to be honest, I didn't expect you to come runnin' back this way, fella. Why, I reckon I 'bout shit myself when I seen you. Anyway, I appreciate you doin' our job for us. Now, why don't you just come on out, save us both some time, eh?"

"You don't want this," the wanderer called back.

There was some laughter then. "Oh, but I think I do," the man responded. "You see, there's a reward on your head, fella, and I don't mind tellin' you it's a fine one. Fine enough that me and the boys, why we're just downright eager to get our hands on it."

"The boys?" the wanderer said. "You mean your three companions?"

"That's right," the stranger said. "I can't imagine what you did to piss Soldier off, guy, and to be honest I don't much care. All I know is, the money he's offerin' as a reward on your head, well, I don't s'pose I'll be the only swingin' dick comes to collect. Not that that'll matter much to you—you see, on account of you'll already be dead.

"Four of you in total," the wanderer said.

"That's right," the man said, sounding impatient, "and what of it? There's plenty more, don't you worry, a bit further on. Searchin' for that sweet little family you been travelin' with."

The wander tensed at that. "What?"

The man laughed. "That's right. You ain't the only one on Soldier's shit list, fella. Oh, I'll admit the reward on them ain't as much as that on you, but then it's still a nice little chunk of change, plenty enough to get out of bed for anyway."

"Not that it'll matter to you," the wanderer said, gritting his teeth. "You'll be dead by then."

The man snorted. "Four on one, I reckon I like my odds good enough."

"You should have brought more men," the wanderer called, trying to buy himself a little time as he thought over his options. If what the man said was true—and considering that he thought himself at an advantage he had no reason to lie—then Dekker and his family were in trouble, not to mention the fact that Veikr's trail was growing colder and colder by the moment.

"Might have brought a few more," the stranger shouted, "only, the thing is, I really hate splitting up money, see? It's just too much of a damned inconvenience is what it is."

"I wouldn't worry about it," the wanderer answered. No sooner were the words out of his mouth than he was stepping out from behind the tree, starting toward the man and his three companions at a dead run. He'd hoped that the man would be the only one wielding a crossbow, and he was gratified to see, revealed in the moonlight as he sprinted toward them, that he was right. It took him only an instant to see that these were not city guardsmen, but street toughs, men who probably spent a fair amount of time robbing and killing others anyway, heard the town crier offer a reward on the wanderer's head and figured they'd earn themselves an easy pay day.

They would learn, though, that some rewards could never be high enough. The men gave a shout of surprise as he charged forward, for whatever they had been expecting, it had not been for him to attack. The leader bared his teeth in a grin, firing the crossbow. The wanderer leapt to the side, lashing out with his sword as he did and sending the crossbow bolt spinning into the woods.

Then he was running again.

The first tough was a giant of a man, as big as Dekker and holding a massive club that few men could lift, let alone wield. Not that it did him any good. The man had counted on his strength and given no thought to his speed, and so it was an easy enough thing for the wanderer's sword to flash out, severing the man's hand at the wrist and sending it—and the giant club it held—falling to the ground. The big man screamed, a sound that lasted for only as long as it took the wanderer to bring his blade back around, driving it up into the man's chin and further still, into his brain.

The man's entire body went rigid, and the wanderer jerked his blade free. Before the body had finished falling he was moving again, charging toward the next man who let out a scream that was a mixture of anger and fear, swinging the rusted sword he held in a wild, unpracticed swing. Perhaps such a swing might have worked on most men and women—if only because they had even less experience with weapons and life-or-death situations than the street tough, but then the wanderer was not like most men.

He had spent most of his life fighting to keep it, and the truth was he knew little else. His sword flashed out, catching the other man's sword on his own. Instead of bringing his blade back around, he stepped into the man's guard, his free hand going to his waist and drawing the small knife he kept there. A short blade, one that was more for utility than combat, but he kept it sharp and so it served well enough, slicing across the man's throat. Blood sluiced out of the rent in the man's flesh, splashing onto the wanderer even as he moved past the stumbling man, dead already, his body just not quite aware of it.

The wanderer stalked toward the leader of the group then, the man hissing curses under his breath as he fought to reload his weapon. The wanderer might have told him not to bother, for he did not have the time. Instead he said nothing, raising his sword to strike. But just then his instincts, honed to a razor-fine edge over the years, kicked in, and he felt more than heard someone approaching him from the side.

It didn't take much effort to figure out who it might have been, so the wanderer immediately leapt to the side. Even as he did, he heard an angry growl, followed quickly by a scream, and he spun to see that, indeed, what he had sensed had been the third man approaching while he was focused on the leader. The man had swung at him with a two-handed strike, aiming for the wanderer's back. But since the wanderer no longer stood where he had, the weapon had only sliced through air instead. At least, that was, until the blade buried itself in the crossbowman's chest.

The crossbowman staggered back, staring in shock at the sword in his chest, taking it with him as he stumbled and fell. Which left the man who had attacked the wanderer weaponless. A much younger version of the wanderer might have left the man alive, feeling as if to attack him now, with him being weaponless, might be unsporting, perhaps even cruel. But the wanderer was not that man anymore. Years spent on the run had taught him that while mercy might be well and good in its place, it could also get a man killed. The easiest way to ensure that a threat to one's life was taken care of was to destroy it.

And so he did, lunging forward, his blade leading. The man, still staring in shock at the crossbowman, his leader, who he had so badly wounded, didn't even notice until the blade entered. But the strike was true, and he had only time enough to let out a soft, bewildered groan before collapsing, dead, onto the ground.

The wanderer pulled his sword free then, turning to regard the leader who stared at him wide-eyed from where he lay on the ground. "P-p-please," he stammered, all traces of his easy confidence gone now—facing certain death had a way of stealing a man's bravado. He dragged himself backward across the ground, wheezing and gasping, the sword still half-stuck into his chest. "P-please, don't kill me."

"You're dead already," the wanderer said as he walked after him. "Your man saw to that. That deep of a wound, you'd likely be dead even if there was a healer nearby, and there is not."

"B-but you could t-take me back to the c-city."

"I could," the wanderer agreed, "but I won't. Anyway, you would likely die before we ever reached it in any case. Now, how many men did you send deeper into the forest?"

"F-f-four. N-now p-p-please, help m—" The man cut off as the wanderer's blade took him in the heart, his eyes went wide for a moment, as if in surprise, and then he slumped to the ground, dead.

"It is the only help I can give you," the wanderer told the dead man. He knelt and cleaned his blade on the corpse's shirt before sheathing it again, then he rose, glancing back in the direction he'd come and then onward. One way was toward Veikr, the other the family. He gritted his teeth, torn with indecision, much as he had been when the Revenants had surrounded the family.

And how had that turned out? he asked himself.

But knowing that indecision would cost him did nothing to help him decide. Veikr was his friend, the only friend he'd had for over a hundred years. Meanwhile, he had only known Dekker and his family for a matter of weeks. A person who didn't know better would have said that Veikr was only a horse, but then that person would have been a fool, for Veikr was much more than that. Was more, in truth, than just a friend.

Despite this, though, the wanderer found his gaze drifting back toward the tree line, in the direction of the family. Dekker was a strong man, powerful, and the wanderer would have given him good odds against anyone save those who had been highly trained in the arts of war. The street toughs, of course, hadn't been. The problem, though, was that if what the man had told him was true, there wasn't one of them but four, and worse yet, it seemed all too easy to think that they might slip up on Dekker and his family unawares.

Between the family or Veikr, he thought that the horse stood a far better chance of escaping any sort of danger he might be in. Which, in the end, made his decision for him. With a frustrated hiss, the wanderer turned and sprinted back toward where he'd left the family.

He moved a fast as he was able through the woods, pushing his body to its limits. He was drawing near the spot where he'd left them, or so he believed, when a roar broke the relative silence of the night. A man's voice and one he recognized as belonging to Dekker.

Please, he thought desperately, *don't let me be too late.*

He had thought he was running as fast as he could, but as it turned out, he had just a little bit more speed left in him after all, and he called on it in that moment. Foolish, perhaps, to go charging blindly forward with no idea of what lay ahead. Certainly it was not in keeping with the lessons he'd received from Tactician, the man who had always pointed out the importance of having a plan, of sticking to that plan, of weighing all your options and making a considered, intelligent choice.

The wanderer knew he was making a mistake, making what might well end up being a fatal one, but he could do nothing else. The thought of something happening to the family was more than he could bear. And so he ran.

In another moment he exploded out of the woods and into the small clearing where the cave sat. The opening was facing the opposite direction and so he could not see anything of the family. He scanned the clearing quickly, though, and in the moonlight, he caught sight of a giant, shadowed form that could only be Dekker. Another shadow lay crumpled at the big man's feet while a third faced off against him, the two circling each other.

The wanderer started forward, meaning to help the big man who seemed to be favoring one of his legs, when suddenly he caught sight of a metallic shimmer off to his right in the treeline. The wanderer spun, narrowing his eyes. The man was well-hidden, blending in with the undergrowth so that, at first, the wanderer did not see him. After a moment, though he found him. But it was not the man which caught his gaze and held it. Instead, it was the crossbow the man held, the one he was currently pointing at the two men, no doubt waiting for Dekker to move around so that he could get a clear shot on the big man, one that wouldn't risk hurting his companion instead.

The wanderer knew that the man might fire at any moment, so he started sprinting in the crossbowman's direction. Even as he did, though, he saw the man tensing, preparing to fire. So the wanderer did the only thing he could think to do—he gave a loud shout. The crossbowman, who had not expected that, started, spinning toward him and firing at the same time so that the bolt went far wide of its mark, shooting off into the forest somewhere between where Dekker fought his opponent and where the wanderer was running.

The crossbowman fumbled at his crossbow, trying to get it loaded again, and he was still trying to do that when the wanderer was on him. He kicked the weapon out of the man's hands then jerked him up by the front of his tunic, slamming his back against the tree he'd been standing beside.

The crossbowman let out a grunt of pain, one that quickly turned into a scream as the wanderer buried his sword in the man's stomach. Then he gave the blade a jerk, dragging it upward, and the man's scream cut off as he died.

The wanderer pulled his blade free and started toward where Dekker and the other man in fight just in time to see the big man lift the other over his head and bring him crashing down to the ground, headfirst, the unfortunate man's neck folding at an unnatural angle that left no doubt that it was broken.

The wanderer could not make out much in the poor light, but he saw the big man stagger after that then fall to his knees.

He rushed forward, kneeling beside him. "What is it?"

"Ungr," Dekker hissed, "you're back."

"Yes. Where are you hurt?"

"It...it's my leg. The first bastard got in a lucky swipe on me, but I'll be alright. Go on—go see about Sarah and El. I'll be along directly."

The wanderer hesitated. He could not tell in the darkness how bad it was, but he could see blood on the man's pants leg, on the ground beneath him too, blood that looked black in the poor light. The big man gave him a tired shove. "Go on, please. Check on 'em for me."

The wanderer gave a nod and turned, drawing his knife in his free hand as he started toward the cave. He was still moving toward the cave entrance when he heard a scream.

"Get back!" A woman's voice, one he recognized and then, a moment later, it was followed by a grunt of pain.

"You bitch," growled a man's rough voice, sounding clearly in pain. *"I'll kill you for that."*

The wanderer stepped into the cave entrance to see that Ella was backed up against the cave wall, Sarah, her little girl, cowering behind her. And in front of them, between them and the wanderer, was a man. In one hand he held a knife. The other was currently clamped to his head where blood was leaking out from a nasty wound. The wanderer noted these things in a moment, just as he noticed that Ella's shirt was ripped, and it did not take much of an imagination to figure out why that might be.

"Seems to me that was your plan anyway, wasn't it?" the wanderer asked calmly. "To kill her, I mean."

The man let out a grunt of surprise, spinning to face the wanderer. "Who the fuck are you?" he demanded.

"That is a bit of a story, and I'm afraid you simply don't have the time to hear it."

The man snarled, rushing toward him. The wanderer watched him come, waiting until the last moment before stepping to the side, ducking under the man's wide swing of his knife. He let his sword go, grabbing the wrist of the hand wielding the knife and brought the man's forearm down even as he drew his knee up. There was a loud *crack,* and the man screamed in pain as his forearm snapped.

The wanderer wasn't done though, his mind not on the man at all but on Dekker—hurt, that much was sure, though how much only time would tell—and on the way Ella's shirt had been torn. He brought his foot down at an angle into the side of the man's knee and there was a loud *pop.* The man screamed louder as his legs gave way beneath him, and he fell to his knees.

The wanderer grabbed a handful of the man's tangled hair, lank with sweat, and slammed his head back against the cave wall.

The man cried out again. *"Please, wait,"* the man said, but the wanderer had no intentions of waiting. Instead, he held the man's head up with his free hand as he slammed the blade through the man's eye, driving it so deep that the leather-wrapped handle fetched up against the bones of the man's face.

His opponent's entire body went rigid, and the wanderer stood there for a moment, regarding him, his chest heaving not just from his exertions but from his anger, too. The blade made a sickening *squelch* as he pulled it free, and the man stayed there for a moment, wavering back and forth, as if his death had come upon him so quickly that it was taking his body a minute or two to catch up. But in another moment, the body collapsed at the wanderer's feet, and he turned to the family.

Ella took a step away from him, a nervous look on her face as she buried her daughter's face in her skirt, the sort of look a person might give to a ravenous wolf they had just watched finish its meal as it turned its bloody muzzle to them.

The look was gone in another instant, though, so quick that the wanderer could have almost convinced himself that he'd imagined it. Almost.

While one of her hands was on her daughter's back, Ella's other still clutched a large stone—the blood staining it marking it as the one she'd used to hit her attacker. But as she stared at the wanderer, the hand holding the stone began to tremble, and she let it drop. "H-h-he came at me," she said, swallowing hard. "S-so I hit him."

She was in shock—that much was clear. It was pretty common when people not normally accustomed to violence were suddenly faced with it. The real question was whether she was in shock because of the man who had attacked her or because of the man who had meant to save her. The wanderer thought, as she stared at him, that he probably didn't want to know the answer.

"You did good," he said and then, as the little girl slowly turned her tear-soaked face away from her mother to face him, "you both did." He raised his gaze to meet Ella's eyes then. "Keep her here—I will return."

"P-please," Sarah said, her little eyes brimming with tears, "y-you can't leave us."

"It's fine, Sarah girl," Ella said, picking her up and holding her tightly against her chest, "everything's alright. Ungr needs to go check on Daddy, that's all."

The wanderer gave her a nod, wondering at the eagerness in her voice, as if she was excited at the prospect of getting rid of him. Not that he could blame her. It was one thing to have a monster save you from another by killing it. It was quite another to have that monster stick around when the killing was done. Monsters got hungry, after all, and even children, perhaps *especially* children, knew well what monsters liked to eat.

He turned and walked out into the night. It didn't take him long to locate Dekker. The big man had dragged himself a dozen or so feet over to a tree, where he'd propped up against it. It was not difficult to find him, not with the trail of blood he'd left in the grass. As he hurried to him, the wanderer saw that the big man's eyes were closed, and his heart skipped a beat. "Dekker?"

At first, the big man didn't answer, and the wanderer was gripped by the thought, the *certainty* that he was too late. Then, slowly, the big man's eyes came open, his head turning toward the wanderer with a loose, unstable quality he didn't like, the way a drunk might look, or a puppet. "Ungr?" he asked in a slurred voice, narrowing his eyes. "That you?"

"It's me," the wanderer said, wasting no more time as he leaned forward and examined the man or, more specifically his leg. It didn't take long to find the source of the wound—a deep cut along the front of the man's thigh.

"How bad is it?" Dekker asked.

"It's not good."

"Did...did I get an artery?" the big man asked. "I...I heard that you got to watch for that, you know, if you get wounded or—"

"No artery," the wanderer said quickly, drawing his knife, so recently used to kill the man attacking Dekker's wife and child, and wiped it on his trouser leg. That done, he began to cut away Dekker's trousers so that he could reveal the wound better.

"How...how can you be sure?" the big man asked in a sleepy voice the wanderer did not like.

"Because you'd be dead already," the wanderer said. "Now stop talking and let me concentrate."

He finished cutting away the rest of the man's trouser leg, then tossed it aside.

"Damn," Dekker muttered, "those were my favorite pair of pants."

The wanderer ignored him, examining the wound. A nasty gash, one that didn't reach the bone but that the wanderer figured wasn't all that far from it either. Blood still oozed from the wound, and Dekker grunted in pain as he pressed hard against it with the palms of both of his hands.

The wanderer had learned some bit of healing over the years—hard not to when you were being hunted by creatures out of nightmares and couldn't go to a healer when you received wounds for fear that they would ask questions, that they might wonder what would leave such claw or bite marks. And so he had been forced to learn how to patch himself up. He had never suffered a wound as bad as this, though, and the truth was that he was out of his depth. Which left one choice.

The ghosts.

He did not want to speak to them, for he was confident that they would have nothing kind to say. But Dekker was dying, and he could not let that happen, *would* not.

He opened the amulet.

Immediately, he was struck with a deluge of voices, not as if twelve spoke at once but as if hundreds did, as if he was haunted by an army of phantoms, all of them disappointed and eager to share their disappointment.

"*Shut up,*" he hissed angrily.

"What's that?"

The voice was not that of one of the ghosts but instead belonged to Dekker, the big man eyeing him strangely. "I was not talking to you," the wanderer said.

"Then who—"

"Save your strength," the wanderer told him. "You will need it."

Then, "Healer," he said as the big man's eyes drifted closed, "I need you."

Youngest, a voice said, but it was not Healer's—instead it was that of Leader. *You cannot linger here. These men were just the beginning. There might well be more and, failing that, there is still the Revenants to think of.*

"I will not leave him," the wanderer said. "Now, will you help me or not?"

Silence then for several moments, and the wanderer began to despair, thinking that the big man would die and he would be able to do nothing about it. In another moment, though, Leader finally spoke. *Very well, Youngest, but you are making a mistake.*

"It is my mistake to make."

Help him, Healer, Leader said, his normally confident, benevolent voice betraying his annoyance. *If you can.*

Youngest? A woman's voice, soft and kind and even in that single word she spoke the wanderer felt some of his anxiety, his fear for the man give way. The woman had earned her name, not just for healing the flesh but the mind, the heart and the soul of those who came to see her.

"I'm here," he said.

This will require a Sojourn. Are you sure you wish to—

"Yes."

Very well.

The wanderer closed his eyes. He did not start by imagining the room. Instead, he started by imagining the door, a door which would lead her into his being, his body and his mind. He swung it wide even as the room began to form around him. She stood there, looking the same as she had the last time he'd seen her, save without the wound that had taken her life. In appearance, she was a woman who seemed to be in her early thirties, beautiful but in a sort of ethereal, natural way that was far removed from Charmer's beauty, a beauty that seemed sharp and precise, deadly and tempting all at the same time.

"Hello, Youngest," she said, giving him a small smile, as if she understood all of his pain, all of his heartache, understood it in a way no one should be able to.

"Hello, Healer," he said. "Please. Come in."

"You are ready, then?"

"Yes."

She inclined her head then stepped across the threshold. Immediately, a jolt went through his body as his control of himself was taken over. It hurt far less with her than it did with the other ghosts, felt far less as if he was ripped away from himself, but it did still hurt. Still, he would accept that pain gratefully, would accept far worse if that was what was needed to ensure that Dekker survived.

So he did his best to hold onto himself, to his identity, an identity that felt like it was blowing away, piece by ragged piece, under the strength of some great wind.

Hold on, Youngest, she told him, the words reverberating in his mind, *I will be as quick as I can.*

The wanderer had been in countless fights, had trained for years and years to become the swordsman that he was, the warrior that he was. A warrior of grace and poise, of speed and strength, and yet watching through his eyes, as the woman worked, he felt...inadequate. Grossly incompetent. For as she worked, cleaning the wound, filling it with a poultice, then stitching it closed, there was not a single wasted movement, nothing frivolous or to no purpose. His hands, with Healer controlling them, moved with an exactness, a confidence that was only possible because of the mind using them, a mind which had spent centuries at its trade and had perfected it—or if not perfected it, had come as close to it as anyone ever would.

He lost track of time as he watched, at once terrified for Dekker and feeling somehow privileged to be able to witness it, the same way a man might feel privileged to witness a master sculptor at his trade. Eventually, Healer sat back, her hands coated in Dekker's blood. *I am finished,* she said, sounding exhausted. *Now, I will give you back to yourself.*

A shudder ran through his body as she stepped out of the door in his mind, and a moment later the room and the door vanished, and he was alone within his mind once more.

"Will...will he live?" he asked quietly, staring down at the big man. Dekker had fallen unconscious at some point during Healer's ministrations.

He will live, she answered, and no sooner were the words out of her mouth than the wanderer felt a great wave of relief wash over him.

"That...that is good. Thank you."

He staggered then, his body and mind both exhausted, as they always were after a Sojourn, and he half sat, half collapsed onto the ground in front of where Dekker still sat propped against the tree.

"Is...is he okay?"

The wanderer turned, surprised to find Ella and her daughter behind him, both of them looking terrified. They looked as if they had been standing there for several minutes.

"He's fine," the wanderer said. "Or...well, he *will* be fine," he went on, glancing back at Dekker. "He is strong."

"You don't have to tell me that much. Thank you, Ungr," she said.

He gave a shake of his head. "It's nothing."

"No," Ella said, "it isn't. But...did you find Veikr?"

"No."

She nodded sadly. "Well...thank you. For coming back. If you hadn't..." She shook her head, bringing a hand to her mouth, close to tears, he could see. Just as he could see that she was doing everything that she could to hold on, to be brave for her daughter so that her daughter didn't have to be.

"Everything's alright," he said. "He will sleep now. Why don't the two of you lie with him?"

"But...but don't you think that we should leave?" she asked.

In fact, he did think that, but he also knew that there was no way they would be able to move the big man for long, at least not without some preparation first, so he shook his head, giving her the best reassuring smile he was capable of just then which, in truth, wasn't much. "We'll be fine—I will keep watch. You should focus on getting as much rest as you can—we will have a long day tomorrow."

She gave a humorless laugh. "Rest. I doubt it," she said. Still, she picked up her daughter, cradling her against her. "But we'll try." She turned and walked toward Dekker and, in another few moments, mother and daughter were lying beside the unconscious man. And despite her words, within five minutes both Ella and her daughter were asleep. No surprise, that. They had slept little in the last several nights and when a person experienced shock such as they had the mind often strove for sleep as a means of escape.

The wanderer left them then to their escape. After all, there were things he needed to be about. First, he walked a perimeter around their small camp, taking his time, listening for any movement in the forest, searching for any sight or sound that might alert him to others coming toward them, slipping through the darkness.

He also took the time to scatter small limbs and dry leaves across the perimeter where there were none so that should anyone approach, it would be near impossible for them to do so without his hearing it. That done, he set about using his sword to hack off several larger tree limbs. Then he used the knife to shave off the bark, rounding out the edges to create what would serve as the two supports of a simple, makeshift travois.

Next, he gathered some of the vines clinging to the trees, pulling them apart and testing their strength. When he was satisfied that he had enough, he brought it all back to the top of the small rise above the cave, so that he might keep an eye on the sleeping family while he worked.

Then he set about the task of lashing the vines across the supports, tying them first to one, then the other so that they formed a sling in which the big man might be laid. He used as much vine as he thought necessary, then he doubled it, to be sure. He was still at the task when he noted one of the sleeping figures shifting, watched it slowly rise and move toward him.

She looked even younger than she was, in the moonlight, rubbing at her eyes, her long golden locks bouncing about her shoulders. The wanderer watched the little girl walk toward him, his hands busily at work all the while. In time, she came to stand within a few feet of him, saying nothing.

"Hello," he said.

"Hi, Mister Ungr."

"Were you not able to sleep?"

She shook her head but said nothing.

The wanderer shifted awkwardly, busying himself with continuing to work on the travois. He knew little of children, for he had never had any of his own, nor any close relatives that had been younger than him growing up and with whom he might have practiced. And so he was unsure of what was expected of him. Normally, he was good with silence, found it, in general, far preferable than the conversations so many men and women felt the need to keep up, as conversations that more often than not meant nothing and amounted to nothing. Even the speakers themselves often seemed not to care what they said, only cared that they filled the silence, as if silence were something to *be* filled, something that *needed* filling.

The truth was that people feared silence. Feared it the same way they feared the darkness. For in the darkness anything might lurk, any demon or banshee, any twisted thing which might pop up and reveal itself. People looked at silence much the same. They used their words the way a man, venturing into the night, might use a torch, holding it aloft, using it to banish the shadows. Pushing away the dark with light the way those words pushed away the emptiness of the silence. A silence that, if left alone, might be filled with something else, *anything* else, and so men and women sought to fill it themselves and, in that way, control it. The same way they hung lanterns at regular intervals along shadowed alleyways and dark city streets in an effort—albeit a vain one—to control the darkness.

But, as the wanderer glanced up from his work at the girl who only stood, saying nothing, just watching him, he decided that perhaps people were not born to hate silence as he had always thought. Perhaps, instead, they grew to hate it, were taught to hate it over the years. But if that were true, then it was clear that whatever lesson imparted that hatred for the quiet, the girl had yet to receive it, for she seemed completely comfortable only standing there.

And despite his love for silence, despite his thoughts on the matter, the wanderer found himself inclined to fill it, found himself trying to think of something, of anything to say. "He'll be okay," he said finally. "Your dad, I mean."

"I know," she said, but it wasn't the sort of "I know" that one expected to hear in such a situation, the sort that someone might say and not really believe. Instead, it was as if the girl took for granted that her father would be okay, that he would always be okay. That, too, the wanderer decided, that faith that things would work out, was something that adults lost as they got older. As a girl or a boy aged, after all, the real world asserted itself, and that simple faith gave way to a complicated sort of practicality at best and, at worst, to faith of another kind, faith that things would *not* work out, that the worst would always happen.

He nodded, unsure of how to answer that, so he turned back to his work. "I'm building a stretcher," he said, "something to carry your dad on."

"I know."

He winced, deciding that while he was bad with all people, he was especially terrible with children. He opened his mouth to say something else, hoping that he might be inspired when he did so. He wasn't, though, so in another moment he closed it again, clearing his throat and resuming his task.

She walked up to him then, and he watched out of the corner of his eye as she sat down on the hill beside him. For a time she only sat there, saying nothing, the only sound that of the crickets of the forest, the rasp of the vines as he snaked them in and out of the two supports, lashing them tighter.

Finally, she spoke. "Do you think Veikr's okay?"

A surge of emotion welled up inside the wanderer at the thought of his horse, his friend, and in that moment he, like so many others before him who had sought to see the silence filled, decided that the silence had been better than that which filled it. "I don't know," he said honestly.

She nodded at that, seeming to deflate, her head hanging low, and he winced, thinking that it had been the wrong thing. It was the truth—but sometimes, most times, really, the truth could be painful. "But I hope he is," he said.

She nodded again. "So do I. I love him."

He smiled in the darkness. "So do I." He took a slow, deep breath. "But Veikr is strong," he said, beginning to recount for her the same reasons he had used in an attempt to comfort himself. "He is strong, and he is fast. They would not catch him."

Assuming, of course, that there had been no Unseen with the Revenants or that other Revenants had not been lying in wait. But saying that would do no good, not for him and not for her, so he left the words unsaid.

"He *is* strong," she agreed. "Very strong."

"Yes."

"And handsome too. He's a pretty boy."

The wanderer smiled at the thought of how Veikr might respond being called a "pretty boy," but the smile quickly faded as he considered that there was a chance—a fairly good one—that he would never see his friend again. "Yes, he is," he managed. *Is. Not was. Please not was.*

"Are you Daddy's friend?"

The abrupt change of topic took the wanderer off-guard, and he turned, looking at the girl. "What?"

"His friend. You know. Like me and Emma Sue. She used to live close to us before..." She cut off, shaking her head. "Anyway, she's my friend. We play dollies and princesses. Are you friends with Daddy like that?"

"Maybe not *quite* like that," the wanderer said.

She nodded, a serious expression on her face. "I see."

"Still," he ventured, "I would like to think that we're friends. Certainly, it would be my honor. Your dad is a good man. Your mom, she's a good woman, too."

"I know," she said. "But I thought Daddy could use a friend. He's lonely, I think...since my grandpa..." She cut off then, leaving the rest unsaid. She turned to him. "Have you been lonely before?"

I have been little else, he thought. "Yes."

"So you need a friend too."

"Yes."

She smiled. "Good. You and Daddy, you can be each other's friends then."

He grinned. "Do you think he'll have me?"

"Sure," she said. "Daddy is nice."

He grunted a laugh at that, nodding. "Yes, he is."

"Mom's nice too," she went on. "Only...she worries too much."

"Oh?" the wanderer said, because he was unsure of what else he might say.

The little girl nodded. "She worries about me, about Da. She worried about Grandpa, too, only...anyway. She worries about everything."

He nodded in return. "It's something that happens, when you get older. You start to worry."

"But why?" she asked. "It doesn't help...does it?"

The wanderer blinked, suddenly unsure of how to answer that. *It doesn't help, does it?* "No," he said finally, "no, it doesn't." After all, worrying about Veikr would not see his friend safe, that much was sure.

"Then why do grownups do it?"

He thought of Veikr, his friend for so many years. "Because...because I think when you get something fine, really, truly fine in your life...like—"

"Like cake?"

He grinned. "Sure. Like cake. Anyway, when you get something fine—like cake—then you worry, you know? You worry that somebody might come along and take it from you, or that you might drop it...something like that."

"*I* don't," she said. "I just eat it. That's what cake's for. I'm going to go sleep. I'm tired. Goodnight, Mister Ungr."

"Goodnight, Sarah."

She started away, then paused, glancing back at him. "Veikr will be back, Mister Ungr. I know it."

"Oh?" he asked. "How do you know?"

She shrugged. "Because I have to know something. So I know he'll be back." She turned without another word, starting back to where her parents slept.

The wanderer watched her, thinking that there were many kinds of wisdom in the world. Wisdom like that of Leader, a confident, high-minded sort of wisdom. But there were other types, too, like Felden Ruitt's earthy, practical wisdom and, perhaps, the greatest of all—the wisdom of a child.

The funny thing, he decided, as Sarah lay down with her mother and father, was that when the girl had first approached him, he had meant to try to make her feel better, to give her what comfort he could regarding their situation. In the end, though, it was she who had given him comfort.

He felt better. Veikr was still missing, but the wanderer felt better. After all, Veikr was no poor, helpless animal. He was the greatest living horse, the last of an ancient breed, known for its power and strength, its courage and cleverness.

He took a slow, deep breath, then set about the task of finishing the travois. When it was done, he considered waking the others and getting started. After all, night might serve to help hide their movements from prying eyes. In the end, though, he decided against it, for while the darkness might conceal them, it would also conceal any who waited in ambush, and by now there was no telling how many or of what type of creature the enemy posing as Soldier had set after them. They might be anywhere, waiting, watching, and he knew that some of those creatures the enemy employed could see in the darkness as well as any beast.

Besides, he thought that the family needed their rest, Dekker in particular. Healer had assured him that the big man would live, but she had also warned him that he would be weak, and that he needed rest. After all, there was no better healer than sleep, that much even the wanderer knew.

And so he did not trouble them, for he had passed enough nights and seen enough sunrises to know that tomorrow would bring troubles of its own.

CHAPTER FIVE

He waited until the sun began to creep above the horizon, pale morning light once more resuming its never-ending struggle against the shadows. Then he rose from where he had spent the night watching over the family and thinking of Veikr and made his way to where the three still slept.

He did not wake them, at least not at first. Instead, he bent to examine the big man's wound, removing the bandages and sniffing it to see if he could detect, by sight or smell, any sign of infection. When he was satisfied that the wound was clear of any such infection, he walked to where he'd laid his pack and retrieved some water. He then set about cleaning the wound once more of what dried blood was there, as well as the herbs he—or Healer, using his body—had applied. When it was done, he repacked the poultice and began bandaging the wound.

He became aware of being watched while he was still working on the bandage. He took his time, pulling it tight and tying it off. When he was finished, he looked up to see the big man staring at him, an expression on his face that the wanderer could not place, though he could see some great storm of emotion in the man's eyes. So intense did that emotion seem that the wanderer half-expected the big man to leap forward in an attack—at least as much of a leap as a man might manage when he'd taken a deep wound to his thigh.

Dekker's face seemed to tremble with the effort of containing that emotion, the muscles of his jaw writhing beneath his skin. The wanderer said nothing, only waited for the man to say or do what he would. In the end, though, Dekker did not attack, nor did he curse the wanderer or shout him down as he half-expected. Instead, the big man turned to regard his wife and daughter, both still sleeping, before turning back. As he did, the wanderer noted something he had not expected—namely, a tear that had begun to wind its way down the leathery skin of the big man's face.

"Mornin'," the big man said.

"Good morning," the wanderer replied.

Dekker's jaw worked for a minute, as if he had something he wanted to say but was finding it difficult to get the words out. "Listen, Ungr," he said, his voice a low growl, "I ain't...that is, I ain't good at this sort of thing."

"It's okay," the wanderer said.

"No. Naw, it ain't," the big man disagreed. "I need you to know, I'm thankful for what you did, comin' back. If it wasn't for you..." He trailed off, his gaze drifting toward his family, still sleeping, a look of such naked love and vulnerability on his face that the wanderer found it difficult to look upon, a pure love that he felt as if he might tarnish simply by being near, simply by seeing it. "Fact is I'm a fool, Ungr," the big man said, "though not so big a fool that I don't know it. Just as I know enough to know that, if you hadn't come back, me and my family...well. I know what you done, that's all, what you did for us, and I know what it cost you too. Know that you had to give up lookin' for your horse to save us. And I just wanted to say thanks. And to say...well, that I'm sorry."

"Sorry?" the wanderer asked. "For what?"

The big man sighed. "As I said, Ungr, I'm a fool. And the way I acted, on the road...you were right, in sayin' I shouldn't have waited. It's just...as I told you, I ain't accustomed to bein' helpless, that's all. Can't say as I much care for it."

The wanderer gave him a small smile at that. "Neither do I."

Dekker snorted. "You, helpless? Forgive me if I disagree with you, Ungr, but from where I'm sittin', you seem like pretty much the most capable fella in the world."

The wanderer shook his head, thinking of Leader, of Soldier, of all the other Eternals too, all far better than him, far more worthy.

He meant to answer the man, but he found that he did not have the words, just then to do it.

"It's fine work, that is. I don't know much about that sort of craftsmanship, but even I can see that. Is it special?"

The wanderer didn't realize at first what the man meant until he came to the realization that, as he'd thought of the Eternals, he'd begun fingering the amulet about his neck. "You'd be surprised just how special."

The big man watched him for a minute. "Don't know about that, Ungr. I'd say I'm just about all surprised out."

The wanderer nodded, thinking that the man was lucky to think that. After all, the world, in his experience, always had another surprise waiting around the corner, and those surprises, when they came, were rarely good ones.

"Well?" Dekker asked.

"Well what?" the wanderer said.

The big man grunted, grinning. "Where I'm from, it's polite to say 'you're welcome,' somebody thanks you."

The wanderer winced. "Listen, Dekker, I really don't deserve—"

"Enough of that," Dekker said. "I won't hear it. You deserve far more than thanks, Ungr, but as that's all I'm in a position to give just now, I'll insist you take it, alright?"

The wanderer nodded. "Right. Well…you're welcome."

The big man snorted a laugh. "I've seen you face down creatures out of nightmare, Ungr, a few different times now, and you seem more comfortable at that than acceptin' thanks."

"Practice, I suppose."

Dekker raised an eyebrow. "Was that a joke, Ungr?"

He gave the big man a grin. "As close as I come, anyway."

Dekker nodded slowly. "Might be you ought to keep at your own job, leave the jokes to the bards."

"Speaking of my work," the wanderer said, grinning, "we had best be leaving soon. We have evaded Soldier's troops so far, but he will not stop looking for us."

"You seem awful sure of that."

The truth was the wanderer was surer of that than he was just about anything. Was more confident that he knew his enemies and their will, their minds far better than he knew anyone else's. And why not? After all, he had spent the last hundred years being chased by them. He only shrugged though.

Dekker seemed to read some of his thoughts in the simple gesture though, for the big man nodded. "I don't mean to question you, Ungr, not so soon after you've saved my and my family's lives, anyway, and that more than once. If you say it's time to go, I reckon it is. Only, give me a minute to wake my girls and—"

"That won't be necessary."

The two men turned to look at the woman and daughter, both with their eyes open, small smiles on their faces. After a moment, Dekker spoke. "Wait just a damned minute," he said. "Do you mean to tell me that you two have been lyin' there pretendin' to be asleep?"

"For a little while," Ella admitted.

Dekker grunted, turning to the wanderer with a look of outrage on his face. "You believe this?"

The wanderer, who had become aware when the two had woken from the changes in their breathing, only smiled.

The big man shook his head, turning back to his wife and daughter. "And just why on earth did you feel the need to pretend to be asleep and eavesdrop?"

"Well, how else are we supposed to make sure that the two of you don't act like complete fools?" Ella challenged.

"*Fools?*" Dekker sputtered.

"Sure, why not?" Ella asked. "After all, you said it yourself, didn't you? Besides, I know how you men are about sharing your feelings, as if having any genuine emotion is somehow a crime, so I thought perhaps it would be best if you were allowed to get on with it in your own, pitiful, stumbling ways."

"It's a damn good thing you're pretty, lass," Dekker said, his face twisting in a mock frown. "And what about you, little one?" Dekker asked. "You think your daddy's a fool too?"

"Only a little," Sarah said, grinning widely then bursting into laughter as Dekker began to tickle her. The wanderer was unaware of the smile on his face until Ella turned to glance at him, raising an eyebrow as if to say *I told you so,* no doubt referencing that Dekker would move past his anger. The wanderer nodded his head to her, a duelist acknowledging a point, and she grinned before turning back to her family.

"Alright, you two," she said, "we need to get moving."

"Fine, alright," Dekker said. "Ungr, you mind givin' me a little help up? Not sure I can stand on my own, though once I get goin' I'm sure I'll be alright."

"You most certainly will *not* stand, Dekker," Ella snapped.

Dekker raised an eyebrow. "My lovely wife, I don't think there's much of a choice. Not, that is, unless you all intend to roll my ass down the road, and I don't imagine that'd be fun for anybody involved."

"Not roll," the wanderer said, "drag."

The big man turned to him, frowning. "What's that supposed to mea—" he began, but cut off as the wanderer stepped out of the way to reveal the travois he'd fashioned the night before.

"You can't be serious," the big man groaned.

"Majesty," the wanderer said with a mock bow, "your carriage awaits."

Dekker did not go into the travois with good humor but, after several minutes of grunting, cursing, sweating work, he *did* go in.

And then the work began in earnest.

CHAPTER SIX

It was noon, the sun directly overhead, when the wanderer finally slowed, allowing the sled upon which Dekker rode to come to a rest. Dust from the hot, dry road billowed up around them, and the little girl, Sarah, coughed as she and her mother walked up to them.

Ella said nothing, only staring at the wanderer in question as she panted for breath. She was exhausted—he understood that well enough, for he was as well. This far south, the sun was not a warm, comforting presence. Instead, it stared down at them with a searing, malevolent gaze, as if it meant to scour the earth clean of them. The dust was another torture all its own, clinging to their clothes, their bodies, and their faces like a second skin, clinging, too, to the inside of their throats, making it difficult to breathe.

In answer to the woman's unasked question, the wanderer turned and regarded Dekker. The man lay on the travois, clearly uncomfortable, his hands grasping his wounded leg, his face, even through the fresh patina of road-dust covering it, a sickly pale. The big man's eyes were closed, his jaw set in a perpetual grimace that seemed a mixture of pain and determination, the way a man might set his jaw when he knew that, for the next little while, he was going to be miserable, and he could only hope to get through it.

"Dekker."

The man had been so intent on his pain, on enduring it, that it took him several seconds to realize that the wanderer had spoken and several more to finally look up, regarding him. "Everything alright?" Dekker asked in a dry rasp.

"Fine," the wanderer asked. "How do you feel?"

"Like an asshole," the big man answered. "Look at me here, ridin' and lyin' about when you're havin' to drag me around like a mule." He tried for an exhausted grin. "Though, it has to be said, a particularly ugly mule."

The wanderer laughed. "Don't worry—you can pay me back later, how'd that be?"

"Can't wait. Anyway, why'd we stop?"

"There's a creek near," the wanderer said. "I thought it might be a good place for a rest."

The big man grunted. "Can't say I'd argue with a cool drink of water just now. I thought, livin' here long as I have, that I was used to the heat, but it turns out I was wrong. Or maybe I'm just gettin' soft in my old age. Still, how do you know a creek's nea—you know what? Never mind. I don't care. I reckon I'll take your word for it. So what's the plan?"

"We need to get you up," the wanderer said. "I don't think it's far, but I also don't want to risk the sled on the forest floor. We could build another if needed, but I don't like the idea of wasting the time to do it."

Dekker nodded, looking at his leg with an expression of trepidation. "Sure thing."

And then they set about it. It was sweaty, grueling work, levering the big man to his feet. There were one or two moments when the thing was very much in doubt, and the wanderer left to think that he was going to find himself with the great mountain of muscle that was Dekker falling on top of him, crushing him. In the end, though, and with the help of a stout tree and the Dekker's wife, they managed to get him to his feet.

By the time it was done they were all sweating and panting for breath. Dekker stood with his back propped against a tree, the wanderer watching him closely as he got his own breath back. If the man fell and they were forced to try again, the wanderer might try to drag the creek to the big man instead of dragging the big man to it, just for an easier time of it.

Dekker remained standing though, at least for the moment, so the wanderer dragged the sled into the forest undergrowth so that it would be hidden from anyone that passed by. When he was finished, he walked back to where the big man waited. "Ready?"

"If I say no, do you suppose a proper carriage'll show up, ready to take me wherever I want to go?"

The wanderer gave a small smile. "I do not think so."

Dekker sighed. "Then I guess I'm ready."

The wanderer nodded, taking one of the big man's arms and draping it across his shoulders. Then they began to slow, arduous process of moving through the forest toward the sound of the water in the distance. Dekker was heavy—far heavier, as far as the wanderer was concerned, than any man had a right to be—and it was slow going, made slower still by the fact that they had traveled half the day and the wanderer was already tired. His arms and legs ached from dragging the sled, and there was a knot in the middle of his back that felt as if someone were digging into it with a rock. He wasn't sure what that someone's goal might be—he only knew that the bastard was persistent.

In time, they staggered past a particularly thick clump of bushes and were rewarded with the sight of a small stream a short distance ahead. It barely even qualified to be called a stream, truth be told, a pitiful thing no more than half a dozen feet across, but that didn't stop the wanderer from feeling a great sense of elation upon seeing it. And judging by Sarah's excited cry the little girl shared his relief. "Can we go in, Mommy, can we?"

Ella turned to glance at the wanderer. He looked at the creek, saw that the water was clear and gently flowing, not stagnant. He gave her a nod.

"Okay, honey, let's go," the mother said, a grin spreading on her own face to match her daughter's as she took the little girl's hand and started toward the stream.

"Come on," the wanderer told Dekker. "Let's get you in the water."

"Why don't you go on in," the big man said, glancing down at his bandaged leg. "I don't much fancy my chances of getting' any swimmin' done just now. Besides, you could use it. I know you're tryin' to hide it, but you look pretty well done in."

"What a pair we make then," the wanderer said. "But you still need to go in. It would be wise to wash the wound. Come—I'll help you."

The wanderer spotted a likely branch, about six feet long, that had fallen from a nearby tree. They moved toward it, retrieved it, and then he and the big man started toward the water. The grass on the bank was soft and lush. And after a half-day of grueling, sweaty travel, the cool wetness of the water was one of the finest things the wanderer had ever experienced.

Ella moved toward them, holding a grinning Sarah in her hands. The big man's wife took one of his arms, putting it over her shoulders, and the wanderer offered the man the branch he'd procured. "A walking stick," he said.

"Reckon why they don't call them what they are," Dekker said, frowning. "Stumbling sticks at best. Shambling sticks, maybe."

"I don't know," the wanderer said, smiling. "Suppose we could write them a letter."

Dekker sighed, taking the stick. "Fine."

The wanderer inclined his head, then started away.

"Just where are you goin'?" Dekker asked.

"I need to gather some herbs."

The big man grunted, as if he knew well that the wanderer sought to give him and his family a moment of privacy to enjoy each other and the cool water. "Fine, but don't be long."

"I wouldn't dream of it, Majesty," the wanderer said, inclining his head. "And I will, of course, see about that carriage you ordered."

Dekker smiled sourly. "Bastard."

"If it pleases you, Your Grace," the wanderer said. The woman and the girl laughed at that, and the wanderer tipped the little girl a wink before turning and walking into the forest.

He remained close, knowing all too well that if someone happened upon the family now, they would not be able to defend themselves. That said, he did his best to give them what privacy he could as he set about the task of gathering the herbs.

He managed to find what he needed within a few minutes, but when he started back toward the stream, he realized something—he was hungry. He had gone days without food before in the last hundred years, too many times to count in truth, but he was hungry. More than that, he was famished. And if he was hungry so, too, were the others. And yet they had not uttered a single word of complaint, likely trusting him to handle things, trusting that if it were safe to stop and get something to eat, they would have done so already.

The truth, though, was that he had simply forgotten. During the last hundred years he'd been forced to endure a variety of miseries and the simple fact was that hunger was one of those easiest to ignore.

Still, they needed to eat to keep up their strength. After all, he had no idea what they would face in the coming days and no way of knowing when they might be allowed another brief moment of respite. That made him think of the snare he had made the night before, but he dismissed it immediately. After all, that snare was miles behind them, and likely even if he had been able to check it, he would have only found it empty in any case. Still, there were other ways he might find food for them.

He set about foraging and found a bush of blackberries, another of blueberries. Shriveled, sad things, no doubt thanks to the oppressive heat, but even in their poor state they would be far better to break one's fast on than air. He took all that he could, wrapping them in several large leaves, then walked back to the stream. The family was farther down, but he could see them well. He set the berries down then waded into the water.

He let his fingers drift loosely as he did. It was not a big stream, but there were fish in it. He'd seen as much when he'd helped the big man get in. It was no easy task, fishing by hand, but he had done it before, had been shown the trick of it by the Eternal known as Ranger. The man had not spoken much in life and even now, a hundred years dead, he did not share the other ghosts' proclivity to constant speech. A man of few words.

The wanderer had asked Oracle about the man during one of their lessons, why he never seemed to speak, even when he was teaching the wanderer, doing so instead by the use of gestures, nods and grunts—of disapproval, mostly. She had told him then that still waters ran deepest of all. He hadn't known what that meant at the time, but slowly, over the years, he had begun to.

Some men who talked often—most men, in his experience— did so because they felt an almost obsessive need for it. A need that did not arise out of inner peace but instead inner turmoil. Men and women who did not feel comfortable with the silence, in simply *existing* and instead felt the need to gain control of their world—or at least pretend to—by imposing themselves upon it, either by action or by speech.

The truth the wanderer had come to learn from Ranger over those months and years training with him was that it was enough simply to *be*. And another truth, too, which was that men could not often talk and listen at the same time. Instead, they chose one to forego the other. And when a man was being hunted, when the slightest sound might betray the predator's approach, or alternatively when he hunted for food, knowing that to fail was to starve, then he learned, over time, to accept the quiet, to allow it, to simply *be*.

The wanderer accepted that quiet now, the quiet of the gently flowing creek, of the wind's slight whisper through the leaves of the trees around him, of the distant laughter of the little girl as she and her parents took this moment to be a family, to love and laugh and appreciate each other. He only stood there, letting the water lull him, closing his eyes and allowing the fingers of his outstretched hands to drift with the current. At first, when Ranger had shown him the trick, the wanderer had tried his best to see the fish, to see them and then attack them, thinking it was a matter of speed, of accuracy. But he had been wrong, of course, and he had learned that wrongness over the weeks and months.

Some things in the world, did not come to a man by desire, by striving, but instead by allowing them to, like a dog that, when threatened would not obey its master's call but, when it felt safe, would approach willingly. Any man or woman staring into water and trying to track the flickering movements of a fish within its shining reflective surface would soon discover that, as was so often the case in life, their perception was wrong. Flawed from the start. Instead, he could only sit and let the fish come to him.

Or not.

The wanderer stood that way for fifteen minutes and was just about to give it up—sometimes, Ranger had told him in one of those rare instances when the man said anything at all, there are fish, and sometimes there are not. But then, something brushed against his finger. A slight, tentative brushing, no more than that, but he found his mouth slowly raising in a grin. He felt the movement of it, the slight change in the water temperature and pressure as it slid past, and he reached out, snatching it up and tossing it onto the bank in one motion. He felt another, an instant later, and reached in again, his hand darting out and closing around the silvery, slick scales before he tossed it up onto the bank next to the first. He opened his eyes then, looking at the two goodly sized fish lying there, and smiled.

He returned to the others, bringing over the fish and the berries. The family had moved to the side of the water, and Sarah was playing in the sand. Meanwhile, Ella was using the hem of her dress to clean her husband's wound, dipping it in the clear blue water of the creek before dabbing at the dried blood. Dekker accepted the treatment stoically, but the wanderer saw the way the man's jaw was clenched against the pain.

They did not notice him for the moment, and he thought perhaps that was best. Let it be only the three of them, if even just for a moment. Let them be a family.

Satisfied that they were safe and occupied, the wanderer set down the fish and berries he'd procured and moved off a short distance, collecting wood and dried leaves to make a fire. Soon he had a solid blaze going. He set several flatter stones atop the flames then laid the cleaned and gutted fish onto them to cook.

He had only just finished when he heard shuffling footsteps and looked up to see the family approaching. Dekker had one arm draped over his wife's shoulders while, comically, the other was draped over his daughter who pretended to strain with the effort of supporting her father's weight.

"Alright, lass," Dekker told his daughter as they came to stand beside the fire. "Best let Ungr help with this bit, if he will. I'd hate to fall on you, squish you like a bug."

"I'm not a bug!" she said, grinning widely.

"Sure you are," he said. "A cute bug, but a bug anyway."

She grinned wider, as if she'd never heard such a compliment, then turned and moved away. The wanderer rose, taking Dekker's other arm. "Let's take our time, alright?" he said. "I don't much care for being squished either."

Dekker barked a laugh and after a minute or two of sweating effort, they managed to leverage him down into a sitting position. With that done, the wanderer examined the man's wound closely, Dekker wincing as the wanderer pressed against the skin around the wound to see how it was healing.

By the time the wanderer sat back, Dekker was sweating profusely. "Well?" the man asked. "Is my leg going to fall off?"

"Not today, anyway," the wanderer said. "It's healing well, and there's no sign of infection."

"Yeah?" Dekker said. "What about the damned itching, then?"

"It's a good thing," the wanderer said.

Dekker snorted. "Sure it is, the same way I've heard it's good luck if a bird shits on a man's head. Mostly, I suspect, because the poor bastard's day can only get better from there."

The wanderer laughed. "The itching means its healing, and I'm afraid it'll likely get worse before it gets better."

Dekker grunted. "Something to look forward to then," he muttered, then turned and regarded the fish lying on the rock and the berry-filled leaves. "Dinner is it?" he asked, and despite the man's obvious effort, he could not entirely hide the note of eagerness in his voice.

The wanderer nodded. "Dinner."

"Great," Dekker said. "Where's y'alls?"

"*Dekker,*" Ella said, her voice a loving mixture of reproval and amusement. "You'll have to forgive him, Ungr," she went on, turning to the wanderer, "it seems that my husband must have suffered a head wound long before his leg, though I doubt this one will heal quite so easily."

Dekker bellowed laughter at that then abruptly cut off, wincing and bringing a hand to his leg, scratching around the wound. "Damn thing," he muttered.

The wanderer nodded. "I'd best reapply the poultice—it'll help with the itching."

"While you're working on that, I'll prepare the food—that fish looks finished to me," Ella said, rising.

"That really isn't necessary," the wanderer said, "I can—"

"I know you can," Ella said, "but you've done enough, Ungr more than enough. You're the one that gathered the food, not to mention looking after Dekker's leg. The least I can do is to serve the meal." And before the wanderer could say anything else to protest, she set about the task, using the large, wide leaves that the wanderer had gathered as trenchers. She separated the fish using the wanderer's knife—after taking a moment to wash it in the creek—then allotted some onto each leaf, along with a handful of berries.

While Ella went about the task, the wanderer saw to his own, mixing the herbs he'd gathered, using a stone to smash them together and rendering them into a fine mash then applying the poultice to the big man's wound.

Dekker hissed as he did. "Feels cold."

"It's supposed to," the wanderer said. When he was finished with the poultice, he re-wrapped the wound, pulling the bandage tight.

By the time he was finished, Ella returned with the meals, handing them out to each of them. "Thank you," the wanderer said as he took his. Dekker also uttered what might have been a thank you, though it was hard to say for sure as he was talking around fish he'd already stuffed into his mouth. Immediately, he hissed, his mouth and tongue doing the delicate dance familiar to anyone who has ever taken a bite of something and found it to be hotter than they'd anticipated. *"Damn, that's hot,"* he said.

"Of course it's hot, you oaf," Ella said, shaking her head, a smile on her face, "it was sitting on a fire."

Dekker grinned at that, and Ella sighed. "Being married, Ungr, is in my experience, a life-long lesson on patience."

"I'll take your word on it," the wanderer said, smiling.

"But surely you must have some idea, haven't you?" Ella asked. "That is, have you never been married before?"

The question made him think of her, standing there in the woods as she had so long ago, the sunlight making her hair seem to sparkle, her cheeks wet with shed tears, her eyes brimming with those yet to come. The smile died on his face. "I...I have never had the privilege," he said.

"But...someone you were close to then?"

"El," Dekker said softly.

"It's...it's fine," the wanderer said, trying a smile, but based on the sympathetic look on the man and woman's faces, being largely unsuccessful.

"Forgive me for prying, Ungr," Ella said, "it's only...well, I feel like you know so much about us, and we don't know anything about you."

"And you wonder if you can really trust a man you know so little about?"

"That's not, I mean—"

"Hey, listen, Ungr," Dekker said, "ain't nobody here sayin' we don't trust you. You ain't ever done anythin' but right by us. We know full well what you've done for our family. I think only, that is, what El means to say is…well…"

"That you have questions," the wanderer said, his gaze moving slowly between the two of them. They both looked embarrassed at that, and the smile came a little easier to his face this time. "It's fine," he said. "I'd have questions too, in your position. In fact, I would be curious if you didn't. And I do not mean to keep you in the dark, I swear. But…the things I would tell you…" He thought of Scholar, then, of those lessons he'd been taught sitting in the man's study or in the great library of which the old man had been the head. He had learned many things, about many people and many places. Yet none of those lessons were what had stuck with him the most over the years. "I had a friend once," he said, remembering the time vividly, almost as if he could step back into that room, where he'd sat at the table in a study smelling of ancient books and manuscripts and the wine that Scholar had always said was his only vice.

"He told me," the wanderer went on, "that truth is a funny thing. It's like a strand a man pulls on, the way a young kitten might tug at a loose thread in a ball of yarn. For small truths, the strand is small, too, and its pulling out does not change the shape of the yarn in any significant way. But there are other strands, other truths. Strands that a man might pull on again and again and again and never reach the end. Truths which, when pulled free, might unravel the ball altogether and, in so doing, unravel the man's very world. There is greatness in truth, he told me, but there is also danger. Knowing this…do you still wish for me to tell you?"

To their credit, the husband and wife took their time, looking at each other, sharing their thoughts by that silent magic that seemed the exclusive purview of those in long, happy marriages. Finally, Dekker gave a nod, turning back to the wanderer. "We would know the truth, Ungr. If, that is, you would share it with us."

"Very well," the wanderer said, "but I will say one thing more and then that will be the end of it—know this. Not all truths are happy ones. The lies of civilization, of the world, the lies we tell ourselves, all serve to mask the worst the world has to offer from us. But behind that mask, darkness lurks, darkness and an evil that you cannot understand fully, not until it has set its gaze upon you. Should I give you what you ask, you will see it, you will know the truth of it, and this evil takes note of the notice it receives."

"What...what do you mean, Ungr?" This from Ella.

The wanderer opened his mouth to answer then hesitated, glancing at the young girl, Sarah, watching with wide eyes.

"Go on, Sarah girl," Dekker said. "Go play. We'll come get you directly."

The girl pouted, clearly not wanting to leave, but she turned and walked away.

The big man watched her for a moment, an expression on his face that was difficult to read, before finally turning back.

"What I meant to say," the wanderer went on, "is that these lies, the ones you've been told all your lives, they hide shadows, and within those shadows, bogeymen. And you see, the thing about these bogeymen is, once you see them, they see you, too. There have been others over the years, understand, others who have become suspicious."

"And what happened to them?" Ella asked, her voice low, soft, a tone in it that told him that she knew the answer already.

"They vanish," he said. "Vanish such that their families are left to wonder where they have gone for the rest of their lives. Are you sure you still want to know?"

The two shared a look again then, finally, nodded.

"But...why?" he asked. It was a genuine question because often, over the years, he had wished he did not know the truth of things, that he could go on pretending as so many others pretended. He had wished, often, when falling to sleep, that he might wake and find that what he had known to be true was all a dream or, if not, to dream himself and never wake. To dream of a world in which he had not watched his friends die, in which good had conquered evil instead of falling to it.

"Way I figure it, Ungr," Dekker said, "evil exists, whether we know it or not. That bein' the case, seems best to me to know it."

He glanced at Ella, and she nodded. Her face was pale, but her expression was one of determination. "I would know, Ungr."

"I cannot talk you out of it?" he asked, looking back at Dekker.

"Not unless you can promise me, Ungr, that not knowin' about the bogeyman underneath the bed'll keep me and my family safe."

The wanderer frowned at that, thinking it through.

"Besides," Ella offered, "it isn't as if they don't see us already. I mean...they've tried to kill us...how many times now?"

"Too many," Dekker agreed. "Wouldn't you agree, Ungr?" They both looked at the wanderer with what might have been smug expressions on their faces.

He winced. "Very well. Perhaps, I should start by telling you that my name isn't really Ungr."

Dekker grunted, and Ella's eyes went wide. "How's that?" the big man asked.

"But...why would you lie? About your name, I mean?" Ella asked.

The wanderer sighed. "You will understand soon, I think."

"So...what is your real name, then?" Ella asked. "The one you were born with?"

"I...do not know," he said.

Dekker frowned. "What do you mean you don't know? Are we supposed to believe you hit your head, got amnesia, that it?"

"Not...exactly," the wanderer said. "Only...if you did not hear your name for many years, for a very long time, would you remember it?"

"Of *course* I would remember it," Dekker said.

The wanderer nodded. "And if you were given another? One that was used in its stead?"

Dekker's eyes narrowed, not in anger, but as if he were trying to solve a difficult puzzle. "I don't understand. Who is 'given' a new name?"

"I was," the wanderer said. He paused, taking a slow, deep breath. "And that name was 'Youngest.'"

They stared at him for several seconds then, not comprehending. He said nothing, only watched them, watched as the truth of it slowly came to their eyes, watched disbelief rise up to meet that truth, watched the two of them war as husband and wife sought to reconcile this new bit of information with what they knew of him. Watched as they overlaid it to see if it would match, turning it this way and that. "You mean..."

The wanderer nodded. "I am Youngest. I am the Thirteenth, the last of the Eternals."

The two drew in sharp breaths then, and for a time neither of them said anything. The wanderer did not speak. He gave them the time they needed to absorb it, to make sense of it, if sense they could make. Finally, Dekker spoke. "So…you mean…all this time…you were him. The traitor."

"Dekker—" Ella began.

'No, El," the big man growled, a sound that turned into a hiss of pain as he tried and failed to climb his way to his feet. "Don't you get it?" he demanded of his wife. "This is him! This is the man who tried to kill the other Eternals. Shit, no *wonder* they came after him, no reason they killed Felden—they thought we were colluding with the bastard! He hasn't saved our lives, El, he's the one who put them in danger in the first pla—"

"*Quiet,*" Ella hissed. "Sarah can hear you."

The big man turned and stared at his daughter who'd stopped in her play to stare at them. "Daddy was just joking, Sarah girl," he said. "You go on back to your playing, alright?"

The girl did, and Dekker slowly turned back to regard the wanderer with open hate in his eyes. "It's your fault," he said. "All of it. Felden didn't die because he was in the wrong place at the wrong time, nor did the Perishables die because Soldier is evil. They died because of you."

"Ungr…or…that is…" Ella paused, wincing. "Is…is that true?"

"It is true that Felden died because of me," the wanderer said, and Dekker let out an angry growl. "But not for the reason you think," he said, holding up his hands to show he meant no harm. "It is my fault for coming to your home in the first place, only I heard a scream and thought the second Unseen—they always travel in pairs—had attacked you and your family. I came meaning to help."

"In pairs…I don't understand," Ella said.

"I understand all I need to," Dekker barked.

"*Dekker enough,*" Ella said, and the big man subsided, content to glare at the wanderer.

"I was attacked a little way from your home," the wanderer said. "I killed one of the creatures there and then, wounded, fled. Only, I saw the smoke of your fire, and I heard your daughter's scream when she and you were playing in the field," he finished, turning to Dekker.

"And I don't guess you just happened to be walking down the road and had some words with it, ended up in a fight?"

"No," the wanderer said, seeing where the man's mind was going and dreading it, never mind that he would be right. "It was hunting me."

"Hunting you," Dekker repeated. "And the other, the one that did for Felden—"

"Was there for me," the wanderer finished.

"*See, El?*" Dekker demanded. "The bastard all but admits it! And why could we expect anything better? After all, he's the most notorious traitor in the whole damned world, the one who turned against his own people and chose those, those *things* instead."

The wanderer found his own anger flaring at that. "You can call me many things," he said, "a coward, a failure, but I am no traitor."

Dekker snorted. "Fella, I hate to tell you, but you're the most famous traitor in the world. There's hardened murderers that'd be offended to be called by your name."

"I know the story you've heard," the wanderer said, "I am well aware of it, have lived with its consequences for a hundred years and more, but that does not make it true."

"A hundred years and more," Dekker repeated, his eyes going wide. "Damn but that's right, isn't it? You Eternals are supposed to live for hundreds, what, maybe thousands of years." He frowned. "Not that you have any right to call yourself one far as I'm concerned, you betrayin' 'em and all."

"I did not betray them," the wanderer said, trying to keep his composure but aware of the way his hand had knotted into a fist. "I have lived for over a century spending little time doing anything but looking back in shame upon that day, that battle, but not for the reason you think. I did not betray them, but I failed them just the same. I failed them and, because of that…because of that…" He trailed off, surprised by the sudden upwelling of emotions within him. He had lived with the hurt of his failure, the pain of it for many, many years, had managed to let the worst of that pain recede back into his mind. And in doing so, he had performed a sort of trick on himself, the way a man with a leg wound might, in sitting, think his leg healed until he went to put weight on it again.

So too, was the pain of that night. He had tried to stand and, in that moment, had found the pain as fresh as it had ever been. It had not healed as he had thought, had not lost its edge. Instead, it had only been waiting for him to reach for it so it might cut him again, waiting for him to put his full weight on it.

"But...that doesn't make any sense," Dekker said, his voice far softer now, for he had seen some of that pain which afflicted the wanderer. "I mean...it can't be true. Can it? That is, why would the Eternals lie and say that you had betrayed them if you had not?"

The wanderer took a slow, shuddering breath, forcing that pain back into the shadows of his mind again. At first, he did not think it meant to go, thought that it would remain there, like a thorn lodged into him, but finally the worst of it subsided. He raised his face, meeting the big man's eyes. "They would not," he said.

Dekker frowned, clearly confused, but it was Ella who spoke. "What do you mean, Ungr? What do you mean they would not?"

"You have heard, of course, of the last great battle? When the Eternals met the enemy head on?"

"Of course," Ella said. "Everyone knows the story. The Eternals won, despite Youngest—that is, your treachery...they beat the enemy, destroyed them."

"That's right," the wanderer said, "and it is just a story. Hear me, for I was there. The Eternals, the greatest warriors, greatest minds of mankind met the enemy in combat...and we lost. The Eternals were all destroyed save me. Leader, in his last moments, told me to flee with the enemy king's sword, a weapon possessing powerful magic, one which he might use to finish conquering mankind, to wipe all of you from the face of the world. Leader told me to flee with it...and so I did. To my great and everlasting shame, I did."

"But...if what you're saying is true," Dekker said slowly, "if the Eternals really did lose...then..."

The wanderer nodded. "Those you have known as the Eternals for more than a century have not been them at all. Instead, they were destroyed, their identities and their kingdoms taken by the enemy. Only I remain to know the truth."

"But…no," Dekker said, shaking his head, "no, that's crazy. That…it's just unbelievable."

"Is it?" Ella asked.

The big man frowned, turning to her. "What do you mean, El?"

She shrugged. "You know exactly what I mean, Dek. Is it really so hard to believe that we've been lied to? After all, you've heard the stories—about how different things used to be, how much better they were. I've heard a thousand stories, most of them told to my father by his father, about how the Eternals would look out for their people, care for them the way a shepherd cared for his flock. But while I've heard the stories, Dekker, I haven't *seen* it. Have you? Have you felt cared for?"

The big man winced. "Stories are just stories, El, that's all. Folks always have a tendency to look at the past finer than it was."

"Maybe," Ella said. "Or maybe the past was better because those in charge actually cared for their people. Look, Dekker, you have to admit things have been bad lately. After all, that's the reason you joined the Perishables in the first place, isn't it? Because you wanted us to live in a better world than the one we have? Because you wanted Sarah to grow up in a better place?"

"You know I did, El, but—"

"I won't argue with you, Dekker. I only ask you to think about it, search your heart and tell me what you really believe. Tell me if you really believe that the Eternals, the great, loving Eternals that are worshipped like gods, those famous for their compassion, would really butcher an entire group of people simply because they disagreed with them."

Dekker considered that, scratching his chin, then finally he shook his head. "No. No, I don't think I do." He turned to the wanderer. "But if what you said is true…and I think I believe you…then…why haven't you done something? Why haven't you…attacked them or…or I don't know."

"Because I would fail," the wanderer said simply. "Do you not see? I watched as Soldier was killed in front of my eyes. Soldier, a man who was better with the blade than I will ever be. He and Leader—who was also a far better swordsman than any you've ever met—and myself, all took on the enemy leader. And we lost. We *lost*," he repeated, his voice ragged with emotion. "No," he said, shaking his head, "I would have no chance against him. Even were it only one against one, and it is not. They are twelve, all more powerful than me. It is all I can do to adhere to Leader's final order, to keep the cursed blade out of its owner's hand, for should he ever retrieve it, the entire race of man would be doomed to fall beneath his might. They would cast off their story, their lies, the way one man might cast off a cloak, and they would kill thousands, tens of thousands, would slaughter and slaughter until there was nothing, until there was no *one* left."

"You mean...that's all you've done?" Ella asked, sounding very close to tears. "For the last hundred years, just traveling the world alone, always hunted?"

"I was not alone," the wanderer said.

"You mean Veikr," she said softly.

He inclined his head in a nod, and she brought her hand to her mouth, turning away.

"So...what you're sayin'," Dekker said, "is that this whole time, we've lived a lie. The Eternals didn't win, they lost, and for the last hundred years we've been fooled."

"Yes."

The big man nodded grimly. "I see. And what of those, those *things* that attacked us at our home and at Will's manse? How do they factor into all of this?"

"They are...creations of the enemy," the wanderer said.

"Creations," Dekker repeated.

"Yes. Since their defeat of the Eternals, they have been trying to find some means of retrieving the sword or, failing that, of ensuring that they might defeat mankind without needing the cursed blade at all. To that end, they began their experiments."

"And those things..." Dekker said slowly. "They looked...I mean, they looked almost human."

The wanderer nodded slowly, watching the big man. "Yes. They would."

Dekker swallowed hard, knowing the truth but not quite willing to accept it yet. "You mean...that those things that attacked us, those monstrosities—"

"Were once humans, as much as you or Ella."

"Or you," Ella said softly.

"Sorry?" the wanderer said.

"You speak of humans as if you are not a part of us," she said, wiping at the tears that had begun to trail their way down her face. "But you are, Ungr...Youngest. You must know that you are."

"Please," he said, "Ungr will do well enough. I have not had a name for one hundred years, understand, for there has been no one to call me by it even if I had. Ungr...I feel that the name was given to me, in a way, by Felden...by your family."

She gave him a weak smile, looking very close to sobbing, and nodded. "O-of course. But that doesn't change anything, Ungr. You need to know that you are one of us. That you're a person, too."

You're a part of this world, he thought, remembering Felden Ruitt's words, *and people, Ungr, need people.* "I do not know what I am," he said honestly. "I know that I was a man, once. Now..." He shook his head.

The woman covered her mouth again at that, letting out a sob before coming to her feet. "I'd...I'd better go check on Sarah," she blurted, then turned and hurried away.

The wanderer and Dekker watched her go. "Is...is she okay?" the wanderer asked. "Did I say something to upset her?"

Dekker sighed. "Seems that a man can live for a hundred years and still be a fool at the end of it," he said, smiling to show that he meant no offense. "She doesn't cry for herself, Ungr," he said. "She cries for you."

"For...me," he said.

"Why, of course," the big man said. "Yours is a sad story, Ungr, and no mistake. Shit, I'm just about ready to do some cryin' myself. Likely I would be, except that, well, I think I mentioned to you, before, about how I wasn't always the sort of man I am now—still a fool, sure, but an honest one."

"You might have made mention of it," the wanderer agreed.

Dekker grunted. "Well. Thing is, I ain't as prone to sadness as my sweet Ella. Me, I'm more prone to anger. And your story, Ungr, while it makes me sad...well, mostly it makes me angry. I don't much care for the thought that my people have been nothin' more than sheep to their rulers, sheep that might be experimented on, if they took it in mind to." The man finished the last in a growl, and the wanderer nodded. After all, he knew well that anger, had felt it himself for many, many years until, in time, it had finally given way to despair.

"You ask me," Dekker said, a menacing expression on his face, "we ought to kill the bastards. Hunt down each and every one of 'em like the fuckin' mad dogs they are."

"I told you," the wanderer said, "I cannot take even one of them."

"Maybe not," Dekker agreed, "but you're assumin' you'd be by yourself. Folks knew the truth of this, Ungr, why...you'd have an army to help you. Thousands, shit, tens of thousands'd fight for you."

"*No,*" the wanderer grated, blurting the word out so abruptly that the big man blinked.

"No? You mean to just have everyone keep on livin' like this? The...the *playthings* of those damned monsters?"

"Yes," the wanderer said, "if it means they *do* keep living."

Dekker stared at him for a moment. "Listen, Ungr—"

"No, Dekker," the wanderer said, "you listen. Do you not think I have had this thought before? Do you think, that in the last one hundred years, I have not run it through in my head, over and over? That I have imagined a hundred, a thousand different ways? Had I even saw a small chance of success, I would have sought my revenge long ago. The Eternals might just be a story to you, Dekker, but they were my friends, my...my family. I would do anything to avenge them. Anything, at least, save for sacrificing the entire world, for failing the task which Leader entrusted to me. I had thought...not too long ago, that I would be glad to have my task finished, even if that meant death, even if that meant failure. I thought that I could accept that, just so long as there was an ending. But I realize now that I was wrong. It is my duty, the *sword* is my duty, my burden, and so I will carry it as long as I am able."

"I'm not sayin' to give it to 'em," Dekker said. "All I'm sayin', Ungr, is that, well, I seen you use that blade, back at Will's family home. I saw what that thing was capable of, cuttin' down those damned things—what did you call them? Revenants? With one slash while they shrugged off any blow from a normal weapon. I say, if there's power in the sword, why not use it yourself? Turn these bastards' weapon against them?"

The wanderer was suddenly very aware of the presence of the cursed blade sheathed across his back. It was as if he could feel it emanating some malevolent energy. He shook his head quickly.

"No. The cursed blade is cursed for a reason, Dekker. I was lucky in not having it take me over, in not being consumed by it. But just because a man running blindly across the street misses the onrushing carriage once, it does not mean that he will miss it again. Or, more importantly, that it will miss him. No," he said, shaking his head again, "the blade is a creation of the enemy and may no more be turned to our purpose than those creatures which he sends against us."

"So what then?" Dekker asked, sounding frustrated. "You mean to run? Just run on forever and ever? That it?"

"Not forever," the wanderer said. "Only for as long as I can." An amount of time which, if Veikr were truly gone, would be reduced considerably. After all, he had long lost count of the number of times the horse's speed or strength had saved his life, or, for that matter, the horse's company kept madness at bay. He thought that he would not be able to survive long with Veikr gone and thought, too, that if Veikr really *was* gone, that was alright with him. Just so long as he saw the family safe or, at least, as safe as he could make them.

"And you think that'll work?" Dekker said. "Just runnin' and hopin' they don't find you?"

The wanderer shrugged. "It has worked so far," he said.

"What a life," Dekker observed.

"Whatever life it is, it is mine."

"But this ain't just about you, Ungr," Dekker said. "Don't you see that? This is about everybody. Every livin', breathin' soul is a slave to the whims of those, those *monsters*. A slave and never mind that they can't feel the yoke about their neck. A yoke you'd keep havin' 'em wear."

"Better the yoke than the grave."

"I ain't so sure about that," Dekker said. "I really ain't. And who are you to make that decision anyway?"

"Who am I?" the wanderer said, suddenly angry, aware that the words had come out in a growl. "Who am I? I am Youngest, Dekker. I am the Last Eternal. That's who I am."

"That's right," Dekker said, "you're the last. But bein' last ain't special, Ungr. Someone's got to be, haven't they? Instead, why don't you try bein' the best?"

The wanderer opened his mouth to speak again, but the big man held up a hand. "That's all I'll say on it, Ungr. I won't argue it no more. We both got our opinions, and I know the fact is you've had a hundred years to figure yours while I've only had minutes to think on mine. Might be you're right. Might be the only way is to keep on bein' slaves. And maybe Ella is right, too. Maybe anger ain't what's called for—certainly it's got me into more trouble over the years than happiness and that's a fact, got me into far more scrapes than out. But if it ain't anger, Ungr, then I guess that just leaves sadness, don't it?"

"I guess so," the wanderer said, feeling as if he'd somehow lost the argument and unsure of how that might be when the man was agreeing with him. "Anyway, it is time we left—there are still some hours left in the day, and we need to take advantage of them."

"Sure," Dekker said.

The wanderer started toward him, and the big man held up a hand, forestalling him. "Let me try," he said.

The wanderer thought it a waste of time, thought it would be far quicker if he helped the big man, but he realized something as he stood there, watching Dekker struggle. The man was not doing it for his pride; he was trying to rise on his own because he was tired of being helpless. The man had a family to protect, after all, and he could do no protecting if he could not stand. The wanderer saw, past the man, that Ella had noticed him trying to get up. She scooped up their daughter and started back, but the wanderer gave her a small shake of his head.

She frowned, as if confused, but he was gratified, at least, to see that she stopped. Dekker growled and hissed and cursed, making use of the walking stick the wanderer had found for him and, in the end, managed to work his way to his feet. He was covered in sweat, trembling, but his mouth split into a wide grin, showing his obvious pleasure.

"Well done," the wanderer said, glancing at the bandage to make sure that the wound had not started bleeding again.

"Thanks," Dekker panted.

"Now," the wanderer said, "when we make it back to the sled, we will need you to ride—it will be faster that way. But as for getting back to it...do you think you can walk?"

The big man grunted as his wife and daughter came up. "Walk? I reckon, Ungr, that if you say it's needed, I can more than walk—maybe I can even run."

The wanderer knew that the man referred to more than just moving back to the sled, that he was also telling Ungr that whatever he chose, he would follow. "Very well," he said, "but for the moment, at least, I think walking will do."

"Thank the Eternals for that," the big man said, then frowned as he realized what he'd said. "Anyway, you know what I mean."

"I do," the wanderer agreed. "Now come—we have wasted enough time already."

CHAPTER SEVEN

They returned to the sled and once Dekker was secure, they resumed their journey. The wanderer had dreaded it, but he was surprised to find that, for some reason, the going seemed to be much easier than it had before their brief respite. He thought at first that perhaps there had been some change in the road, that they were going down a decline or that the trail had gotten smoother. But a quick examination showed him that neither was the case. The path they traveled was, if anything, steeper than it had been before. As for the state of the road itself, it was as it had been, dry, hardpacked earth that rose up in clouds of dust as they moved across it.

His next thought was that he was rejuvenated from the rest, the food and water or some mixture of the three, but while those things had been nice and had indeed given him some more energy, he knew that they could not account for the change. It was as if somehow Dekker had gotten lighter, as if he had shed a hundred pounds in the space of an hour. But after a few moments' thought, the wanderer realized the truth. Dekker had not gotten lighter—he had. Or, at least, the burden which he had carried on his shoulders for so long had. And why not? After all, he had spoken of it, spoken of it for the first time to anyone save the ghosts or Veikr.

He had shared his past, the weight of worry and fear and shame that had dragged at him for a hundred years and, in so doing, he had lightened his own burden. He felt…renewed. He still had his burden, of course, still had his duty, but for the first time in a very long time, that burden seemed…bearable. And so he bore it, continuing on at as fast a jog as he could manage while still allowing Ella, carrying her daughter against her chest, to keep up with him. But had it not been for waiting on them, the wanderer thought he could have almost run.

They continued on that way for another hour, until they finally reached the top of the gradual rise. Ahead of them, the thick trees and undergrowth of the forest—which had flanked them on either side—gave way to rolling hills as far as he could see. There was a stream that ran along the left side of the field, and he did not think it was only his imagination that the grass looked far greener ahead of them than where they now were.

The wanderer found himself pausing, staring out at the world. It was strange to him to think that while the world was dangerous, often cruel, even after so long traveling upon its surface, a refugee, an exile, he still from time to time caught glimpses of its beauty. Beauty like that he now gazed upon, the wide rolling fields of grass swaying in the wind, stretching on for miles as far as he could see and beyond. The world was beautiful—there was no denying that. But then, he knew that the intricate designs and patterns of some snakes were also beautiful, beautiful enough to attract the unwary, beautiful enough to cause their prey to abandon their caution and walk willingly to their own doom. He only hoped that he was not doing the same and bringing the family along with him.

"Everything okay, Ungr?" Ella asked from beside him.

He nodded. "Good—let's go."

They traveled on for another thirty minutes, and despite his fear that he was making the wrong choice or that he was leading the family into a trap, no danger presented itself. And he comforted himself with the knowledge that if anyone or anything was lying in ambush, he could not have helped but to see it, for the entire area around them for miles was visible save that part of the ground occluded by the hills in front and behind them as they traveled up and down the rolling landscape.

A slight breeze had picked up, rare this far south, and it was cool against the wanderer's hot skin. It even began to rain. Just a little, but a little was more than it had done in the last two days. The water felt like a blessing upon his face and arms, and he found a slow smile spreading across his face as he ran. He had only just decided minutes ago that he'd been wrong after all and that it had not been a trap, when they were running up a rise and Ella spoke.

"Ungr?"

He paused, glancing at her, his smile still in place. "Yes?"

"What...what do you think that is?"

The wanderer turned to look behind them where the woman indicated, as did Dekker, grunting as he craned his neck in the sled. Ella did not have to explain what she meant, for it was clear enough. In the distance, at the forest's edge, was a rolling cloud of dust, similar to those they had caused when running across the dry ground, but different in that it was far bigger. The wanderer watched that dust, hoping that perhaps it was only kicked up by the wind, but he knew that that was not true. The slight breeze would not have been anywhere near enough to have caused the dust to move in such a way. Indeed, his fear was proven true a moment later when figures on horses began to emerge out of the cloud.

He could not get a specific count, not from so far away, but he judged there to be at least twenty riders, perhaps more.

"What is it?" Dekker said. "Damnit, I can't see anything from down here."

"Riders," the wanderer said, his eyes not leaving the distant figures.

"How many?"

"Twenty," the wanderer said, "maybe as many as twice that."

"Is it possible they have nothing to do with us?" Dekker asked grimly.

The wanderer watched them for another moment then slowly shook his head. "I don't think we can take that chance."

"What should we do, Ungr?" Ella asked, her tone betraying a fear that she was doing her best to hide from the little girl.

The wanderer looked to either side of the road. Nothing but fields, on and on and on, and the comfort that open area had provided had, in seconds, turned to despair. There was nowhere to hide, for if they went to the fields the riders would only see them sooner. He turned and looked in the direction they'd been traveling. In the distance, he could see the tree line as the woods resumed, but he decided after some brief calculation that there was no way he and the others would make it there before the riders caught up to them.

But what choice did he have? None, that was the truth of it. He turned to Ella, his gaze taking in Dekker as well. "We run—as fast as you can."

The woman nodded, but it was clear that she was exhausted from carrying her daughter the distance they'd already traveled, and it did not look like she had any running left in her. "Sarah," he said, "can you do me a favor?"

The little girl who, up to that point, had sat with her head buried in her mother's shoulder, turned to regard him. "Of course, Mister Ungr."

"Can you go and sit with your father?" he asked.

She looked at Dekker as if for permission, and the big man frowned. "Ungr, look, are you sure—"

"I'm sure," he said. "Go on, Sarah," he said, offering the girl a smile, well aware that every moment they wasted brought the riders closer. "It will be fun."

"But…Ungr, you can't mean to drag both of them," Ella said.

"I do."

She swallowed. "But…Maybe I can help. I can carry one end or—"

"You can help, Ella," he said, "by running as fast as you can."

"But—"

"*Go,*" he said. "*Now.*"

The woman glanced at Dekker and her daughter, her worry clear on her face, but then thankfully she did, turning and starting down the path once more at a fast clip.

"Look, Ungr," Dekker said, "I know you're strong but…you sure you can do this?"

"What choice do we have?" the wanderer asked, raising an eyebrow. "Unless, that is, you want to stop taking a rest, maybe drag me for a change."

The man winced. "Maybe later."

"I'll hold you to it. Now, you just keep a grip on to Sarah—it's time."

Before the big man could say anything else, the wanderer turned, picking up either end of the supports once again, the callouses that had formed on his palms and fingers during the day aching painfully. He did his best to ignore the ache, just as he tried to ignore the pain of his arms and shoulders, the burning in his lower back. He gritted his teeth, lifting the supports up, and then started forward—or at least, he meant to. Perhaps it was the girl's added weight or, more likely, that the brief pause had broken his rhythm. Either way, for a moment, the sled did not move, and he was suddenly overcome by a powerful conviction that he would still be struggling—and failing—to move it when the riders came upon them.

Finally, though, with a growl of effort, he dragged the sled forward, and it began to move. Reluctantly, at first, as if it meant for him to be caught, but as he strained against it, it began to pick up speed. He continued down the trail, his muscles crying out in protest, his shoulders burning as if someone had set a torch to them, but he clenched his jaw and continued on—sometimes, oftentimes, it seemed to him, that was all a man could do. To just keep going.

And so he did. He kept going up the slowly increasing incline until he reached the top of the next rise, and then he did it again. The third time, he did not know that he would make it, felt as if at any moment he might fall over, but he continued to put one foot in front of the other, taking it one step, one heaving effort at a time, and eventually they were at the top of the third rise. He risked a glance behind him and saw that the riders were unsurprisingly gaining on him. In less than an hour they would catch them up.

And that was assuming he was even able to continue for that long, a fact which remained in doubt considering how exhausted he felt.

"What do we do, Ungr?" Dekker asked.

The wanderer glanced down at the big man, behind them where he could still see, in the distance, the dust trail of the approaching riders. Still a way off yet but getting closer.

No time to run and nowhere to hide. That left only one choice. "Can you stand?" he asked.

Dekker grunted. "We been through this—'course I can stand." But despite his words, he looked far more unsure now than he had when they'd first started. No surprise that, for the bumps and jostles of the sled no doubt pained his wound.

The big man suited action to words, though, and with a bout of hissing curses worked his way to his feet. He was out of breath by the time he was standing, his daughter's hand in his.

"Dekker? What's happening?"

The wanderer and the big man turned to see Ella coming back toward them along the road in a weary half-jog, half-shuffle.

"I'm not sure yet, love," Dekker said, glancing back at the wanderer.

"You can walk?" the wanderer asked the big man.

"Of course I can walk," Dekker said. "I told you before, Ungr, if it's called for."

"Show me," the wanderer said.

The big man frowned, glancing at the wanderer then in the distance from where the riders approached. After a moment, his eyes went wide. "You mean to fight them," he said, his voice incredulous.

"Yes," he answered.

"And…what? You think you can win? Against so many?"

The wanderer said nothing, only watching the big man who grunted. "I see. I don't like it, Ungr. I could help—"

"You can help by getting your family as far away as you can," the wanderer said. The big man started to open his mouth, obviously preparing to argue, but the wanderer held up his hand. "Please, Dekker," he said, meeting the man's gaze with his own. "I've done things in my life that I am not proud of, things which I regret. I would not have your family be one of them."

The big man winced then, after a moment, held out his hand. "It's been an honor, Ungr."

"For me as well," the wanderer said, taking the hand and giving it a shake.

"Good luck," Dekker said. "Come on, love," he said, turning to his wife who was staring at the two of them with an incredulous look on her face. "It's time we left."

"B-but, you can't mean to-to *abandon* him," Ella said.

"That's exactly what I mean to do," Dekker said, glancing back at the wanderer. "Because he asked it of us. Now come."

He started away then, apparently confident that his wife would follow with their daughter.

"You're sure?" she asked.

"I am," the wanderer said. "Go, Ella. Take your daughter and go." He glanced back at the road where Dekker made a slow, shuffling progress, leaning heavily upon the walking stick the wanderer had found. "It may be, Ella," he said, "that you and your daughter can outpace your husband. I would, if I were you, to give you the grea—"

"I go where my husband goes, Ungr," she interrupted, a fierceness to her tone as she met his eyes. "Wher*ever* he goes."

The wanderer nodded. He had expected as much, but for the sake of the woman and the girl he'd had to try. "Go," he said again. "There is little time. And please, take this," he finished, lifting the cursed blade from his back and offering it to her. The woman stared at it as if it was a snake that might bite her, an opinion that would serve her well, if she was to carry it for any amount of time. Then, slowly, she took it, draping the sword over her shoulders. She stared at him for a moment then, with tears in her eyes, but it was Sarah who spoke. "W-we can't leave him, Momma," she said. "We can't—"

"Come, Sarah girl," Ella said, her voice rough as she lifted her daughter. "Mister Ungr will catch up with us, won't you, Mister Ungr?"

The girl turned to him with eyes brimming with tears. "As soon as I'm able," he said. It was not a lie, not exactly, but he felt the guilt of it just the same.

"Come on, Sarah girl," Ella said, picking her up, "it's time we left." The wanderer watched as they started away after Dekker.

He continued to watch for another moment until he was sure they would continue. Then, he turned back and regarded the distant cloud of dust, growing closer yet seeming, at the same time, not to move at all. It approached the same way that a man's death approached, by degrees, coming nearer seemingly only when he was not looking. A slow, unseen approach, but one that was inevitable for all that.

He did not despair as he watched it come, as many men might when facing their death. He had thought of this moment often over the years, had considered it and, like all men, had from time to time, feared it. Unlike most, he had also, from time to time, hoped for it.

But it was here now and neither hope nor fear would change its coming. And what worry he felt was not for himself but for the family. He worried also, for Veikr, his friend. Oracle had told him once, that it was a man's worries, more than anything else, his fears, which made him human. Perhaps she had been right—certainly the wanderer was in no position to argue. But he did not need to be human, not now.

He needed to be better.

And so it was not the advice of Oracle to which he clung but that of Soldier. A man must enter a battle with a clear mind, for if it is muddied with worries and fears and errant thoughts, then his form will also muddy in accordance with his mind.

He lifted his scabbarded sword off his back and moved so that he stood at the apex of the small rise. Then, he sat, crossing his legs in front of him and placing the sword lengthwise along them.

The wanderer stared out at the distant riders, taking slow, deep breaths. He perused his mind, lifting each worry, each fear, and examining them one by one. He examined them the way a man, stepping into an attic he had not entered for years might reacquaint himself with its contents, brushing away the dust and the cobwebs to see what was underneath, turning it this way and that so that he might know it. Because it was only in knowing exactly what he had that a man might know whether to keep it to his good or to throw it out. For a man, Soldier had told him, was like a work horse who started the day with a light burden, an empty cart, but over the course of the day, his life, his burden grew as one thing after the other was tossed inside. And as his burden grew, the horse, the man, grew slower until, weighed down by his burdens, he could barely move at all.

The wanderer closed his eyes, taking slow, deep breaths and began to discard those things that would not serve him. Worry for Veikr—thrown aside. Either his friend was okay or he was not. Either way, the wanderer could do nothing for him. His shame at his failure—thrown aside. Shame would not help him, not now, if it ever had. Guilt, fear, hope, it was all cast aside in those moments. He visualized each thing as it was thrown away, discarded, all of them remaining close enough that, should he survive, he might pick them up again, but he did not think that would be a problem. It was not a question of survival anymore.

Requiem for a Soldier

It was a question of time. He was selling his blood, his life for the family, for time. All he could hope was that he would get a good price.

When he was finished, when all that could be thrown out had been, he opened his eyes, feeling lighter than he had in a very long time. The riders were closer now. Fifteen minutes away, perhaps, certainly no more than that. He rose, glancing behind him to check on the family. He could see them still. They had traveled farther than he'd expected but nowhere near as far as he had hoped.

He turned back to look at the riders, close enough that they were resolving from a sort of vague blur of man and horse to individuals, close enough that he could see that his estimate of twenty had been off. There were forty at the least, far too many for him to be victorious against.

But then...he had never meant to be victorious.

He drew his sword from its scabbard, aware, in the relative silence only broken by the distant clomp of horses' hooves, like low, rumbling thunder, miles away yet but coming closer, of the sound of the metal as it left the scabbard. Aware of the feel of the leather grip in his hands. How many times, he wondered, had he drawn the blade? A thousand? A thousand, thousand? Too many to count, even if he had cared to, and he did not. What mattered wasn't how many times he had drawn the blade. What mattered was that now would be the last time.

He did not replace the scabbard in its customary spot upon his back. Instead, he tossed it to the side of the road. He lifted his blade in front of him, watching the way the sunlight played on its surface. It was beautiful, but then the world's most deadly things often were its most beautiful.

He let the sword drop so that he held it at his side, at a downward angle to the ground, rolling his shoulders to work the tension out of them, flexing his fingers. He considered opening the amulet, speaking to the ghosts one last time, but he decided against it. He faced his death, there was no denying it, and like all men, he must face it alone. And so with nothing left to do, he watched that death come, waited for it.

He let everything else drift away, carried by the slight breeze. He did not think of the family, not anymore, nor the fields of green to his left and right. He thought only of the riders, only of the sword in his hands. There was nothing else.

Until there was.

But what encroached upon his mind was not worry for his friend or for the family, nor was it nervousness. Not the feel of the breeze against his skin or the sound of the clomping of the horses as they drew closer. It was instead a different sound.

A neigh.

But not just any neigh. Instead, it was one he recognized, and how not, for he had heard it often over the last century. He turned slowly to look in the direction, thinking that surely he must have been dreaming, that the sound was no more than a conjuring of his mind as it prepared itself for the end. He thought, he was *sure* that he would turn and look down the road only to find that there was nothing there. He didn't, though. There was something. A horse. And not just any horse, *his* horse.

"Veikr?" he asked, the word coming out in a dry, disbelieving croak.

The horse was charging toward him through the field, running at a line diagonal to the road. And the wanderer was left to marvel at the sight of him, marvel and stare in disbelief as the giant horse galloped toward him at a speed his contemporary brethren could not hope to match.

And then, in less than five minutes, Veikr was there, standing before him, the horse lathered in sweat from the exertion. The wanderer reached out a tentative, trembling hand, sure that he would try to touch the horse but instead touch only air, and in that moment the horse, a figment of his mind and nothing more, would vanish.

But his fingers touched more than air, instead they stopped on the horse's muzzle, and he breathed a great, shuddering sigh of relief before hugging the horse tightly, running a hand along his muzzle. "You're alive," he said.

Veikr snorted, as if to ask how the wanderer was so foolish as to think he could be anything else. He was still holding onto his friend when Veikr stomped his hoof, and the wanderer pulled away. "Right," he said. "Not if we stick around here for much longer."

He walked to where he had discarded his scabbard, then bent and retrieved it, returning it to its customary spot on his back. He sheathed his blade then turned back to Veikr, noticing for the first time that there was a long but thankfully shallow cut down the horse's flank, the blood dried. He wondered if this was the wounding that had made Veikr utter the scream he'd heard when the horse led the Revenants away and thought that likely it was.

He would see to it, later. For now, though, he picked up the hope he had discarded and climbed into the saddle. "Come, Veikr," he said. "There is a little girl I know that would be very happy to see you."

The horse gave a whinny, needing no more urging than that before he turned and started down the road. It did not take them long to catch up with the family, all of them looking one more step away from falling over but grinning just the same as they watched them ride up.

"Well, wonders never cease," Dekker said. "Seems to me I recognize that giant horse from somewh—"

The big man never got a chance to finish what he'd been about to say, though, for his daughter—who'd looked like she was going to fall asleep standing up an instant before—suddenly gave a shout of glee and burst forward, wrapping Veikr's muzzle in a tight hug. "Oh, Veikr," she said, "I missed you so much. I love you."

Veikr whinnied, as if to say that he loved her too, and the wanderer looked down at his horse, shaking his head.

"Come here, Sarah girl," Dekker said. "You can love on Veikr later." He paused, glancing at the wanderer, then past him. "Well, seems to me we still need to be about the process of fleeing. Or did those riders up and decide to turn around?"

"No such luck, I'm afraid," the wanderer said as the girl reluctantly walked back to her parents, her head hanging so low he thought it a wonder her forehead didn't scrape the ground.

Veikr gave a sad little neigh of his own, shaking his head as if in protest, and the wanderer grinned, giving the horse a pat. "Never knew you to be so sentimental," he said. The horse glanced over his shoulder, meeting the wanderer's gaze with a look that seemed to say that if he were more like the little girl maybe he would have. Which, he supposed, was fair.

"So what's the plan?" Dekker asked.

The wanderer climbed down from the saddle. "You three will ride on Veikr."

Dekker glanced at the horse doubtfully. "The three of us? I know we did it outside the city but...you sure he'll be able to keep it up with all of us on at once?"

The wanderer glanced at Veikr who seemed to roll his eyes before giving a shake of his head, making it clear what he thought of that. "He will be able to keep it up as long as he needs to," the wanderer told the big man honestly.

"No offense, understand," Dekker said to the horse, who looked at him with an expression that somehow conveyed offense.

The big man cleared his throat, taking a step back. "Remember," he said, jerking a thumb at Sarah, "that's my daughter there."

"And what of you?" Ella asked, looking at the wanderer.

"I will run."

It was the woman's turn to look doubtful. "Run," she said. "You mean to keep up with a horse out of legend?"

Veikr seemed to stand a little straighter at that, and the wanderer gave a soft laugh. "If he takes it easy on me," he said. He turned and glanced behind him. Thanks to where they stood on the rise, he could not see beyond it to the riders, but he knew they would be fast approaching. "Come," he said. "We'd best hurry. Ella—the blade."

The woman nodded, removing the scabbarded weapon from where it had hung from her back and offering it to him with no small amount of relief on her face. It was a relief the wanderer understood, for none knew better than he the weight of that burden.

Then, in another moment, husband and wife were sitting atop Veikr's broad back, their daughter between them. "Now then, Weakest," the wanderer said to his horse, unable to keep the smile from his face, "show us your strength. And whatever you do—do not wait for me."

And then they were running.

Thanks to the blessings he'd received to become an Eternal, the wanderer was far faster than a normal person, stronger, too, and possessed of an endurance unmatched by any other. At least, any man. As fast as he was, the wanderer was no match in speed for a horse, and a glance back over his shoulder showed him that the riders were gaining on them. Slowly, but gaining just the same.

He looked back to the forest, far in the distance, and it did not take him long to realize that they would not make it in time. Worse, based on the fact that they were suddenly coming faster than they had been, the riders had seen him and the others, something he'd been hoping to avoid for at least a little while longer.

He found his eyes drifting southward then, toward where, in the distance—but closer than the forest ahead—he could see the thick, untraveled wilderness which marked the border of the Untamed Lands.

Do not even think it, he told himself. *The Untamed Lands are all but certain death.* And that was true enough, for he had heard the stories from the other Eternals, including Soldier himself. He had seen the haunted look that came over their faces, had heard the pain of the memories in their voices as they recounted those things which they had faced when pushing the wilderness back, each foot of ground upon which the men and women of the kingdom now lived bought and paid for in blood. And those things which had drawn that blood, which had extracted that blood, lay beyond those trees, in the Untamed Lands.

All but certain death to venture into the Untamed Lands, or so Soldier and the other Eternals had told him, and he believed them. But then, to continue to flee to the western wood was not near-certain death—it *was* certain. Which meant that even the grim possibility of entering the Untamed Lands was better.

"*Veikr,*" the wanderer called, "*turn southward.*"

The horse did not hesitate, turning immediately, leaving the road behind and charging into the grass. The wanderer followed.

"South," Dekker yelled to him from atop Veikr, "but...you don't mean to go into the Untamed Lands, do you?"

"I do."

The big man's jaw clenched, and the wanderer could see the man's nervousness clearly writ across his features. And that was just as well, for he should be nervous. Any man with breath in his lungs ought to be unnerved with the thought of venturing into the Untamed Lands. Dekker, though, did not argue. Instead, he glanced back at the riders chasing them then gave a grim nod, clearly coming to the same conclusion that the wanderer already had. Going into the Untamed Lands was not a good choice—it was the only one.

Which didn't banish the feeling of trepidation the wanderer felt. Were it just him and Veikr, he would feel differently, for he was confident that he and the horse could avoid most of the dangers the Untamed Lands might pose and, even if they could not, it would only be the two of them who would suffer for it. Now, though, he was bringing the family as well, and should some terrible fate befall them, it would be his choice that brought it upon them.

Still, they ran on, the wanderer pushing his body for every ounce of speed and strength it could muster to reach, more quickly, a place he did not want to go. They were halfway across the field when he glanced back to check on the riders only to see that they had just now crossed into the field in pursuit, swords waving in their hands as they pushed their horses to their limits.

Not some of the enemy's creations, not these, but simple men and women. Likely they, like the crossbowman and his fellows that the wanderer had encountered in the woods, had been tempted by the reward the creature posing as Soldier was offering. But unlike the crossbowman, the leader of this group had come with enough men to be confident of getting the job done.

He saw, also, that it would be a close thing as to whether he and the others might reach the Untamed Lands before the riders caught them up. *"Ride on, Weakest!"* he shouted, slapping the horse's rump. Veikr responded instantly. No longer constrained by trying to remain at his side, Veikr leapt forward in a gallop that would have left the pursuing horses behind him in a matter of moments as he surged toward the tree line.

The wanderer followed along as fast as he could but the distance between him and Veikr increased by the second.

Which was the least of his concerns. Of far greater concern was the distance between himself and his pursuers, a distance that had grown small enough that the wanderer could hear a shout from one of the riders clearly. *"Don't let them get into the Wilds—fire!"*

Fire.

The word resounded in the wanderer's mind, tearing away his certainty that the others were safe.

He spun in time to see that at least half a dozen of the riders at the front were holding crossbows, displaying a surprising amount of dexterity as they took aim with the weapons, all of them pointing them in the direction of Veikr and the family riding on his back.

The wanderer didn't stop to think. He leapt so that he interposed himself between the riders and the family, spinning to face the crossbowmen. No sooner had he done so than the riders let fly with their missiles. His sword was in his hand in an instant, and he did not hesitate before he drew the cursed blade as well, knowing that he would need it. Then the missiles were flying at him, but though they seemed impossibly fast at first, as the power of the enemy's weapon surged through him, they seemed to slow, not to a crawl, but slow enough that he was able to keep track of them, eleven in all, not twelve as he had first thought.

Gritting his teeth as raw power ran through him from the cursed blade, feeling as if he stood in the center of some great inferno, the wanderer swatted first one then another crossbow bolt out of the sky, counting them as he did.

*Seven...eight...nine...ten...*and then, with a desperate leap, extending himself full length in the air to reach it, *eleven,* the very tip of his sword striking the bolt enough to deter its flight, flight that would have unerringly struck Dekker in the back where he rode atop Veikr.

The wanderer had a brief moment of relief, but before he hit the ground pain suddenly lanced into his left arm, and he cried out as he was spun by the force of whatever had struck him. The graceful roll he'd intended, one that would carry him easily to his feet, instead turned into a bone-jarring, bruising tumble. Finally, he managed to get control of the wild roll, coming to his feet. He glanced at his shoulder and saw that he had been right the first time—there had been twelve missiles after all. Not so difficult to deduce considering that a crossbow bolt, or at least what was left of it after his brutal roll, was sticking out of his shoulder. He glanced back at the riders, and saw that they were close now, close enough that he could see the expression of shock on the face of the rider at their front, a man with a thick black moustache and who the wanderer took as their leader. He watched as that shock turned into anger and the big man jabbed his sword in the wanderer's direction. *"Kill that bastard!"*

Even had he not been wounded, the wanderer could not have taken on half so many. As it was, his left arm was already numb from the bolt, and the thing would be over quickly. He started away, meaning to sprint toward the woods, much closer now, then paused as he realized, with a stab of fear, that he no longer held the cursed blade in his left hand. A wave of intense fear overcame him then, and he cast his gaze about frantically until, a moment later, he saw the blade lying a short distance away. He rushed forward, sheathing his sword, and picked up the cursed blade, then turned and sprinted at the tree line as fast as he was able, each step sending a fresh stab of agony into his wounded shoulder, demanding his attention, his thought.

And that was fine, for a man did not need to think to run. And so he ran. He ran as fast as he could, ran as his breath rasped in his lungs, as his legs ached from the pain of it. Blood leaked from his wound, staining his shirt and running down his arm until he dribbled a trail of crimson from his fingertips as he moved.

And still he ran on.

He'd nearly reached the tree line when he heard the sound of a horse's hooves behind him, close, and more on instinct than any rational thought, he ducked. A moment later, a sword flew over his head as the leader of the riders surged past on his horse, his blade slicing through the air where the wanderer's neck had been a moment before.

But the horse did not surge far, for the beginning of the woods, of the Untamed Lands, lay only a few dozen feet ahead of them now. The horse seemed to know it, or perhaps was responding to its rider's fear when it reared, letting out a squeal of terror and nearly sending the rider spilling from his saddle.

The wanderer could have cut the leader down then, but he was well aware that more riders were coming up from behind him, would be on him any moment, so he ignored horse and rider both, sprinting toward the trees.

He reached them a moment later, going a short distance farther to put some obstructions between him and his pursuers before turning to check behind him.

He needn't have worried, though, for a quick look was enough to see that none of the riders had followed him. Instead, they had stopped at the forest edge, the riders and their horses prowling back and forth in front of the tree line like jungle cats peering into the tall grass for their quarry.

It was as if they had struck an invisible barrier, one which would not permit them to enter. Which, the wanderer knew, in some ways, they had. Only, this barrier was not one made of stone or wood, but instead of their own fears. Fears which, he knew better than most, were completely justified. No doubt, living so close to the border to the Untamed Lands, the riders had grown up on stories about them much as Dekker had, had no doubt been warned again and again by their parents to avoid the woods at all costs. Yet despite those warnings, children would be children, and the wanderer doubted if there was a single person among those riders currently glaring in at him who had not lost someone who had dared ventured into the woods at some point during their lives.

He remembered well the time he'd spent in Celes, and although he'd spent the vast majority of his years there training, even he had heard the stories. A furious growl drew his attention, and the wanderer turned to see the leader of the riders. The mustached man had dismounted, and he stood just outside the woods, pacing back and forth like a dog who wanted nothing more than to sink its teeth into something it had spotted only to find itself come up short as it reached the end of its leash.

"*Come on out, you bastard!*" the man shouted. "*Come on out and let's get this over with.*"

The wanderer did not answer, at least not with words. Instead, he let his answer come in the form of him turning around and starting toward where Veikr waited along with the family some distance farther in.

"*Last chance, fella!*" the man shouted after him. "*If you're going to die, at least let it be by a man—better that than the ghosts and the monsters that lurk in there!*"

Still, the wanderer said nothing, only continued to where the others stood. They barely seemed to notice though, for the husband and wife were both gazing about them as if expecting ghosts to come floating down out of the treetops. As for the little girl, she had eyes only for Veikr, petting the horse's muzzle while Veikr visibly preened at the attention.

"Relax," the wanderer told Dekker and Ella, "the true dangers are farther in."

The husband and wife both turned away from the trees to regard him, and Dekker let out a hiss when he saw the arrow. "Damnit, Ungr, you're shot!"

The wanderer winced, propping one hand on a tree to keep from wavering on his feet. "I noticed."

Ella hurried forward. "I can take a look, maybe—"

"Later," the wanderer said, glancing back at the riders, still waiting in the field beyond the trees, watching them. "We'd best get moving."

"Why?" Dekker said. "Those bastards don't look in any hurry to come in, if you ask me. Why, I expect we could sit down and have us a good jaw, and we'd still find them there when we finished."

"It isn't them I'm worried about," the wanderer said, meeting the big man's eyes, "but what Soldier will send when one of them reports back that they have us cornered in the Untamed Lands. Not that they'll need to report, for I drew the cursed blade, and so he—and the others of his kind—knows exactly where we are."

The big man frowned. "I don't much care for the way you think, Ungr."

"Neither do I," the wanderer admitted.

"So what then?" Dekker asked. "Travel farther into the Untamed Lands? A place—" He paused, glancing at his daughter before moving closer, talking in a low whisper so that the little girl might not hear. "A place that, according to the stories is so damned haunted ghosts are too afraid to come here?"

"It's not ghosts you need to worry about," the wanderer said. "In the Untamed Lands, the things that will kill you are all too alive."

The big man grunted. "Sounds like you speak from experience."

"Yes," the wanderer said. "Just not my own. The others, they told me of the Untamed Lands."

"The other Eternals, you mean."

"Yes."

The big man shook his head. "Don't suppose I'll ever get used to that."

"Me neither," the wanderer said, offering the man a smile.

"Either way," Dekker said, "I want to say thank you, you know, for doin' what you did back there. You saved us. Again." He sighed. "What is that? Three times? Four? Keep this up, I'm liable to lose track."

"Let's hope you don't have to," the wanderer said.

The big man nodded grimly. "Anyway, I'm sure it won't hurt if we take a few minutes, let El look at that shoulder—I'm no healer," he went on, glancing at it, "but that's a lot of blood."

"There'll be more if we tarry," the wanderer said. "You've seen how fast the Unseen can move when they've a mind to. No, we need to put as much distance as we can between us and this spot, as fast as we can."

"Papa, can't we rest? I'm tired."

They all turned to look at Sarah, the little girl rubbing at her eyes, her exhaustion plain on her face. Dekker and Ella looked helplessly at the wanderer who gave the girl the best smile he was capable of with his shoulder throbbing sickeningly. "We must go a little farther, I'm afraid, but you can ride on Veikr."

The girl glanced down at Veikr. "But...he's hurt, isn't he? I don't want to bother him."

"What, that little scratch?" the wanderer said, glancing at the horse's flank and waving a dismissive hand. "Veikr's stronger than his name implies—that is nothing to him. Isn't that right, Weakest?"

The horse snorted, giving a shake of his head. The girl giggled at that. "Alright, if it's okay with Veikr."

In another minute, they were moving, the little girl riding on Veikr's back while Dekker and his wife walked along beside the wanderer to give the horse a break.

Traveling was harder here, and they made poor time. The Untamed Lands had earned their name. There were no roads, no real pathways as such, not even those poorly-maintained, hard-packed trails of earth that could be found among the outskirts of civilization from one small hamlet to another. And that was as it should be, perhaps, for civilization and all its trappings, all its comforts and protections, had no place in the Untamed Lands.

Still, the wanderer had been trained in woodcraft, and after some searching, he located an animal trail, one likely used by deer and the creatures which spent their time hunting them. Not much, but likely the best they were going to get. The trail itself was thin, too thin to allow them to walk abreast and so they proceeded in a line, the wanderer at the front, Veikr coming up next with the little girl on his back, then Ella, and last, Dekker.

Such a formation made conversation difficult, and the wanderer thought that was just as well, for he did not feel much like speaking then. In truth, his shoulder throbbed sickeningly. He felt nauseous, dizzy, and it was all he could do to keep putting one foot in front of the other, to use his sword to occasionally swipe away some vine or limb which had grown to block the path upon which they walked. It took every ounce of his strength, every ounce of his will to keep going.

But he *did* keep going, just as he had kept going for the last one hundred years. For he knew that now, like then, to stop was to die. To fail.

While they walked, the wanderer listened for any signs of pursuit from behind but also for anything up ahead, for each step carried them farther into the Untamed Lands—danger was not coming. It was already here. But he heard no sounds of anything approaching from out of the thick undergrowth on either side of the path, which was just as well as, right then, he did not think he would have put up much of a fight against a temperamental squirrel.

The path lay before him, his path, and so pain or no pain, he walked it. There was nothing else a man could do. He took one step down it, his vision blurring. Then he took another. His head spinning, his feet uncertain beneath him, as if he stood not on the solid forest floor but on the deck of some ship cast wildly about in a powerful storm.

He took another step, not sure he *would* manage to take it until he did.

"Ungr? Is everything okay?"

The voice sounded as if it came from a long way off, and the wanderer turned, glancing back to see that Veikr and the girl, Sarah, were no longer behind him. Instead, it was Dekker, though what sort of expression was on the man's face he could not tell for his face, like the rest of him, was little more than a blur.

"Of course," he said, focusing on saying the words clearly and not swaying drunkenly. "Why?"

"No reason," the big man said, and the blur shifted, what the wanderer took as him shrugging his massive shoulders. "Just was wonderin' is all, you know as you've been standing here, not movin', for the last...say, two minutes?"

The wanderer blinked, turning to glance at Veikr in surprise, but the horse was little more than a white smudge in his sight, so could confirm the man's words one way or the other. *Two minutes*, the wanderer thought. Two minutes squandered when seconds wasted might mean their deaths. The creature posing as Soldier would not be content to leave them to the Untamed Lands, not so long as the wanderer carried the sword. He would send some of his servants to get it back. Likely, he already had. And if that danger was not enough then there were the denizens of the Untamed Lands themselves to think about.

They needed to move, quickly, needed to find shelter, none of which would be aided by worrying the family unnecessarily.

"Everything's fine," the wanderer rasped. "I was only thinking, planning our next move."

"Thinking," Dekker repeated.

"Yes," the wanderer said, opening his eyes wider in an effort to see the big man better. It didn't help.

"I see," Dekker said. "So what is it then?"

It felt as if a great fog had settled over the wanderer's mind, concealing his own thoughts from view, making it difficult to grab hold of one. Finally, though, he managed it. "What's that?"

"Our next move," Dekker said. "What is it? I mean, you said that the real dangers of the Untamed Lands are farther in, right?"

"That's right." *I think...isn't it?*

"So what's our next move?"

The wanderer gave the man a small smile, or at least tried to. He felt odd, disconnected from his body, and he had no way of knowing whether the expression ever actually made it into his face. "Simple," he said. "We go further in."

"But Ungr, are you sure you can—"

"*I'm fine,*" the wanderer croaked.

With that, he turned on his heel and, suiting action to words, started deeper into the Untamed Lands. Or, at least, he meant to. Certainly, *part* of him—namely, the upper part, from his waist and above—started forward. The rest though, his legs and feet—the parts that were inarguably the most important for activities like walking—decided differently. And then one thought made it clearly through the hazy fog filling his mind. And that thought was...*falling.*

He was falling, falling, falling, and then with a jarring, teeth-rattling, *oomph* not falling anymore but fallen. More than that, though, not conscious anymore either but decidedly not.

CHAPTER EIGHT

He drifted then. Drifted on currents of memory, currents in which he saw her face, the woman he had loved and who had loved him. But hers was not the only face rising out of the deep. There were others. Many. The Eternals, his brethren, his mentors, his heroes. Their visages rising out of the dark waters upon which he floated like phantoms and that was right, for they were that, that and nothing else. They did not speak and that, too, was right, for the dead had no voices. They only watched him, their expressions unreadable. Not blank but unreadable, and there was a profound difference, for it seemed to him that those faces felt something, *said* something. Yet it was as if they spoke in a language he did not know, perhaps one that he *could* not know.

Were they ashamed of him? Were they proud? Indifferent? Loathing, disappointed, supportive? They could have been anything. They could have been nothing.

Dozens, hundreds of faces, their unreadable expressions floating before him, as if waiting for him to speak, but what would he say? What *could* he say to justify his actions for the last several days, how he had risked the entire world, a world which all the Eternals had given their lives to protect? How could he justify the last century?

***

"How is he?"

Ella glanced away from her work, looking over her shoulder to see Dekker standing there. She resisted the urge to snap in annoyance at the interruption—not the first—as she turned back to the unconscious man.

Ungr's face was pale, his skin feverish, and from time to time he shivered in his sleep never mind that his forehead was so hot that when she touched it her first instinct had been to jerk her hand away. None of which was a good sign and none of which would do anything to comfort her worried husband.

And he *was* worried, that was certain. She needed only note the way Dekker kept shifting his weight from foot to foot, anxious to help, to do *something*. It was why she didn't snap at him for interrupting her again, for looming over her like he was. After all, the man was nearly six and a half feet tall—he really couldn't help but to loom. And whatever annoyance she might have felt vanished when her glance had shown her just how worried he was. A big man, her husband, fierce, protective, one that would take on an army if he thought they meant harm to those he loved and that without hesitation. She didn't know the specifics of his past—he'd tried to shield her from that, the fool—but she did know, from the scars he carried, that he had fought for his life and more than once.

A brave man then, if a fool, but now his worry for Ungr had made him like a child who wore his fear on his face for any to see as he waited for her answer.

"He's breathing," Ella said, which was just about the best comfort she could offer him, giving her husband a small smile before turning back to the unconscious man again. "Now, please, Dek. Let me work, will you? Why don't you go check on Sarah?"

"Ah, right. S'pose you don't want her walkin' up while you're workin' on him. I imagine she'd want to talk and it'd be distractin'."

I don't have to imagine, Ella thought. "Yes. Thank you," she said as she bent forward, putting a hand to Ungr's forehead. She was aware of a slight hesitation—perhaps as her husband realized the irony in what he'd said—then he turned and walked toward where Sarah was still, Ella hoped, asleep.

She frowned as she checked Ungr's forehead and discovered that it was still hot, though whether it was warmer than it had been before she couldn't tell for sure. She let her gaze travel down to the man's shoulder again, meaning to check on the wound. Dekker had managed to get the unconscious man's shirt off so that she might better access the wound and now, like the first time when she had cleaned and bandaged it, Ella found herself hesitating as she stared at the dozens, perhaps hundreds of scars on the man's wiry, naked torso.

So many that there was far more of him that was scarred than was not. So many scars that they came together to form a sort of map on his skin, a map of over a century of pain, of sacrificing himself, of *selling* himself one piece after another in order to buy the world—her and everyone else in it—a little more time.

Tears rose unbidden to her eyes then, and Ella, frustrated with herself, ran an arm across her face. Her tears would not help the man, yet faced with proof of such suffering, how could anyone with a heart not cry? How could anyone stare at that marred flesh, covered in scar-tissue, realizing that those scars had been gained while spending a solitary existence trying to keep the world safe, and not be moved to tears? It was not a matter of being tough, for Dekker was the toughest man she had ever met, and even he had hissed at the sight of Ungr's uncovered torso, nor had she missed the tears that had gathered in his eyes. No one could stare at so much evidence of pain and suffering and not be moved.

It was not a matter of being tough.

It was a matter of being human.

But those past scars, however bad, however many, would not kill him. Instead, it was the one on his shoulder, the one he had gained while protecting Ella and her family that would do that. So she gave her head a shake, took a slow, deep breath in an effort to steady herself, and leaned forward, untying the makeshift bandage she had used to cover the wound in Ungr's shoulder little more than two hours ago.

She was surprised to discover that the bandage was dry. The wound had bled a lot—proof of that could be seen easily enough staining Ungr's discarded shirt—had still been bleeding when she'd finished poulticing it and applying what medicine she could and began wrapping it.

She had expected the bandage to be soaked through by now or nearly so—it was the reason she'd thought to check it again—but there was no blood on it at all. She frowned, slowly peeling away the bandage and hoping for some answer to that.

But when she had finished unfurling the bandage covering the man's shoulder, she was not left with any answers but, instead, only more questions. *"How...how?"* she managed in a dry rasp, though the words were in a low whisper and meant only for herself.

Yet, despite that, she got an answer. "The Rituals," a voice said.

Ella let out a gasp of shock and would have screamed had she any breath to do it. She recoiled and then realized that the voice she'd heard had belonged to Ungr. Not that that did anything to lessen her surprise. The truth—the one she had been doing her best to hide from Dekker, had been doing her best, in fact, to hide from herself—was that she had not expected Ungr to wake again. The man had lost a lot of blood, after all, and he had certainly looked like he was, if not dead, then well on his way. In fact, he still did.

Ungr winced. "Sorry," he said. "Didn't mean to scare you, only—"

"*Ella*," a voice said, and there was a loud thudding on the ground as Dekker approached like a herd of buffalo, "*what is it? Are you alright?*"

Ella got over enough of her surprise at Ungr's recovery to turn as Dekker approached. "I'm fine, Dek," she said. "Really."

"What is it then?" the big man said as he lumbered up to her. "I mean, for the Eternals' sake, El, you scared me half to—" The big man cut off with a grunt as he stopped beside El, staring wide-eyed at Ungr.

The other man gave him a pained smile. "Not *Eternals*, I'm afraid," he said. "Just the one."

Dekker let out a sound that was somewhere between a hiss and a grunt and then rushed forward, pulling the wanderer into an enveloping hug before Ella could warn him off. Ella could see the smaller man's head peeking over her husband's boulder-like shoulder. There was a curious expression on his face, one that was a mixture of pain and contentment as he patted Dekker awkwardly on the back. "It's alright," he said. "I'm alright."

"*Ha!*" Dekker said, leaning back and clapping the man on the shoulder, which Ella was thankful to see was at least his unwounded one. "See there, El?" he said, turning to her with a smile that took up pretty much his entire face. "I told you he'd be okay, didn't I? Didn't I tell you?"

In point of fact, he hadn't said anything of the sort, had instead just asked her one question after the other, rapid fire, the way a child, looking to be comforted might. But Ella loved her husband, and she smiled. "Of course, dear," she said. "And I'm as happy as you to see that Ungr is doing well. Still...if we mean to keep him that way, I think maybe it's best you don't do anymore celebrating."

"What do you mean?" Dekker asked, frowning.

"What I mean, Dek," she said, "is that I've seen lumberjacks who are easier on the trees they're cutting down then you are on a man you're glad to see alive."

Her husband cleared his throat, coloring as he turned back to Ungr. "Sorry, Ungr, I didn't mean—"

"I'm fine," Ungr said. "No harm done." He gave a small smile then. "Or, well, at least not much."

"Good," Ella said, "now, if we've got that out of the way, I'd like to take a closer look. I don't know what miracle it is that's kept you alive this long, but I'd just as soon not tempt fate, not if I can help it."

"Not a miracle," Ungr said. "Magic. Specifically, the magic of the Rituals."

"Magic," Dekker repeated before Ella could say anything. Then her husband grunted. "Well, if it's magic that'll let you survive a crossbow bolt, maybe I need some of that for myself."

Ungr gave him another small smile. "There is always a cost in this world. And the Rituals...they are no different. It is why there are so few Eternals, for most of those who are selected are not...chosen." He gave a small shrug then winced in pain as the movement pulled on his wound. "Or, at least, that is how it was explained to me."

"What sort of Rituals?" Dekker asked.

Ella found herself leaning forward, eager to hear the other man's answers. After all, the Eternals had always been more like gods than men and women, and she, like nearly everyone else, had been taught to pray to them from a young age. A child, studying for a test from their tutor, might pray to Scholar for knowledge. A young woman, attending a village dance, might pray to Charmer for grace and poise even while her parents prayed to Oracle to grant her the wisdom necessary to make good choices. Even now, she could hardly believe that she knelt in front of one of those noble visages.

If what Ungr had said was true—and she had no reason to doubt it—then he hadn't been an Eternal for long before tragedy had struck, but he had spent time with the greatest, most powerful men and women alive. In fact, he *was* one. Oh yes, she was curious about the Rituals, and there were a thousand other things she might have asked. But while he might have been nearly a god, just then, Ungr was a man, a man who was wounded and very close to death, one who had received his wound by saving the lives of her family, so Ella brushed away her curiosity.

"Ask him your questions later, if you'd like, Dekker," she said. "For now, I need to see to his wound."

"Oh, of course, of course," he said, shaking his head. "Damn, I'm a fool. I'll leave you to it."

As he started to leave Ella looked away from her work and at her husband for the first time since he'd approached. She blinked. "Dekker?" she asked.

"Yes, love?" her husband said, turning back to her.

"Is that a tree you're carrying?"

The big man glanced over at what he was carrying with an almost guilty expression. "Well...that is, it's only a little one. I just...well, you screamed and..." He trailed off, looking sheepish.

"Right," Ella said, feeling at once exacerbated and overcome with a deep love for the man in front of her. "Well, maybe it'd be best to get rid of it before you go huggin' Sarah."

"Of course," he said, tossing it aside then walking away.

Ella turned back to see Ungr staring after her husband, a look of awe on his face. "The Eternals are not the only ones capable of incredible feats," he said softly. Then he turned to her. "Just how strong is he, really?"

"Here's hoping none of us ever has cause to find out," Ella said, meaning it. "Anyway, sorry about that. Dekker can be a bit...protective."

"The world being what it is," Ungr said, "I can think of worse things."

"Yeah," she agreed, looking lovingly at her husband where he knelt beside Sarah. "So can I." She gave herself a shake then turned back to Ungr. "Anyway, I suppose it's time we see about that wound of yours. Not that there *is* much of a wound," she finished as she leaned forward and examined it more closely, seeing that her first, shocked observation had been accurate. The "wound" which, hours ago, had been a nasty, puckered hole in the man's shoulder, one that had looked hideous even after her best attempts at sewing it back together, had now nearly completely closed. No one, seeing it, would have guessed that an archer had sheathed his crossbow bolt in the man's shoulder only hours ago. "I'm beginning to understand how you have survived as long as you have," she said. "Anyway, there are no signs of infection that I can see. I'll reapply the poultice and put a clean bandage on. How do you feel?"

"Like a man who's been shot with a crossbow," he said with a smile.

She shook her head. "Right, sorry, I'm a fool and that's a fool's question."

"Between the two of us," he said, "I'd guess I'm the fool—after all, people rarely end up with crossbow bolts in their shoulders from being exceptionally clever."

"Maybe not," she agreed. "But they do when they risk themselves in order to save someone else."

He fidgeted, clearly uncomfortable at that, and she sighed, shaking her head. "Men. I swear. Always so eager to be heroes and then so embarrassed when someone recognizes you as such."

"As I said, I'm a fool." He smiled. "One that would have been dead a long time ago if it hadn't been for Veikr and—" Suddenly his eyes went wide, and he let out a grunt, a panicked expression coming onto his face. He started toward his feet, hissing in pain as he did, but Ella thrust out a hand, stopping him.

"Just what are you doing?"

"I have to get up," he said, "Veikr, he was wounded, I need to—"

"Veikr is *fine*," she said quickly.

He froze at that, then turned to look at her. "Fine? But...how do you know?"

"I know," she said slowly, "because I saw to him myself. The cut on his side was long, but it wasn't deep. He's faring well, far better than you will if you push yourself too hard too fast. I don't know much about Eternals and magic Rituals, but I do know that if you looked like death that'd be an improvement."

He gave a soft laugh, easing back again. "I'm beginning to think that Dekker's toughness is a survival mechanism."

She rolled her eyes. "I can flatter your ego, Ungr, or I can keep you alive. Guess which I choose?"

He nodded slowly. "Thank you, Ella. For seeing to Weakest. He...he is..."

"Your friend," she said. "I know."

"Yes," Ungr said. "He is my friend." His eyes went wide again at that as he seemed to have another thought. "The blade, the cursed blade, it—"

"Is safe," she interrupted. "Dekker has it taken care of."

"Dekker," he said, "he didn't touch it, did he? It is cursed, the blade, and it—"

"He didn't touch it," she said.

He eased back again, breathing a heavy sigh of relief. "Good," he said. "That is good."

"Now if you're done panicking," she said, "why don't you sit back and relax. I've got to finish tending to your wound. You should get some sleep, if you can. After all, there is no better healer than sleep."

"There is no time for sleeping," Ungr said. "As soon as you are finished, we must leave. I will be alright and, anyway, we dare not squander anymore time than we already have on my account. Soldier will be sending his creatures after us."

"As you say," Ella said. She continued her work then and in another ten minutes, when she was finished, she was unsurprised to find Ungr sleeping. Despite the man's words, he needed his rest and so, satisfied that she had done all that she could for him, she rose and left him to it, walking toward where her husband and her daughter lay.

CHAPTER NINE

It was dark when he woke. What little light there was came from the rare splashes of moonlight that managed to make it through the snarl of branches and tree cover overhead. His fever had passed, that much he knew, and he was on the mend—he had been on it enough to recognize it.

The worst of the pain was gone, the magic imbued in him during the Rituals combined with Ella's attentions proving its worth. True, he was tired. Exhausted, really. But then, he had been tired before. He used the tree upon which he'd been propped to help work his way to his feet. Once there, he set about looking for Veikr.

The horse was lying down, sleeping, but as the wanderer approached his ears gave a twitch, and his eyes opened, turning to regard him.

Veikr gave a soft snort, coming to his feet, and the wanderer smiled as he shuffled forward, running his hand along his muzzle. "I'm alright," he said.

Veikr nudged him in his chest, making a contented sound, and the wanderer grinned. "I'm pleased to see you, too. Weakest, listen, I just want you to know, when you left, I—" He cut off then at what sounded like a mixture of a piercing scream and a wail. It sounded almost like the scream of a mortal woman or, perhaps, like the sound of a mountain lion, only it was too powerful to have come from either. He frowned, gazing off into the night. The sound had seemed to come from far away, but then in the woods sound often traveled strangely. Besides, many of the creatures of the Untamed Lands, according to what the other Eternals had told him, could travel great distances in shockingly short amounts of time. It had made them brutal adversaries during the war and it would serve them well enough should they decide to hunt the wanderer and his companions.

Veikr gave a soft neigh, turning to regard the figures of the sleeping family.

"I know," the wanderer said. "And you need not fret, Weakest. We will protect them." *At least as long as we can.* "Come. We had best wake them, and quickly."

***

Fifteen minutes later, after waking the family and assuring them—at least a dozen times, the wanderer suspected—that he and Veikr were both fine, they started out. At Dekker and Ella's repeated insistence, the wanderer rode on Veikr's back with Sarah, their daughter, while the husband and wife walked along beside.

The wanderer had tried to argue the point, but the truth was that while his body healed faster than a normal man's, he knew it would serve him well to give it a little while longer to recuperate. So, in the end, he had acquiesced, and they had started on their way once more.

He was tired, it was true, but he knew that the world cared nothing for a man's excuses, that it would come at him tired or not, weak or not, and so he listened closely as they rode, for any sound of something coming upon them out of the wood. His eyes scanned the surrounding trees, and he rode with his left hand, still weak from his wound, gripping Veikr's reins, the other holding the handle of his bared blade. Normally, he might have left it sheathed at his back, but he knew that his exhaustion would rob him of some of his speed, some of his strength, and if he and his companions encountered any of the creatures the Eternals had told him about he would need all the advantages he could get.

The girl sat behind him, her head pressed against his back, and he was aware of her, of the need to protect her, in a way that he had never been aware of the world when he had set about trying to protect it. He could not save the world, after all. It was huge, far too big for one man to shield it from harm, even should he use his own body to do it. The girl though, was small enough. He hoped that she was small enough.

Thinking of advantages, of how they were in the most dangerous place in the world, one that he did not know as much about as he wished and him wounded with a family needing his protection, the wanderer thought of the other Eternals, found himself idly fingering the locket hung at his neck.

He had not given the ghosts leave to speak in some time, and he knew that should he do so now, they would have plenty to share regarding his decisions of late, particularly him traveling to the Untamed Lands. But then they were ghosts, after all, and he had yet to ever hear of a pleasant haunting. He did not want to speak to them, to hear the recrimination in their voices, the anger, the disappointment, yet he knew that if he wanted any chance of making it out of the Untamed Lands with the family alive, he would need their help. And so, the choice was one that made itself.

He opened the locket.

The voices came at once, a deluge of scorn and frustration. The wanderer only remained silent, accepting it, letting it wash over him the way a man, seeing a wave come and knowing he could not avoid it, might brace himself.

Warned you not to get involved with those Perishables, though their name at least is apt, for—Tactician's voice, sharp, like a dagger plunged at him again and again.

—was ill-considered, Youngest, to tie your fate—and thereby the fate of the world—to this family. As foolish as a man, hanging from a cliff by one hand that refuses to let go the man he holds in the other so that, in the end, they can only both fall to their doom. That was Scholar's voice, sad and ancient and possessed of a quality that made everything he spoke ring with truth.

—And to draw the cursed blade not once but twice in your flight. Do you not see, Youngest? It is not only that it alerts the enemy of your whereabouts, though there is that. The blade is cursed for other reasons, for a fell guise lies upon it, one that has begun to work in you even now— Oracle's voice, not sounding angry so much as she sounded afraid, worried. Not for herself, for the dead were beyond saving and therefore beyond worry. Instead, she seemed worried for him, and he found himself listening,

wondering how she might finish, only she did not manage it before her voice was drowned out by another.

Hope you know what you're doing, Youngest. The Untamed Lands are called so for a reason—I would not venture into them, even with an army, if given a choice. This was Soldier's voice, not scolding, but matter-of-fact. Honest and simple in its honesty.

Enough, all of you. This from Leader, his voice resonant and commanding as it always was, and the others went silent. *Soldier is right, though, Youngest. It was a desperate choice, for you to come here to the Untamed Lands.*

"I am a desperate man," the wanderer said, low enough that he hoped Sarah would not hear.

Indeed, Leader said. *And I am correct in supposing that you are aware that you might yet escape your predicament?*

That was true, of course. After all, if he were to abandon the family to their fate—a fate that was not in question, not here in the Untamed Lands—the wanderer could take Veikr and flee. With only him and the horse, he was confident they could make it out of the Untamed Lands safely, could evade the creatures and troops Soldier had sent after them. After all, they had done it many times before. "I am aware," he said quietly.

Leader, perhaps hearing his resolve, did not bother asking the next obvious question. Instead, he spoke on. *So what is it then, Youngest? You have obviously not come to us seeking our counsel, at least not on this, so what is it you want?*

There had been a time when the wanderer had respected Leader above anyone in the world, had thought that, in many ways, he sat as far above the other Eternals as the Eternals sat above the rest of the world. He possessed a keen intellect, one to match Scholar's, a wisdom to match Oracle's, a creativity to match Alchemist's, a physical prowess to match Soldier's, and compassion to match Healer's. And yet, he had never been vain or arrogant, had lived not to be served but to serve.

Until he hadn't.

A great man, the best of men, and to hear the disappointment in his voice, even in the voice of his ghost, was a terrible thing to bear.

"I...I have only done what I thought best," the wanderer said, suddenly feeling the need to justify his decision.

Yes, Leader agreed, *but best for whom?*

That caught him off guard and, for a moment, he had no answer to give. Or, at least, he did not like the one he had. He had not made the choices he had over the last days for the world, that much he knew. After all, he had risked the cursed blade many times, and so had risked the world. He wanted to believe he had done it for the family, but even that he was not sure about. Had he done it for the family, or had he done it for himself? Done it not to protect them, but to protect the way they made him feel—that he belonged, that he was a part of the world again, feelings he'd not had in a very, very long time? Was all of this, in truth, no more than some selfish need to drive back the loneliness that had grown over the years? To feel wanted? To feel *needed?*

"I don't...I don't know," he answered honestly, and his voice broke at the last.

Very well, Leader said, his voice softer, full of compassion. *The choice is made, and that is what matters. So, Youngest, tell us what you need.*

He felt lost for a moment, felt confused and foolish, like a man who attacks a figure looming out of the darkness, dodging its return blows even as it dodges his, only to realize that in the end, it was his shadow and that he had only been fighting with himself.

He gave his head a shake, forcing the thought away. He could worry at it later, if he liked, could take his time at it, the way a dog might worry at a bone, but first they had to survive the night. "I need information," he said back quietly. "You have all dealt with the dangers of the Untamed Lands, and I have not. I would ask that you be my eyes and ears."

Eyes and ears, Tactician said sharply. *You must be ki—*

Very well, Youngest, Leader answered. *We will offer you what help we may, though you must understand that there is no way that you might be made safe, not while you are in the Untamed Lands. Each moment that you spend here brings you closer to your death. For there are things which lurk in the great expanses of the Untamed Lands that have not been seen in generations. Beings, creatures from ancient times, many of which are the originators of some of the worst legends, the most terrible stories the world has.*

"I understand," the wanderer said. "All I ask is that you offer me what help you may—whatever happens, it is my fault and mine alone."

I'm sure that will be a great comfort to that family of yours when they are being made something's meal, Tactician said.

Enough, Tactician, Leader growled. *He is aware of the danger and yet still chooses to press on. Aid him or be silent.*

Tactician, at least for the moment, chose silence, and the wanderer only hoped that he would not remain that way. For while he might have been difficult to deal with, there was no denying that Tactician was a genius, a prodigy even from a young age, or so the legends regarding him said, and over the centuries which he and the other Eternals ruled he had proven his aptitude again and again. If the wanderer and his companions had any chance of making it out of the Untamed Lands, they would need Tactician's help.

He thought of saying something to soften the blow, to help Tactician's pride. The problem, though, was that he had never been good at such things. So, thinking that anything he said could only be the wrong thing, he chose to say nothing instead, traveling on in silence.

A moment, Youngest.

This came from Ranger's voice in his mind, and the wanderer did as requested, pulling Veikr to a stop.

"What is it, Ungr? Everything alright?" Dekker's voice came, sounding pained as he looked up from where he propped heavily on the walking stick the wanderer had procured for him.

The wanderer held up a hand. "A moment, please."

To your right. Along the tree.

The wanderer turned the way Ranger said and regarded the large tree standing there. "What of it?" he asked, seeing nothing unusual that might have drawn Ranger's attention.

Move along the side.

Frowning, he dismounted Veikr, moving to the side of the tree. He was surprised to find that, on this side, the bark of the massive tree had been deformed. But staring at it, he realized that "deformed" wasn't the right word. His hand tightened on the grip of his sword as he understood that what he had first taken for some odd growth of the bark or, perhaps evidence of some injury the tree had taken when it was much younger were, instead, claw marks. Four in total, running at a diagonal down the tree's surface, as if a cat had been stretching here, digging its claws into the tree. Only, to have made the marks he was staring at, those claws would have had to have been as large as both of his hands put side by side. Each.

"What made these?" he asked quietly.

Best not stick around to find out, Youngest, Tactician said in his mind, his voice grim. *The tree, the claw marks, they're a way of it marking its territory.*

"You've...you've seen it before?"

Not I, Tactician said. *Berserker did, though...the poor bastard. Time to go, Youngest. Quickly—but quietly, mind. The thing that made those marks, it isn't just its claws that're big but its ears too, understand?*

The wanderer didn't understand, at least not completely, but he thought he understood enough to be getting on with. He turned back to the family then held a finger to his mouth, motioning them, and Veikr, farther down the trail.

Thankfully, none of them said anything, even Sarah. Instead, they only complied, and they all moved quietly through the undergrowth. Then, suddenly, there was another sound in the wood, a groaning, wooden sound, and the wanderer turned slowly, gazing into the forest. The trees were thick here, blocking much of what lay beyond them from his view, but he saw, in the distance, trees bending aside the way bushes might give way to a man walking through them, creaking as they did, some smaller trees snapping altogether.

At first, the wanderer could not see what caused this disturbance but then, for a brief moment, he did, or at least he saw part of it—specifically, a furred leg, one that disappeared somewhere into the trees but one that was, without doubt, taller than he was himself. He didn't see much more than that, but then he didn't really need to.

He turned back to see that the family had frozen, all of them staring into the woods, the little girl, Sarah, with both her hands clasped over her mouth, as if she were straining to hold the top on a bottle lest its contents—in this case, screams—spilled out. The wanderer understood, for he wasn't all that far from screaming himself.

They stood that way, barely daring even to breathe, as whatever it was stalked farther into the forest. The wanderer caught sight of patches of fur here and there as the giant figure moved away from them. He waited until it was out of sight, the disturbance it caused no more than a distant sound...then he waited some more.

Finally, he turned back to the family, giving Dekker a nod. The big man and his wife, along with Veikr and the small girl riding atop him—who was currently still staring out at the woods, her eyes impossibly wide—started down the path once more.

The wanderer studied the woods for another few seconds then slowly turned and followed behind them.

They proceeded on quietly, no one daring to break the silence. When the wanderer was sure—or at least as sure as he was likely to be—that the creature did not mean to attack them from behind, he moved to the front of the procession, taking up the lead.

As he did, he allowed Ranger to guide them, for the ghost, like the man he had been, was an expert at woodcraft, able to notice in a glance a hundred small details that a normal person could not and, further, to know what those details meant. The wanderer followed him completely, as he had when he'd trained with him. He expected that the family must have thought it strange, the way he led them off the path from time to time, taking a wide detour into the woods only to return to it a short while later.

The wanderer, though, did not question, for beneath the boughs of great trees, among the bracken and the bushes littering the forest floor, he knew there was no one more capable than Ranger. Hours passed, and the day came on in full as they traveled, the sun rising high above them, chasing away many of the shadows which had clung to the tree trunks. Many, but not all, for some shadows were more persistent than others, lingering despite the dawn.

Still, while the sun might not have completely rid the world of the darkness lingering within it, it seemed to do a pretty thorough job of wiping away that darkness which had grown in each of them during the night. It was a gradual change, but one the wanderer could not help but notice. Where, hours ago, after they'd seen the monstrosity, Dekker and his wife had moved like two people headed toward their own execution, now they seemed lighter, their steps easier. And once, the wanderer glanced back and even caught sight of Dekker holding a branch back so that his wife could pass through, bowing deeply, Ella smiling and shaking her head as she walked past him.

It did the wanderer good to see that, and a quick glance at Veikr's back showed that, by the smile on the little girl's face as she watched her parents' antics, it did her good as well. And as he walked, the wanderer found that his own steps began to feel lighter too, his body stronger. Part of this, he knew, was due to the Rituals, but not all. Still they did not speak, all of them, he supposed, feeling much as he did, like a child tiptoeing past his closet in the darkness, confident that, just because he did not see the monster lurking within it, that did not mean it wasn't there. And knowing that should he be too loud, should he draw attention to himself, then it would prove its presence quickly enough.

So they tiptoed in silence, but they smiled as they did it, and while the wanderer knew, like that child, that evil existed, that it *lurked,* waiting, he was also reminded of another truth, one he had forgotten over the last century. Evil existed, yes, but so too did good. Good was often quieter than its counterpart, not shouting to be seen, not pointing accusatory fingers, or shaking its fist. No, good came upon a man when he did not expect it, in the sound of a child's laughter, in a quiet moment shared between two people who loved each other. Sometimes, a man had to look for the good, but it was always there, waiting to be found, even beneath the boughs of the wild trees of the Untamed Lands.

Strange, perhaps, to feel the most at peace that he had felt in a very long time while traveling in the most dangerous place he had ever been. And yet…he did. The wanderer did not understand that feeling, but neither did he question it, choosing instead to allow it to buoy him up as he walked.

At least, that was, until he became aware of a smell. Faint at first, but terrible, nonetheless. It made the wanderer think that perhaps an animal had died nearby, and that the odor he detected was its body decomposing.

But as they continued on, he discarded that theory. For one, while the smell did remind him of something dead, there was more to it than that. He thought also that it reminded him of body odor, as if someone had been at hard, sweaty labor for days and not bothered to clean themselves. But that was not the main reason he gave up the idea. The main reason was that the smell was getting stronger, *closer,* and if dead animals could be counted on to do anything, it was to remain still.

He was still puzzling over it, trying to figure out what it might be, when there was a splintering of wood and something seemed to appear in the tree beside him as if by magic, sticking out of its trunk. The wanderer examined the object in an instant, taking in its characteristics. It appeared to be made of bone, three pieces of bone about six inches each which had been sharpened to points and lashed together with what might have been vines.

Alarm bells suddenly began to sound in his head, and the ghosts began to all talk at once. He could not make out what they said, but then he didn't need to, for he understood their tones clearly enough—fear.

Shit, he thought.

He spun toward the family. "Get on Veikr. Now."

"Ungr, what is—" Dekker began.

"*Now,*" the wanderer snapped. "There is no time."

Then, as if his words were a cue, there suddenly came a loud *whooping* sort of sound from nearby. Then another, and another, the woods suddenly coming alive with the strange, animal-like calls. The wanderer scanned the woods, his sword still in his hand, then turned back quickly to check on the others.

The family had mounted Veikr and they were all now staring into the trees with faces pale from fright.

"What...what is it, Ungr?" Ella asked.

There was a crash of sound from beside him, and the wanderer ducked in time to narrowly avoid an axe, fashioned of bone, that was swung at his neck. The weapon embedded itself in the trunk of the tree beside him, and the wanderer spun to take in his attacker, realizing that his first thought on what might be coming had been right and wishing it hadn't been.

The Accursed who'd attacked him snarled and spat, bloody foam coming from his mouth as he forewent his weapon and clawed at the wanderer with long, yellow nails. The wanderer's mind was still trying to catch up, to understand, but thankfully his sword arm needed no such time. It reacted immediately, his sword flashing up, and in another instant his attacker's hand, severed from his arm at the wrist, was hurtled away into the undergrowth.

His attacker, though, didn't seem to notice at all, not even hesitating before he lunged forward, snapping at the wanderer with his teeth like an animal. The wanderer backpedaled, at least for the two steps he was able before his back struck the trunk of a tree. The one-handed Accursed pursued him, leaping forward, and in desperation the wanderer brought his leg up, kicking the creature away.

The Accursed flew backward, striking the ground and going into a roll before coming up on all fours. Or, at least, he would have had he not been missing a hand. As it was, he crouched on his feet and one hand, the bloody foam pouring down his chin as he gnashed his teeth over and over again. His eyes were wild, inhuman, and once again the wanderer was reminded of some feral beast.

The Accursed rushed him again, and this time the wanderer stepped to the side of the charge. The Accursed managed to pivot in midstride and lunge forward at the wanderer, his mouth open wide, meaning to take a bite out of him. But the wanderer's sword was already moving and instead of getting a bite of flesh the Accursed got a mouthful of steel as the blade slid into his mouth and out the back of his head before striking a tree trunk and digging deep into it, pinning him there.

The wanderer was aware of Sarah screaming as he stared at the creature still struggling, uncaring about the sword sticking through it and out the back of its head just as it was oblivious to the way its one remaining hand was being cut to ribbons as it grabbed at the sword, trying to free itself so that it might come at him again.

The wanderer stepped toward the creature, making sure that his back would block most of it from the little girl's view, assuming her parents had not yet made her look away. Then he drew the knife he kept at his waist. The creature did not seem to notice the knife or, if it did, to care. It only continued to paw at the sword as the flesh of its hand hung in tatters. The wanderer felt a wave of disgust and something else—pity, perhaps—wash over him, then he took the knife and slid it across the Accursed's throat.

The creature continued to struggle for a few seconds but then its struggles finally ceased and it died.

"By...by the Eternals," Dekker breathed. "Is...is that thing a man?"

"No," the wanderer said as he sheathed his knife and ripped his sword free. "It's believed they were, once, but not anymore."

"More of the fake-Eternal experiments?" Dekker hissed.

"Perhaps," the wanderer said, "but if so, then they are the first experiments, for the Accursed were around long before we knew of the enemy's presence. But enough of that—where there is one Accursed, there will be others."

No sooner had he said the words than more *whooping* began, seeming to come from everywhere at once. The sound echoed strangely so that there might have been only a dozen or hundreds, there was simply no way to tell. And the truth was that the wanderer had no intention of waiting around to find out.

"It is time to run again, Weakest," he said to Veikr. "With me."

He was running then, and he did not check behind him to see if Veikr was following, knowing that he would. The whooping calls were coming from all around them now, and several more of the strange, sharpened bone weapons flew at them out of the trees, one coming so close that the wanderer was forced to deflect it with his sword, the blow so powerful that it nearly knocked his weapon from his grip.

He careened through the trees, completely unaware of where they were going, only following Ranger's barked directions, trusting the Eternal ghost to help him avoid the other Accursed pacing them on either side through the trees. He did not catch many glimpses of them, but what he did showed some swinging from vines, others leaping from tree branch to tree branch and still others loping through the woods on all fours. Anyone staring at them would have thought them more animal than men, and they would have been right to do so. He had told Dekker true—the Accursed had been men once, or so it was believed. But whatever they had been, they were men no longer. Far stronger, faster than men, possessing the grace—and viciousness—of animals.

Had Veikr been given free rein to run, the wanderer knew that the horse would have easily outdistanced their pursuers, if not as easily as he might have normal men and women. The problem, though, was that he was not given leave to run, for the woods were choked with trees and undergrowth, not to mention the fallen trees they came across from time to time, barriers that slowed them down as they had to navigate their way around or over them, costing them precious seconds, seconds they could not afford to lose.

The wanderer was aware of the number of the creatures around them growing as more and more caught up.

"*Ungr*, above!"

Dekker's voice, and the wanderer looked up immediately to see to his surprise that one of the Accursed had flung itself out of the tree like a chimpanzee. It was hurtling toward him, its teeth bared in a rictus of a grin, holding a bone-shard dagger in one hand and a rock in the other. The wanderer pivoted, leaping to the side in an abrupt gesture that sent a spasm of pain through his ankle and knee, lashing out with the sword as he did. It dragged a deep furrow across the Accursed's chest, sending it off course so that it struck the ground hard, going into a roll and fetching up against a tree with bone-jarring force.

The wanderer heard something crack, the creature's back perhaps. He was moving forward with the intent of finishing it when Dekker shouted again.

"Behind you!"

He spun in time to see another of the strange throwing weapons hurtling toward him. He leaned to the side, and the missile sailed past, within inches of striking him, then off into the undergrowth. The creature who had thrown the missile was right behind it, loping forward in that strange, monkey-like movement, then leaping at the last moment in time to receive the wanderer's blade through its chest.

The Accursed were strong, seemingly capable of ignoring pain, if they felt it at all. They were fast, too, but no amount of strength or speed changed their biology, and while they might not have been men, their hearts were, at least, in the same place. Proof of that could be seen the moment his blade pierced the creature's chest, and the light of life vanished from its eyes in an instant. It crumpled to the ground, and the wanderer ripped his sword free, turning and starting back toward Veikr and the others only to come up short as another Accursed stepped in front of him.

This one was large, larger even than Dekker, and up to that point the wanderer would have thought it unlikely that he would ever meet anyone bigger than the other man. The figure, like the others of its kind, was completely naked, giving the wanderer a clear view of the corded muscle all along his body, as well as dozens of scars.

The creature's face, too, was scarred, with raised ridges where it was clear he'd suffered several deep lacerations, only these formed into a sort of looping, whirling design that made the wanderer think that they had been intentional.

The figure only stood, staring at him, while others of its kind appeared out of the trees on either side, surrounding the wanderer but keeping their distance. The figure in front of him bared its teeth, and the wanderer saw that every single one had been filed to a dagger-sharp point.

Well aware that they were running out of time, that soon, any moment, there would be enough of the Accursed surrounding him and the others that they would have no chance of escape, the wanderer rushed forward, meaning to deal with the creature as quickly as possible. The creature only stood, waiting, its thick arms folded across its barrel chest, its sharpened teeth bared in a too-wide grin.

Even when the wanderer drew within only a few feet of him, still the Accursed did not react—which was fine by the wanderer. If the creature wanted to stand still and die he had no issue with it, for he would need all of his energy to ensure that they made it out of the encircling Accursed anyway.

He lunged forward with a strike that would take the creature in the chest, that *had* to take it in the chest.

Only...it didn't.

The Accursed moved. Its right hand came up, slapping the wanderer's blade away with a contemptuous ease, hitting the blade-side and yet its skin did not feel like skin at all but like thick hide, and the sword did not cut into it. Instead, the wanderer's blow was knocked wide, and he stumbled at the unexpected, weaponless parry. He was still trying to regain his balance when the creature moved, bringing its other hand around, knotted into a fist.

The Accursed's blow was aimed for his face, but the wanderer managed to pivot at the last moment so that it struck him in the shoulder. Which was just as well as the attack landed with shocking force, sending the wanderer crashing to the ground, his shoulder, his entire left arm, numb. So powerful was the blow that he found himself dazed, feeling more as if he had been struck by a carriage or kicked by a horse than hit by a creature that resembled a man.

The wanderer tried to get some grip over the immense pain and the blow had caused, was lying there trying to do exactly that. Until he wasn't. Before he knew what was happening he was being lifted into the air, and he stared groggily at the creature, realizing that it had picked him up with one hand with seeming ease, its sharp-teethed smile still well in place. Then it pivoted, swinging its arm, and he wasn't floating in the air anymore at all but flying through it.

He tried to orient himself, was still trying when he struck something with teeth-rattling force, and the breath exploded out of him in a *whoosh* as he collapsed to the ground.

He lay there, wheezing, gasping for breath, and took stock. A cracked rib, he thought, maybe two, and a left arm and shoulder that would not be useful anytime soon. No time to worry about that though, for if he hesitated any longer he'd have much more than some pained ribs and a hurt shoulder to worry about.

He had at least managed to hold onto his sword, which was something. Though if the rest of the creature's hide proved as effective in warding off its edge as its hand had then he did not know what good that would do him. Still struggling to get his breath back, straining and hissing with the effort, the wanderer worked himself to his knees, using his still-working right arm to prop himself up.

In front of him, the Accursed with the sharpened teeth was walking forward, taking his time, clearly in no hurry. But it was not him upon which the wanderer's eyes caught. Instead, it was Veikr, Veikr and the family. They were near the edge of the encircling Accursed, all of them watching him. Groaning, he stabbed his sword into the ground, using it to lever himself up. He was standing then, if only just.

He did not possess the strength or ability to fight the creature moving toward him and certainly not those other Accursed—numbering in the dozens now—in the clearing. Which left only one choice. "*Run!*" he roared at the family, at Veikr. "*Get them out of here, Weakest!*"

He didn't have time to say anything more then or to see if they listened, for in another moment the Accursed, who'd been taking his time, suddenly burst forward. He did not carry a weapon, but he did not seem daunted in the least by the fact that the wanderer was armed and he was not. He charged forward, his massive hands balled into fists, coming on in a flurry of blows.

Still struggling to get his balance, mentally and physically both, the wanderer backpedaled away from the relentless assault. His back fetched up against something he hadn't noticed, and he hissed as the Accursed swung a meaty fist at him. The wanderer ducked, nearly falling, and lunged away. The creature's powerful blow struck the tree, tearing a large chunk out of its trunk.

The wanderer took a moment to glance back where Veikr and the others had been and was relieved to see that there was no sign of them. They, at least, had made it out which was good, for he realized that he was going to die here. He could not beat this creature, not in his current state, and even if he was able to somehow manage it, it would make no difference. There were plenty more to finish the job, and the wanderer doubted that the other Accursed surrounding him would be willing to let him walk away if he somehow defeated their leader.

His death had finally found him, then. It had taken well over a century, far longer than it did to find most, but then that was the thing about death. A man might evade it for a time, might stay ahead of it, but it would hunt him always, that death, and sooner or later, it *would* catch him. In time, it would have him, and it seemed that, for the wanderer, at least, that time was now.

So he squared his shoulders, calling on what strength remained to him, and watched the Accursed approach, seemingly none the worse for wear for punching a tree. Standing there, though, the wanderer realized something. He was not satisfied with running from death anymore, not content to let his death come to him. And so, with a roar, he charged toward the creature. The Accursed tensed, seeming surprised by this action, as well it might have, as surprised as the cat to find a mouse racing toward it in fury. The wanderer swung his sword, a darting blow at the creature's neck, but the Accursed knocked the blade aside with its forearm, suffering perhaps the smallest of knicks for its trouble.

It swung in a counterattack, but the wanderer dodged the blow, pivoting and spinning, his sword coming toward the creature's side with all the strength he could muster with one arm. Only, the blow never landed. The Accursed caught his wrist, stopping the attack less than six inches from its side. The wanderer strained against its grip, but he might as well have been a child struggling against a fully-grown man for all the good his efforts did.

He abandoned his attempts to wrest the blade free, letting it go instead. He punched the creature in the face, then a second time, its head rocking back against the forces of the blows only to come up again, still smiling, still baring teeth that were now bloody. Growling with anger, the wanderer reared back to hit it a third time but before he could the creature moved its hand forward, almost casually, almost *gently,* and gave him a shove.

But while the Accursed's movement might have seemed gentle enough, the force of the shove most certainly did not, and the wanderer let out a shout of surprise as he was sent hurtling backward. He stumbled, trying to catch his balance, but his feet went out from under him and he fell.

Groaning, he lifted himself up on his elbows to see the creature still standing where it had been, his sword lying on the ground beside it. It knelt, lifting the blade and staring at it the way a grown man might stare at a child's improvised toy, wondering what pleasure he could possibly derive from it. Then it looked back to him, grinning wider, and tossed the blade so that it landed beside the wanderer.

"That's how it's to be then?" the wanderer asked, wheezing.

The creature said nothing, only watched him, waiting for him to take the sword, to rise. Left with no other choice, the wanderer obliged. Ignoring the dozens of pains and aches demanding his attention, he worked his way to his feet, having to use the sword like a cane to keep himself there. "Come on then, bastard," he said.

Say this for the creature, at least it had no intention of making him wait. No sooner were the words out of his mouth then the

Accursed rushed forward, its bulk moving deceptively fast. The wanderer gritted his teeth and held his sword out in front of him, thinking that, if he were lucky, perhaps the bastard would impale himself. He'd heard of men killing bears in such a way, using their own weight against them, and the Accursed was nearly the size of one.

He was not so lucky, though. The creature dodged his sword, and the wanderer growled, swinging, knowing he would be too late, seeing the creature pivot out of the corner of his eye and knowing that this blow would land and then it would be over.

But the blow did not land, and the wanderer was not sent crashing to the ground or hurtling through the air once more. Instead, it was the creature that went flying. It hit a tree—perhaps even the same one the wanderer had hit, he was too disoriented to know for certain—and the giant trunk snapped in half, sending the top half of the tree, and the Accursed, crashing to the ground.

The wanderer blinked in shock then turned to see that the creature had not been struck by a god after all but by a two-legged kick from Veikr who stood there looking at the wanderer expectantly.

The wanderer took in the horse's empty saddle and glanced around, feeling a panic. "The family?"

Veikr gave a soft neigh, and the wanderer breathed a sigh of relief. "Safe then. That's good. And thanks...for coming back. Now, we'd better get out of here. That was their leader, but while he might be dead, I doubt the—"

There was a great roar, like some giant beast, and the wanderer stopped talking, turning, along with the horse, to see the broken tree moving on the ground, shifting.

"Impossible," he breathed, and Veikr gave a soft neigh beside him as if in agreement.

But impossible or not, the giant tree was thrust aside and, in another moment, the Accursed leader was climbing its way to its feet. The wanderer blinked in disbelief, watching the creature gave its head a shake as if to clear it. He had never seen anything shrug off a kick from Veikr—a kick that could break down a brick wall. The wanderer knew for he had seen it. Yet, the creature seemed largely unfazed as it started toward them again. "But...how?" he asked.

He was still staring in shock at the creature when Veikr gave him another neigh, pushing him with his muzzle. "Right," the wanderer said. "Better we don't stick around to find out."

It was an effort, pulling himself into the saddle with only one good arm, his entire body throbbing with pain, but he managed it.

The creature, apparently only just becoming aware that he meant to escape instead of stand there and die, gave another roar and rushed forward.

"*Go, Veikr!*" the wanderer shouted. The horse obliged, exploding forward with such a burst of speed that the wanderer nearly went flying over the back of the saddle, only just managing to hold on. Suddenly the forest was alive with the *whooping* calls of the Accursed as they protested his and the horse's attempts to flee. They reached the edge of the encircling creatures in moments and several moved as if to block their way. Veikr did not try to dodge them, choosing instead the expedient of making use of his great size and strength to plow through them, sending them scattering—at least, the fortunate ones. The unfortunate ones ended up beneath the horse's thundering hooves as they rode past.

Then they were through, Veikr rushing around the trees, showing that his line of horses, extinct save him, were not just strong or large but possessed of a grace and agility far beyond any other beast.

They traveled that way for a few minutes, Veikr weaving a path through the woods, and soon the Accursed were out of sight somewhere behind them, only their whooping calls proof that they were still following.

Veikr came to a stop by a large tree and, after a moment, the family appeared from behind it.

"Thank the Eternals," Ella said. "Ungr, are you alright?"

The wanderer gave her a pained smile. "I've been better, but then I could have very easily been far worse. Now come, you must all climb on Veikr—we're not out of danger yet."

"What about you?" Ella asked.

"I will run," he said, starting to dismount the horse's back.

"Bullshit," Dekker said. "Look, Ungr, you're barely able to keep your saddle—a blind man could see that. You've got no chance of running, and I'm sure that horse of yours agrees that he didn't risk goin' back for you just for you to commit suicide five minutes later."

The wanderer hesitated, preparing to argue then deciding from the look on the man's face, on *all* of their faces, that there would be no point. Mostly because they were right. "Very well," he said, "then I will ride as well. All of you, climb up."

"All of us?" Dekker asked, surprised. "But...that is, are you sure?"

The wanderer gave the man a tight smile. "It would be impossible for a normal horse, yes, but then Veikr is no normal horse. He will be able to bear the burden, at least long enough."

"Long enough for what?" Dekker asked.

The wanderer met the man's eyes and gave a small shrug. The man seemed to understand, grunting and nodding at his wife and child. "Go on then. Ladies first."

In another minute they were all in the saddle, and Veikr started forward, toward the north, only to be greeted with more *whoopings* from that direction. "There is no choice, Weakest," the wanderer said grimly. "We must go south."

The horse turned then, and they were moving again. As they set out, the wanderer reached up to the amulet, which had snapped closed sometime during his fight with the Accursed and opened it again, thinking that any advice from the ghosts would be welcome. For Veikr could not keep up such a pace forever, not with so great a burden on his back. Soon, the horse would tire and then the Accursed would catch them.

"Anybody got any advice?" the wanderer asked quietly but the ghosts, for once, were silent. It seemed that they, like him, could see no way out of his current predicament.

There was nothing to be done then but to continue forward, to run their race against the Accursed, even if the wanderer knew it was a race they could only lose. He was still casting about for some answer—and still coming up empty, the calls of the Accursed seeming to grow closer by the moment—when Veikr burst out of the undergrowth into a clearing. And beyond the clearing, towering before them, was a mountain.

The mountain, Tactician hissed, *head toward it.*

"Toward it?" the wanderer asked.

You heard me, the Eternal said. *At best, you might find some network of tunnels or some cave that you might hole up in.*

"And at worst?' the wanderer asked, frowning.

At worst the steep ground will slow them, and you might find something to put your back against, so that they cannot all come at you at once.

The wanderer didn't much care for that—for if they ended up with their backs against something with so many Accursed after them, the result was all too clear and never mind how much time they bought themselves.

Still, it was better than his own idea—mainly because he didn't have one—so he gave Veikr's reins a snap, and the horse started forward, though he didn't think he imagined the weariness beginning to creep over the giant mount. A normal horse would have already been terribly wounded underneath the burden Veikr carried, assuming it could carry it at all, and the wanderer knew that they did not have long before even the legendary strength of Veikr's line failed him.

But weak or not, Veikr continued on, thundering across the ground. They were three quarters to the base of the mountain and the scree-covered trail leading up it, when the wanderer glanced back and saw the Accursed emerging from the forest. One at first, then another, and another until there were dozens of them, all of them covering the ground with surprising swiftness.

He turned back to check on Veikr's progress toward the mountain and no sooner had he done so then they reached the bottom of the mountain trail. They were just starting up when Veikr suddenly whinnied as if afraid, rearing up and nearly spilling them from the saddle.

The horse's front hooves came down again, and he paced to the side as if avoiding something—only there was nothing there. "Come on, Weakest," the wanderer said, glancing back at the approaching Accursed, moving surprisingly fast. "There is no time."

Again the horse started forward to move up the mountain path and again it shied away, jerking away as if burned.

"What is it?" Dekker asked. "What's happening?"

"I don't know," the wanderer said. "Stay here."

He dismounted, doing his best to stifle the groan of pain that threatened to come as he did. Dekker grunted. "Where else we gonna go?"

The wanderer nodded, shuffling toward the path. Suddenly, a terrible feeling of foreboding overcame him, and he, like Veikr before him, jerked away. His heart was hammering in his chest, his hands slick with sweat. He swallowed hard, telling himself the fear was irrational, that there was nothing to be afraid of.

Hesitantly, aware of time slipping away from them, he reached out tentatively. At first, he felt nothing, but, abruptly, a terrible feeling of sickness and foreboding overcame him, and he jerked his hand away.

A beguilement. It was Oracle's voice in his mind. *One made to keep others out, and whoever cast it knew their work.*

"Can you…take it down?" the wanderer asked, panting.

No, the Eternal said. *To take it down would be the work of days, for it was weeks, perhaps months in the making. No, I cannot destroy it, and considering what is at our backs I am not sure that I would want to. I cannot break it but…perhaps…I can bend it. Bend it enough to allow you and your companions in, though I warn you, Youngest, that the spell might be damaged, if I do so.*

"Fairly sure we're all going to be damaged if you don't," the wanderer said.

Very well, the Eternal said. *Reach out. Touch the beguilement again and, this time, do not pull away.*

Easy for you to say, the wanderer thought, but he did as he was told, reaching his hand out and tensing, his jaw locking as that terrible feeling washed over him again. Only this time, he weathered it, refusing to pull away, his entire body trembling with the effort.

He did not know how long he stood there—it might have been seconds or hours, he knew only that it took everything within him not to be moved. But he was aware of the family sitting atop Veikr, a short distance away, counting on him to save them. And so he stood, stood until he could no longer, until he collapsed to one knee, his hand still outstretched.

Then, finally, Oracle's voice came. *Now,* she said. *Quickly.*

"Forward," the wanderer croaked, and then he suited actions to words, stumbling to his feet and staggering forward.

For a moment, the wanderer felt resistance, as if he walked into a sheet, perhaps, one held on either end. He continued forward anyway, and in another moment that feeling vanished, as if whoever had been holding the sheet had abruptly dropped it, and he stumbled, nearly falling as that pressure disappeared.

He looked back and saw, a moment later, Veikr and the others following him.

Quickly, Oracle said in his mind, a strained sound to his voice.

"*Faster, Weakest!*" the wanderer shouted, and the clearly exhausted horse surged forward. No sooner had he done so than the first of the Accursed reached them, charging at them in the characteristic run on its hands and feet the way he'd seen others of its kind move. The wanderer tensed in expectation as it reached the spot where he knew the barrier had stood and was shocked to see it move past it.

He crouched, readying for its assault, and the creature let out an eager, bestial roar, flying toward them only to freeze in the air the way a fly might when suddenly finding itself ensnared in a spider's web. The creature's eyes opened wide at that in a very human-like look of confusion.

"What...what happened to the damned thing?" Dekker asked.

"I...don't know," the wanderer said, moving forward slowly, carefully, the Accursed's eyes tracking him, its body trembling with a desire to attack him but obviously unable to move as he moved closer.

Aware of the creature's fellows coming up fast, the wanderer staggered toward it, coming to stand within a foot of the creature, examining it. He reached out carefully with one hand toward the spot where the Accursed had become stuck. His stretched fingers were only halfway to the spot, though, before the creature's eyes widened, it let out a hostile growl that quickly became a panicked whimper. Then, abruptly, it was flung through the air as if fired from an enormous—and invisible—version of a slingshot like the one the wanderer's father had made him when he was a child.

The creature sailed dozens, hundreds of feet into the air until it was little more than a speck in the wanderer's sight, until that speck began to fall, vanishing somewhere in the distant forest beyond the clearing.

The beguilement reasserts itself, Oracle said, quite unnecessarily as far as the wanderer was concerned.

"And that with finality," he agreed.

"Damn," Dekker said, letting out a low whistle as he came to stand beside the wanderer, staring off. "Don't reckon we'll be seein' that fella again."

Parts perhaps, the wanderer thought. The other Accursed reached them then, striking all along the barrier in front of the wanderer and the others, all of them hissing and snarling and spitting in their frustrated inability to get at him and his companions. All, that was, save for the one who had very nearly killed the wanderer minutes ago. This one stood watching him, its teeth bared in what could not even loosely be considered a grin, its massive arms folded across its massive chest, its knuckles stained with the wanderer's blood.

That put the wanderer in mind of his numb arm, and he tried to flex the fingers of his left hand. Tried and, largely, failed. Just as well that the barrier was in place then, though if what Oracle had told him were true there was no knowing how much longer that might remain true. "We need to go," he said. "Now."

"S'pose I can leave all this fun behind," Dekker said, turning and starting toward where Sarah stood, pointedly keeping her daughter turned away from the Accursed beating against the barrier.

The wanderer looked at the leader for a moment longer, a mixture of animal and man, cruel and strange and unnatural, and while it might not have been beating senselessly on the barrier like its counterparts, he saw its hatred for him in its eyes.

And that was okay. Thanks to the lie the enemy had told of his role in the final battle the entire world had spent the last hundred years hating him, thinking him an abhorrent traitor. Every man and woman old enough to have heard the story, hated him, everybody walking the face of the world except him…and sometimes even him.

Hate he could deal with for it, like pain, was known to him. Not a friend, perhaps, but an acquaintance, a house guest that dropped by often and without warning. He turned and moved back to the others. "Ready?"

"More than," Ella said in a troubled voice as she regarded those Accursed still flinging themselves at the barrier and having no more luck than they to start with. The wanderer could only hope that remained the case, that the barrier held. He hoped, but he could not make himself believe it. After all, if there was one thing that could be said of the world, one truth that no philosopher or scholar or holy man dared refute, it was this—things fell apart. It was, in the end, what they were best at.

"Come," he said. Then they were moving, the little girl riding on Veikr, her mother and father walking beside her, and the wanderer taking up the rear as they followed the circuitous mountain trail which led ever upward.

As they walked, the wanderer tried to flex the fingers of his left hand again. He felt some small movement, but he judged that it would be several hours yet before he was able to use the limb effectively at all. Not a big deal normally, perhaps, but when you were venturing into the Untamed Lands, past a barrier the purpose of which was still unknown with Accursed at your heels, it was far from a comforting thought.

He pulled the left shoulder of his tunic back with his good hand and was unsurprised to see a giant black bruise already formed along his shoulder in an ugly patch.

"Thing packs a wallop, eh?"

He glanced to the side to see that Dekker had fallen back to walk beside him and the wanderer quickly covered his shoulder once more. "You could say that," he agreed.

"How's the arm then?"

The wanderer gave the man a small smile. "Still attached, I think. Anyway, it's been better."

The big man grunted. "Imagine so."

They walked on in silence for a few minutes until the big man spoke again, glancing back at the path behind them. "Those things, you called them the 'Accursed,' is that right?"

"That's right."

Dekker nodded grimly. "A bloodthirsty lot, that's for sure."

"Yes," the wanderer said. The big man was trying to make it appear as though he were just having idle conversation, but the wanderer did not think so. He suspected that many allowed Dekker's size and plain, open way of speaking to convince themselves that the man himself was simple, but the wanderer would not so easily fall into such a trap. It was clear that the man was driving at something, and so he walked on in silence, waiting for the man to approach it the way he would.

"Just one thing that keeps botherin' me," Dekker said.

"Only one?" the wanderer asked, giving the man another small grin.

Dekker barked what might have been a laugh. "Right. Well, maybe not. Anyway, I just keep wonderin', you know, about how we made it through that barrier back there, for instance."

"With the help of the Eternals," the wanderer said. "Oracle, specifically." The big man glanced at the pendant around his neck, the pendant that, in that moment, the wanderer realized he was holding in one hand.

"I see," Dekker said slowly. "So...you talk to 'em then. Through that?"

"Yes."

The big man didn't seem satisfied, though, only frowning deeper. "There is something else concerning you?" the wanderer prompted.

"Thing is, I was once on wall-crew for Celes—pretty much doin' exactly what it sounds like. Patchin' pieces of the wall, cleanin' it, repairin' it, that sort of thing. Anyway, from time to time, parts of it'd be so fouled up we'd have to tear a whole section down before we could build 'em back. Tear it down and move through it, understand, like the way we moved through that barrier yonder."

"I understand," the wanderer said.

"Only, when we would tear such a whole through, that wall, it didn't fix itself. Didn't *get* fixed until we done it, puttin' each piece back bit by bit, a process a whole lot more time-consumin' then the tearin' down had been in the first place."

The wanderer glanced over at the man, seeing that his mind had driven to the number one worry concerning the wanderer himself and that without any assistance from the ghosts of Eternals. He found himself shaking his head in wonder, annoyed and impressed at once that he had underestimated the man's intelligence after all. "You wonder if the spell will hold."

"I do," the big man said. "Wasn't as simple a thing as you might expect, Ungr, tearin' those holes in that wall, fixin' em. We had to be careful, see, on account of a hole in the wrong spot might bring the whole damned section topplin' down, or so I was told. It was for that reason that we always had an engineer from the city with us, along to make sure we didn't shit the bed on the whole thing. An expert, understand, on the wall, one who knew every damned thing about it, knew it as well as if he were married to it—I s'pose maybe even better. Wasn't that big a fan of the man—arrogant in a way he didn't have a right to be, if you ask me, and in that way like most folks—but he knew that damned wall. Was an expert on it and that was sure. So…I guess what I'm askin' is…" He trailed off.

The wanderer sighed. "If I am such an expert on the wall—the beguilement—we traversed."

The big man gave him a smile of his own, shrugging.

"No," the wanderer said, "I am not. Neither, I'm afraid, is Oracle. She could be, if given time enough to study it, but there was no time."

"I ain't complainin', understand," Dekker said quickly. "You saved us, and that's a fact, a sort of habit you're fallin' into it seems. But…"

"But you worry about the wall," the wanderer said. "About it falling."

"Aye," the big man said. "And about what might happen, when it does."

"So do I," the wanderer said honestly.

Dekker nodded. "Was afraid you'd say that." They traveled on in silence for another moment until the big man shrugged, clearly doing his best to put on a lighter tone. "Anyway, what'll happen will happen, and we'll deal with it when it comes. For now, though, do you have any idea of where we are?"

The wanderer gave the man a small smile, shaking his head. "None, I'm afraid."

"Or where we're goin'?" Dekker said.

The wanderer winced. "Up?" he asked, glancing back at the winding, inclined trail.

The big man studied him for a moment then barked another laugh, giving a nod. "Up it is, then."

They continued on in silence. They did not talk much, the wanderer with his own dark thoughts, Dekker clearly struggling with his wounded leg, even with the help of the walking stick. In time the path they trod became increasingly steep. The wanderer from time to time caught signs that someone or something had been through before, such as a snapped twig from a foot or scuff marks that were clearly unnatural. Signs, but not enough to help him determine who—or what—might have passed through here, only enough for him to know that none had done so recently.

He wasn't sure where he expected the trail to lead. Some monster's den, perhaps, or a feeding ground for strange creatures out of nightmare. But when they reached the path's end, coming to the top of the mountain which revealed a large plateau, he found that he had been wrong. Not a feeding ground or a den—at least not of the kind he'd expected. Instead, it was a town. And those which he saw moving around its buildings from where he and the family stood staring at it, were the strangest creatures of all creation—men. Men and women and children, too.

It was no great city, was little more than a hamlet, in truth, one probably consisting of a few hundred souls and no more. Yet, seeing it there, in the Untamed Lands, made its dusty wooden buildings and the single road—a path of packed earth—that ran between them look, to the wanderer, at least, like some great gilded city of the gods, unexpected and wonderful, an oasis in the desert that was the Untamed Lands.

"I'll be damned," Dekker breathed from beside him.

"Blessed would be closer to the truth, husband mine," Ella said, glancing back at them with a grin.

"Sure it would, love," Dekker said, grinning himself. "Only, it doesn't have the same ring to it, does it?"

The wanderer understood their joy, a joy like that of children waking up to an unexpected present from their parents. He understood it, for he felt it too, only his joy was tempered by over a century's worth of disappointments and frustrations, so he stared out at that village not with a smile.

But, at least, with hope.

They reached the outskirts of the small village a little while later and no sooner had they done so than there was a shout.

"Careful!"

The wanderer spun at the unexpected voice, his hand going for the sword at his back. Then he saw the cause of the shout and instead brought his hand down, catching the ball that was flying at him.

He examined it for a moment, saw that it was no weapon or danger, just a child's toy.

Half a dozen children, boys and girls, had run up and stopped a short distance away, watching him warily. The wanderer wasn't surprised. He was stained with blood from his fight with the Accursed, his clothes ripped and torn from the several fights he'd been in and from making his way through the dense woods of the Untamed Lands. But even had he looked his best, still he thought they would have hesitated. Children often did, when dealing with adults, and more's the pity, they often had cause to. He glanced at Sarah, the little girl's gaze slowly shifting between the kids and him, and the wanderer offered the toy to her. "Would you like to return it?" he asked.

The little girl took the ball, a childlike mixture of excitement and nervousness on her face, then turned to her parents. Both smiled. "Go on then, lass," Dekker said. "Best give 'em their ball back."

Sarah nodded, then swallowed hard before turning and moving slowly toward where the small group waited. "Here's your ball," she said, offering it.

"Thanks," said a boy, one who appeared to be a year or two older than the others, and he took it. He started to turn away then paused, glancing back at her. "What's your name?"

"I...I'm Sarah," she said.

"I'm Elliot," the boy said. "Do you want to play?"

The girl glanced back at her parents, clearly eager to say yes, and her parents, in turn, glanced at the wanderer. "Probably not, right?" Dekker asked. "More important things to do and all that?"

"No," the wanderer said slowly as he glanced back at the little girl and the other children. "No, I don't think there are more important things. Why don't you two stay here, watch after her? It's getting late—I'll go and see about securing rooms for the night."

Dekker grunted, husband and wife sharing a look of hopefulness similar to their daughter's. "You sure?" he asked.

"I'm sure," the wanderer said, giving him a smile. "They look safe enough."

"Mister Ungr, you're leaving?"

He turned to where the girl Sarah was looking uncertain again, sad at the prospect of him leaving, perhaps, but more likely at the thought of Veikr's absence, a thought confirmed by the way she glanced at the horse. "Veikr can remain—I do not think I will need a ride, not for so small a town as this."

She smiled, clearly relieved. "But...but you're leaving?"

He wondered at that, if it was for his benefit, to make him feel better, and if it was, he decided that it worked. He grinned. "Yes, but I will be back very soon."

"Promise?" she asked.

"I promise," he told the little girl, offering her a smile. She returned the smile, then turned, following the group of children a short distance away, all of them friends in an instant, the way only children could be, laughing and giggling and continuing the game.

The wanderer turned to the husband and wife. "You'll be alright?"

Dekker raised an eyebrow. "I think maybe we can take a gang of seven-year-olds, if it comes to it. If not, I s'pose we can always run away on that horse of yours. Still, you sure want to go into town alone?"

The wanderer glanced back at the small, sleepy town, looking like some artist's rendering of a peaceful mountain town, then considered the barrier, a barrier clearly meant to keep the worst of the Untamed Lands out, to create inside of it a bubble of civilization, of peace. Then he turned back to Dekker, nodding. "I think I'll be alright," he said.

"And you'll be back soon?" Ella asked, clearly still uncertain about the plan.

The wanderer gave her a comforting smile, much like he had her daughter moments ago. "I'll be back soon," he agreed. Later, he would think of that, would think of how the world seemed determined, when a man made a promise, to make him break it.

For now, though, he did not know what would befall him, what events lay in wait, and so he gave the husband and wife a confident nod before starting into the village. It was, as he'd first thought, a simple village. As he moved down the village's main—and only—

thoroughfare, the wanderer caught sight of a carpenter's, a blacksmith's, and a baker's. He did not see the butcher's, but he could smell it and expected it was on the other side of one of the buildings.

He passed some people making their way down the road, others tending to small gardens outside the houses. But all of them, no matter what activity they were about, paused in the doing of it to watch him pass. Some watched with hostility, others with fear or suspicion, others with simple shock. But all of them, without fail, watched.

The wanderer did his best to look non-threatening—not a particularly easy task considering that his clothes were spattered in blood and he had two swords sheathed at his back. He avoided eye contact, continuing on until he spotted a building he thought was likely the village's tavern. It was not easy to tell for certain for there was no sign marking it as such.

Still, he wanted to get off the street, was aware of the stares of those villagers still watching him like an itch between his shoulder blades. Under that scrutiny whatever sense of relief he'd felt at discovering the small village was beginning to fade. He was beginning to think it might have been foolish to leave the others alone after all and now wanted to finish his business as quickly as possible.

He stepped through the door and the inside of the building revealed itself to be the common room of a tavern as he had hoped. A dozen or so people sat scattered about the room, talking quietly. Or, at least, they were, until he stepped inside. Their conversations abruptly cut off and they began studying him as intently as those in the street had. The wanderer did his best to ignore those stares, walking toward the rough-hewn wooden bar where a thin man who appeared to be in his fifties stood. He held a glass in one hand, the rag he'd been using to polish it in the other, but he was not using it now. Instead, he, like the rest of the common room—like the rest of the village, come to that—had frozen at the wanderer's appearance and now stared at him with his bushy gray eyebrows furrowed, as if the wanderer had just posed him a particularly difficult riddle.

Left with nothing else to do, the wanderer walked up to the bar and sat at one of the three stools positioned there. "Good evening," he said.

"Evenin'," the man said, the word seeming to come out of his mouth of its own volition while the rest of him still remained frozen.

The wanderer glanced behind him at the common room, those men and women still watching him, then back to the barkeep. "I take it you all don't get many visitors."

The man snorted, a sound somewhere between genuine amusement and disbelief and shook his head. "None'd be closer to the truth, stranger."

The wanderer nodded, and the man said nothing, only continued to stare. Finally, the wanderer decided the silence had dragged on long enough. "Well," he said. "You don't suppose it's the location, do you? You know, being in the Untamed Lands and all."

The man blinked at that, then, burst into wheezing laughter. "Location, he says. I tell ya, fella, I don't know who you are, and I can't for the life of me imagine how you come to be here, but seein's as you *are*, I s'pose I'd just as soon you be funny. Fact is, I'm surprised you managed to make it all the way through town without somebody tryin' to give you a good poke, see if you were a ghost or not."

"I think there were some that weren't all that far from it," the wanderer admitted.

"Well, that ain't no surprise."

"Right," the wanderer said, deciding that he didn't want to get into a deep conversation with the barkeep. After all, Dekker and his family were still at the other end of the village, and while none of the villagers had been openly hostile, he didn't feel comfortable in continuing to leave them there any longer than necessary. "Anyway, I was going to inquire and see about renting a couple of rooms for the night."

"A couple of rooms for the night," the man repeated as if the wanderer had spoken in a different language or told the beginnings of a joke, and he was only waiting for the punchline.

"That's right," the wanderer said, frowning. "I took that this was the village's inn, or am I wrong?"

"I don't know what you're playing at, stranger, but if it's a joke, it's an odd one. Anyway, I guess you could say that my place here's the closest to an inn our little hamlet of Alhs has."

"Alhs," the wanderer repeated slowly. "That's an interesting name. Does it mean anything?"

The man grunted. "If it ever had a meanin', stranger, it don't no more. What it means is our place in the world, the only place anybody here ever sees, and a place only seen by those who live here or are born here. Or...at least, that is, until you come along."

"So," the wanderer repeated. "About the beds?"

"Now, if it's beds you're after," the man said, giving him a knowing, conniving sort of smile that immediately made the wanderer dislike him, "that I have. Rooms for the night, that's a different story. Ain't no cause for an inn in Alhs. As I told you, the only folks ever here are the folks born and raised and livin' here, and those folks already got rooms for the night, don't they?"

"Then what *are* the beds for?" the wanderer asked, genuinely curious.

The man leaned forward, his eyes sparkling. "Well, see, folks might have their bed, but that don't mean they got nobody to warm it, does it? They come here, maybe they can talk to a lady'd be happy to do that, for a price. One of 'em gets to stay warm on the cold nights, the other gets to make her purse a little heavier—both walk away happy."

The wanderer blinked. A whorehouse. Of course. If it was a riddle, it was not a particularly difficult one, and he could only blame his exhaustion and the wounds he'd suffered for it taking him so long to catch on. "I see," he said, then started to rise.

"Where you off to then?" the man asked.

"I don't know," the wanderer said honestly. Which was true enough. All he knew for sure was that he wanted to get back with the others as quickly as possible, felt that he had already wasted too much time talking to the brothel owner.

He started to turn then but paused as the man spoke. "Might be I know a place you could stay."

"Oh?" the wanderer asked, turning back to meet the man's gaze.

The man nodded. "*Might* be, understand," he said. "As I said, we don't get visitors to Alhs. Just doesn't happen. But might be I'm in the way of knowin' there's a woman who's got some spare room in her barn. Not first-rate accommodations, maybe, but I reckon the hay'll be dry and a sight softer than the ground with a roof over your head 'case it decides to rain."

"What woman?"

The man gave him a small smile, a slyness in his gaze, and the wanderer's dislike for him was reinforced. "Well now," the man said, "seems to me that's the sort of information might deserve a bit of a reward…call it a finder's fee."

"A finder's fee," the wanderer repeated. "For the woman's name."

"Sure," the man said, licking his lips. "A small thing, maybe, but then it's the difference between sleepin' on the hard ground and in a warm barn, ain't it? Reckon you'd like that little tidbit of information like a man in the desert'd like a sip of water." He shrugged as if apologetic. "Supply and demand, that is."

The wanderer sighed, starting to reach for his coin purse, then froze at the sound of a woman's scream. It wasn't the first he'd become aware of since he'd realized the type of establishment in which he stood, but this one was far different than the muffled, excited—and obviously feigned—screams and cries he'd heard so far. For this scream was not one of pleasure, faked or otherwise. Instead, it was one of pain and fear.

The wanderer spun, looking at the stairs leading up to the brothel's second floor, the place from which the scream had come.

The barkeep gave a nervous sort of laugh. "Oh, don't mind that. Sometimes, the fun gets a little rough that's all, but no real ha—" He cut off at the sound of another scream, and then that of a door being swung open.

"Get off her, Clem, you piece of shit!" shouted a woman's voice, sounding older than the one that had screamed.

"You cut me, you bitch!" A man's voice, bellowing in fury and pain. *"I'll kill you for that!"*

There had been a time—one not so very long ago—when the wanderer would have forced himself to ignore such cries, convinced that when fighting a great evil, a man could not bother himself with all the smaller ones. The truth that he'd come to learn, that Felden Ruitt had taught him, was that evil was evil, all a piece, and either a man fought it or he did not. He'd have felt guilty about it, but his guilt would do nothing to help the person he abandoned to their fate. Now, though, he found his feet moving toward the stairs at a run even before he was aware of it.

"Hey, hold on a minute now," the barkeep shouted after him. The wanderer had once been a man who could turn a blind eye, who *had* turned a blind eye—countless ones—toward another's grief, but he was that man no longer. He was a part of the world, and so he ignored the barkeep's shouts as he charged forward.

He took the stairs two at a time and in another moment reached the second-floor landing. He followed the sounds of struggle down the hall to a door that had been thrown open. He stepped through, taking everything in at once. A woman who appeared to be in her early twenties cowered in the corner, one hand clutching a sheet to herself which only did a moderate job of hiding her nakedness while the other hand covered her face and, judging by the blood seeping through her fingers, a broken nose.

She took no notice of the wanderer. Instead, her attention was focused on the man standing, naked, in the middle of the room. He was six-and-a-half feet tall at the least, with the broad shoulders and the hard, corded muscles of a man who spent his days at manual labor. While the woman in the corner was focused on him, the big man was too busy looming over a second woman, his hand raised in a fist.

The first thing the wanderer noticed of her was her hair, long and fire-red, seeming to blaze around her, her emerald green eyes blazing, too. This woman was older than the first, attractive perhaps in her late thirties or early forties, and also unlike the first, she did not seem scared—instead, she seemed angry. Fierce. She was clothed in no more than a shift, the top of which hung down where she had also clearly been previously engaged in her craft, but the woman didn't seem to mind. She squared off against the giant man as if she were a duelist in a ring, only she carried no rapier or foil but a knife, stained crimson with the man's blood from a wound the wanderer noted along his cheek.

The man towered over her the way a bear might tower over a child, yet she stood with her teeth bared like some furious animal, her body tense. She reminded the wanderer of some wild jungle cat, danger and grace, beauty and ferocity all rolled into one. But despite her fierceness, she was sporting a large, fresh bruise on her face, and knife or no, the big man's size would tell in the end, or so the wanderer suspected.

Either way, he had no intention of waiting to see how it would go. He had waited enough in his life, avoided enough. He was done with that now.

"Tell me," he said, "do you get charged extra for being an asshole?"

All three had been so busy regarding one another that they had not noticed the wanderer's arrival and so all spun to him, clearly surprised.

The red-haired woman recovered first, giving him a fierce nod. "Damned right we do, and we charge it in blood," she hissed, her chest heaving.

"The bitch cut me," the man said, sounding like a sulking child. "Now, you get on out of here, fella. This ain't none of your damned business."

"Maybe I think it is," the wanderer said.

"That so?" the big man growled, sounding angry now, a child who'd gone from sulking to petulant and was now ready to take his anger out on someone else.

"That's so," the wanderer agreed. "Say that I'm a concerned citizen, curious about what all the fuss is I heard from downstairs."

"The *fuss,*" the man snapped, "is that the bitch cut me."

"So you said," the wanderer said calmly. "And her?" he asked, glancing at the girl—for despite the fact that she was a woman grown, he found that he *thought* of her as a girl—cowering in the corner.

The man's face twisted in rage, his whole body quivering with it, and the wanderer prepared to interpose himself between him and the girl should the man make a move toward her. In the end, though, the man turned back to the wanderer. "Bitch laughed at me," he spat.

"I-I didn't, honest," the woman said, "just...just giggled, is all, I didn't mean anything by it."

"I...don't understand," the wanderer said. "She...laughed at you and for this you hit her?"

The big man said nothing, his chest heaving with anger, and the older woman spoke. "It's on account of she seen his pecker," the woman said, sneering at the big man. "What little of it's there to see, anyway. Can't blame her for laughin'—there's folks that'd go to freak shows and pay good money to see such a thing. Looks like a third thumb dangling down there, if such a thing could be said to dangle at all. It's a wonder you can find it to take a piss."

The big man howled in fury then, rushing toward the red-haired woman. Or, at least, he meant to. The wanderer had seen his kind before—sometimes, he despaired that the world was full of little else—and so knew how the man would react to the woman's words, likely before the man knew himself. So while the woman had been talking, he'd been edging around the room and so when the man started toward her, the wanderer stepped forward, interposing himself between the two of them and interposing his *sword* between himself and the large man. The man froze as the blade's tip came to rest inches from his throat. As people do.

"Just who the fuck do you think you are?" the big man demanded in a drunken slur.

"Does it matter?"

Judging by the man's response, it didn't. He was fully in the grips of his anger now. He roared, his eyes dancing wildly with a madness born of rage and started to lift his hand.

It would have been an easy enough thing for the wanderer to let his blade finish its path, driving it into the man's throat. The simplest thing in the world, but then killing, or dying, for that matter, was rarely complicated. At least when it came to the act itself.

What *was* complicated, though, was that he and the others had just arrived in town, had just found this sanctuary in the middle of the Untamed Lands, a sanctuary which was not accustomed to visitors and whose residents were already viewing him with outright suspicion. He doubted they would trust him and the others more if one of the first things he did when he arrived was commit murder.

In general, the wanderer wasn't against killing—some people just had a sickness, and a blade through the heart was, if not the only cure, certainly the surest. However, he *was* against alienating an entire village that seemed to consist of the only beings for miles who didn't want to kill him and the others.

So instead of letting his sword do its work, he allowed the big man to slap it away. The big man rushed forward then. The wanderer could have evaded the man's tackle, but the red-haired woman stood behind him and all the fierceness in the world wouldn't stop her from being squished flat by the man's massive form. So instead, he stood in place and was struck by the man's onrushing attack. He did his best to slow him—which mostly consisted of grunting in pain as the wind was knocked out of him—and then he, and his tackler, careened across the room, the woman barely leaping out of the way in time. That quick dodge left only the wall for them to hit—and hit it they did, with enough force that a sharp shiver of pain ran up the wanderer's back, and he groaned.

"Teach you to stick your nose where it don't belong," the man growled, rearing a fist back. The wanderer saw it—in truth, he saw two versions of it, the real one and the one caused by his double vision at the blow he'd just taken—but seeing something coming and being able to get out of its way were two very different things. Anyone who'd lived life for any amount of time knew that much.

He was dazed and hurting from his previous wounding, his ribs still aching terribly, and the man's other hand held onto the front of his shirt like a vice, and so the wanderer was unable to evade the blow. The man tried to hit him, and he was hit. Hard.

Hard, but far from the hardest the wanderer had endured over the years, and so while he *was* thrown to his knees by the force of the blow, he was *not* thrown into unconsciousness. At least not completely.

He crouched on his hands and knees, the floor seeming to tilt and pitch beneath him. He was still crouching there, focused on getting his breath back, when a boot struck him in the stomach, hard enough to lift him off the ground and hurl him over onto his side.

The big man loomed over him, and the wanderer watched as he raised his foot, clearly meaning to stomp his face into the floor. As he watched, gasping for breath and trying to decide just how many of his ribs were broken, he knew he couldn't get out of the way in time.

But before the man's foot could come all the way down, there was a shout from the doorway. *"Just what in the shit is going on here?"*

The big man froze, turning toward the door, and the wanderer followed with his own blurry-eyed stare to see a sandy-haired man standing in the doorway. Continuing with the naked or nearly so theme, the newcomer wore no shirt. He had on a pair of trousers he'd obviously hastily pulled on and wore a single boot on his left foot, his right bare. He held a wooden truncheon in one hand while his other held onto the waistband of his trousers which, lacking a belt to secure them, kept trying to slide down.

The wanderer meant to answer, or at least to hear the answer someone else gave, to make sure that the newcomer, some sort of village lawman by the badge he clasped desperately in the hand pulling at his trousers, heard the truth. The problem, though, was that the big man's strikes, combined with the wounds he'd previously received at the hands of the Accursed leader, were simply too much.

The wanderer *did* listen intently for anyone's response.

At least, that was, until he passed out.

CHAPTER TEN

He woke to a splitting headache, as if someone had taken his head and clamped it in a vice and was slowly tightening it, bit by bit. He did not open his eyes at first, but then he did not need to open them to know that something had changed. He was not lying on the same hard wooden floor he had been when unconsciousness had claimed him. Instead, the floor upon which he lay, while hard, had some small bit of give, and his fingers, did not feel wood but hard-packed earth.

Voices were coming from nearby but he did not open his eyes to check. He was weak, at the mercy of whoever had brought him here to this place. He was injured and a second's subtle questing showed him that he was unarmed. He thought that, at least he ought to hold onto the element of surprise. Not that it would likely do him much good—after all, his whole body hurt. Not much use surprising someone if the biggest threat you could muster was a harsh word. He thought it best to wait, to bide his time. After all, there was always time to die terribly later. So instead of trying his bonds—too much to hope the man or woman who had tied him had done a poor job of it—or opening his eyes to scan his surroundings and likely give himself away, he lay quietly.

And he listened.

"...*telling you*, Sheriff, I ain't never seen nothin' like it. Why, shit, accordin' to Clem, he was mindin' his own business, enjoyin' a little bit of leisure time and not hurtin' anybody, then this fella comes in wavin' a sword around like some sorta madman." An excited, nervous voice, one that the wanderer recognized as belonging to the man who had burst in on his and the big man's fight—if him getting the shit kicked out of him could be called a fight.

"That so, Ward?" another voice asked, this one sounding older, more in control, not bored, not exactly, but far from the level of excitement exhibited by the first speaker. "I only ask on account of I know Clem, just as I know the girls he's taken it in mind to beat on in the past, and in my experience, Clem's enjoyment *comes* from hurtin' somebody."

"I know we've had run-ins with Clem in the past, Sheriff, but he's turned over a new leaf, he has. Left his violent ways behind him."

"If he did, he left 'em within reach," the sheriff responded dryly. "Look, Ward, I know that you and Clem are pals—if this is gonna be a problem for you, maybe you ought to go on home for the day while I figure this all out."

"What's to figure out, Fred?" the other voice said, still sounding excited but angry too. "Some stranger comes busting into town, waving his sword around, why Clem was just doin' us a service is all. You ask me, we're lucky he ran into Clem and not some innocent, upstanding member of Alhs."

A soft snort. "Oh, sure, we're all very thankful for Clem, not least those women he beats on when he's in his cups."

"*Whores,*" the younger voice said, sharp with anger.

"*Women,* Deputy Ward," the sheriff repeated, a warning in his laconic tone. "And that'll be Sheriff Fred goin' forward, Ward. I'll give you one pass as Clem's your friend and he's all wrapped up in this, but one's all you get. As for those *women,* they're just as much members of Alhs as you or I. Folks got to eat, that's all, and who are we to judge how they get food on their table? Besides, it seems...well, a bit hypocritical, don't it? You hatin' 'em as you do? Seems an awful lot like the farmer hatin' the donkey as pull his plow or the lumberjack hatin' the axe that gets the choppin' done."

"What...I'm not sure what you mean," the voice spluttered.

"That's alright there, Ward, don't throw a fit, I don't feel like haulin' your ass all the way to Doc's on my own. My point is, maybe you ought to leave off on all that 'whore' business. 'Less of course, you want to tell me—in detail, mind—how you were on hand at the scene so quickly."

"Just happened to be passin' by," the deputy murmured.

"Sure," the other voice, the sheriff, said, "just the same as we're goin' to pass by actin' like Clem's a saint."

"But I don't know how else we're going to—"

"Now, there was other folks there too, wasn't there?" the sheriff asked.

"I don't follow you," the younger voice said slowly.

"If not, it's on account of I'm goin' somewhere you don't want to go, Ward," the sheriff said. "See, thing is, we ain't got to take Clem's word for what happened—just as well as I'd count myself pretty well damned if that were the case. He ain't the only one that was there, is he? There was that fella there, of course, he as seems to be enjoyin' our accommodations mightily—"

"A stranger!" Ward said. "Not local. I don't see how you can think on trusting him, a fella that came into Percy's and immediately went about tearin' up the place."

"I'm less worried about Percy's brothel and more how he came to be in town in the first place, just as you ought to be," the older voice said, a slight reprimand in it now. "After all, it ain't s'posed to happen, ain't s'posed to be *able* to happen. You know that as well as I."

"All the more reason to make him disappear, Sheriff. Ain't as if anybody'd miss him."

The wanderer tensed at that, preparing to defend himself or, at least, to make a show of it. The way he felt he didn't think it'd be all that much of one.

"Careful there, Ward," the sheriff said, his voice stern. "Why, somebody happenin' by, not knowin' you as well as I do, might hear that and think you're recommendin' killing a man outright just on account of we don't know his name. Don't think folks would take kindly to the idea of that. Don't think *I* would take kindly to it."

"No, no, of course I don't mean that," the voice said quickly, sounding nervous. "I just...well, honest, Sheriff, I don't know that we can take the word of a man who carries not one but *two* swords. As if one ain't enough for whatever he's got planned."

"Oh, I don't know," the older voice said. "I been thinkin' lately that it'd come in handy havin' backups. Speakin' of, remind me later to look into hirin' a second deputy. Anyway, it ain't just this fella, but Joan, too, who was there. And young Isabella. They'll both need to be questioned, too, once Doc's done seein' to 'em that is."

"Be a whole lot easier to question 'em if you'd have hauled 'em in and put them both in a cell like I suggested," the younger man said, pouting.

"The same could be said for your buddy Clem, I imagine."

"He ain't the one that pulled a knife and cut someone's face, Sheriff."

"No, he ain't," the sheriff agreed, "but it seems to me that Joan was doin' what she always does, her best to protect the other girls. Anyway, what would you have me throw young Izzy in a cell for? For the crime of lettin' Clem beat on her?"

"We don't know that's what happened," Ward said quietly.

"No, and we don't know that the sun is in the sky where it's always been, but I expect that it, and Clem, will continue to act accordin' to their natures. Now, I'd just as soon get this all sorted, so why don't you go down to Doc's and see about gettin' Joan and Isabella over here."

"But Sheriff what if he wakes up?"

"Well, if he wakes, I imagine he and I'll have a bit of a chat."

"You sure it's safe? I mean, to be here alone with him?"

"If it ain't then I'm going to have some serious complaints for Rosco. After all, if that fella's able to bend bars that are s'posed to be solid steel then I'd say our village blacksmith's got some explainin' to do, wouldn't you?"

"Still, I think it's best I stay here."

"Well, now, that's the nice thing about orders, Deputy Ward," the sheriff said, and although he spoke casually, the wanderer could detect a hint of menace in his tone, "they don't much care what you think's best. All they care about is bein' followed. Do *you* follow?"

"Yes, Sheriff," the second man responded, his voice tight with anger, and the wanderer heard the man rising from his chair and moving away. A moment later a door opened, a bell ringing as it did, then it closed again.

For a few seconds, there was only silence, then the sound of wood scraping against the floor, another sound of footsteps, taking their time, moving toward the wanderer's cell. They paused where he suspected was outside of the bars. "Well," a voice said. "You gonna just lie around all day or what? Though, fact is I suppose I could do with a nap myself—not that I'd be able to sleep a wink. I've you to thank for that, in case you're wonderin'."

The wanderer opened his eyes and slowly rose to a sitting position, wincing at the pain in his ribs as he did.

"There we are," the sheriff said smiling. "How was your rest?"

The wanderer studied the man sitting outside the cells. Slightly overweight, probably in his mid-fifties, with gray hair and a long gray moustache. He didn't look particularly threatening, but then there was an intelligence in his eyes that was enough to remind the wanderer that looks could be deceiving. "My rest was troubled," he answered, "but then it always is."

"Well. I imagine gettin' the shit kicked out of you by the town giant didn't help matters."

"No, I don't imagine it did."

The sheriff nodded. "Clem ain't much of a conversationalist; leastways what talkin' he does he tends to do with his fists."

"So I saw," the wanderer said, rubbing a hand at his jaw where a definite bruise had formed.

The sheriff leaned back in the chair he'd dragged in front of the cell, drawing a small leather pouch from his pocket. He opened it, and the wanderer was greeted with the strong smell of tobacco as the man reached in, pinched some out and began to place it into a small pipe he took from his pocket.

"Word is that stuff will kill you."

"Some things are worth dying for," the sheriff said, giving him a wink. "Anyway, you get my age, stranger, you have to start facin' the reality that death's comin' to visit whether you want to entertain him or not. The best a man can do is determine the manner of his visit, and to me there seems to be worse ways than this." He paused as he leaned forward to light the pipe on a candle then leaned back. "Ways like maybe strangers who come to town with two swords strapped across their back and not seeming all that reluctant to use them."

"I didn't come to town looking for trouble."

"Just a knack for findin' it then?"

The wanderer considered the course of his life and, finding that he could not rightfully disagree, chose a noncommittal grunt instead.

The sheriff gave a small smile. "I figured as much. S'pose I always had the knack myself—it's why I went in for bein' sheriff. Figured if I was goin' to be runnin' into trouble on a full-time basis I might as well get paid for it."

"Do you regret it?"

The sheriff considered that for a few seconds then finally shrugged. "Been sheriff for thirty years now. Guess it's about all I know."

"Which isn't really an answer."

The man gave him another smile. "No, I s'pose it isn't. Still, a man spends his life tryin' to smooth out the world's wrinkles, it keeps him busy. My experience, there's plenty enough trouble to go around for anyone wants a go at tryin' to get rid of it."

"And have you? Gotten rid of it, I mean?"

The sheriff took a long pull of the pipe, the smoke drifting lazily into the air. "Some, but then that's the thing about trouble, ain't it? There's always more lurkin' around the corner. See, trouble ain't a *thing*, it's a product. One that's manufactured, like horse-shoe nails or stirrups, only trouble's made by every man, to one degree or another. Every woman too, so far as that goes. Any person, walkin' around breathin' the air is a trouble-smith, that more'n anythin' else. Can't get rid of trouble, not really, not without gettin' rid of people." He leaned forward then, watching the wanderer. "Which brings us to you, the latest wrinkle that needs ironin' out."

"A wrinkle, am I? I wonder, do you talk to all the townspeople so kindly?"

The sheriff raised an eyebrow. "Only those who bust in brothel doors and start trying to kill my constituents."

"If I'd wanted to kill him, he'd be killed."

The sheriff watched him for a moment, frowning, not angrily, but thoughtfully. "I think maybe I believe you," he said. "But then that does a poor job of answering my questions and a fine one of making more."

"You wonder how I came to be at the brothel, in the man, Clem's, room."

"I wonder how you came to be in Alhs at all," the sheriff said bluntly. "But how about we start with Percy's—that's the brothel you were workin' on tearin' down—and we'll go from there."

The wanderer was impatient, wanted nothing but to get out of the cell and find Dekker and the others. He thought they were okay, but thinking wasn't enough—he wanted to see them with his own eyes, Veikr, too. And more than that, he was worried. Worried about the suspicious townsfolk, sure, but that was only part of it, and not even most. Mostly, he was worried about the barrier around the village. Oracle had been able to get them past it, had unwoven enough of it that they could get through. The problem, though, was that the wanderer had lived in the world long enough to know that when things—things such as barriers protecting mountaintop sanctuaries from the depredations of the Untamed Lands—started to fall apart, they rarely stopped.

Still, the man sitting before him, lounging, really, was the one in charge of whether or not he got out or rotted away in the cell for the interminable future, so he took a deep breath. Doing his best to gather up his patience, he recounted everything that had happened since they'd arrived in Alhs. It wasn't as if he had much choice.

The sheriff listened quietly, not interrupting once. When the wanderer was finished the other man sat back in his chair, making a slow, thoughtful sound as he tapped at his chin. "Huh," he said finally. "Well, s'pose that's about what I expected."

The wanderer blinked. "That's it? I'd have thought you'd have questions. Or doubt my story, maybe."

"Oh, they're comin'," the sheriff said. "As for doubting your story…I don't. Why would I, when I'm gettin' it right from the horse's mouth? Particularly when I know Clem's a right horse's ass who's never shown all that much reluctance to raise his hand to a woman, little pecker or not."

"If you know he's like that, why haven't you done something?"

The sheriff frowned at that. "Easy there. Just because I'm inclined to believe you doesn't mean I intend to listen to a lecture on how to be a lawman from a man who appears to be, what, in his thirties? Either that or you've aged pretty damned well."

"You'd be surprised," the wanderer said dryly.

"Maybe," the sheriff said, "but let's hold off on any more surprises for now, how'd that be? Instead, why don't you tell me—" He cut off as the bell hung from the door rang, announcing someone's arrival. Only, the person who came through the door didn't so much "arrive" as storm through. It was the red-haired woman from Percy's, her hands fisted at her sides, a look of pure fury on her face as she stalked inside.

"Joan," the sheriff said, "what an unexpected pleasure," but his sarcastic tone did a fine job of belying his words.

The woman spun to regard the sheriff, and even though there was a wall of steel bars separating the wanderer from her and even though her attention was not on him at all, the wanderer found himself wanting to take a step back at the fury dancing in her eyes. Dangerous and beautiful all at once, like some great storm. "You can keep your lies, Fred," she said. "I spend my workday pretending for men; I don't mean to do it now. How about instead you tell me what you're doing?"

The sheriff blinked, glancing at the wanderer before back at her. "Why, I'm investigating, Joan. That's *my* job."

"Investigating," she said, making the word a curse. "Seems to me like you're just sitting around."

"All part of it, I assure you. As a matter of fact, I was just asking Mister—" He paused, glancing at the wanderer. "Now that I think on it, I haven't yet caught your name."

The woman gave an angry snort. "Some investigating."

"Look, Joan," the sheriff said, "I was just asking him about what happened, was gettin' ready to ask him how he come to be in Alhs in the first place until you burst through my door like you had a grudge against it."

"Who gives a shit who he is or how he came to be here?" she demanded. "You're interrogating some, some *stranger* when the only question you *should* be asking is where the nearest noose is so you can hang that bastard Clem by his neck until his toes stop twitching."

The wanderer blinked at that, the sheriff seeming just as taken back. "Damn, Joan," the sheriff breathed. "Seems a little much, don't it?"

"Does it?" she demanded in a challenging tone. "If it were up to me, Fred, that bastard would suffer before I gave him the privilege of being hanged. Seems to me that's what anybody with any decency'd do. So tell me, Fred, you lose your decency somewhere?"

"Must have left it in my other pants," the sheriff said dryly. The woman's face turned red at that, and she opened her mouth, clearly preparing to administer a tongue lashing. The sheriff, likely seeing it coming and meaning to avoid it, held up his hand. "Let me assure you, Joan, that everything that can be done *is* being done."

"That so?" she said. "Because you don't look in any particular hurry, Fred. And I wonder why that is. I don't suppose that has anything to do with the fact that the person that bastard was beating on is a whore, does it?"

"Now, Joan," Fred said, "listen here, you know that—"

"No, *you* listen, Fred," the woman snapped. "I told you the last time that bastard touched one of the girls that it would *be* the last. If you don't do something about it, I can damn sure promise you that I will. Once that bastard's in the ground you can sit around and talk to strange men as much as you'd like."

"Joan," the sheriff said warningly as he rose from his chair, "I've tried to be patient with you, knowin' what you and the girls have to put up with ain't no small thing, but if you—"

"Ungr," the wanderer said, and they both turned to him.

"What?" the woman asked.

"What?" the sheriff asked.

"My name," he said. "It's Ungr. And as for being a strange man…well, I suppose I'm no stranger than most."

They continued to stare at him for several seconds until the woman finally snorted. "No stranger than most. Not sure if I'd agree with that. I've met some odds ones—pricks, mostly—and as odd as they've been, I've never seen any stand there and get the shit kicked out of them the way you did."

The wanderer gave her a small, humorless smile. "All part of my master plan."

"Sure," she said, some of the anger leaving her face now to be replaced by a grin, "just so long as your plan was to get knocked unconscious."

"Who knew victory tasted of blood?"

She stared at him in wonder for several seconds, then shook her head and turned to the sheriff. "You've got you a strange one here alright, Fred, and never mind what he says."

"Lucky me," the sheriff said. "Anyway, I thought you were s'posed to be lettin' Doc see to you, Joan? That's an ugly bruise."

"I've had worse," she said. "Don't worry about me—worry about Isabella. Clem broke the poor girl's nose, the worst break I've ever seen. She'll be lucky if she doesn't starve to death for lack of work."

"Starve? Come now, Joan, that's a bit dramatic, isn't it?"

"Is it?" she demanded, staring at the sheriff, some of her venom coming back. "And do you know a lot of folks that'd be keen on fucking a whore with a nose as twisted as Clem's sense of morality?"

The sheriff winced. "I'm still lookin' into things here, Joan, but if Clem's behind it—and I don't doubt he is—" he went on quickly before the red-haired woman could speak, "then I'll make sure he pays for it."

"The son of a bitch can't pay enough as far as I'm concerned," she spat. "Leastways unless someone cut that little pecker of his off—be doing all the girls at Percy's a favor, not just the ones he beats on."

The sheriff sighed heavily. "Righting wrongs, that's my job, Joan. Will you let me do it?"

"Sure," she said, giving him a smile as sharp as an assassin's blade, "but maybe I'll stick around anyway, you know, to make sure it doesn't turn into some boys' club, help you avoid temptation and all that."

The sheriff frowned, clearly not pleased by the insinuation that he was corrupt, and he opened his mouth to speak. Before he could, though, the door burst open once more. The wanderer turned, hoping to see Dekker and the others, expecting to see the other woman from the brothel, Isabella, they had said her name was. But he was destined to be disappointed on both counts for the man that burst through the door, sweaty, his hair disheveled, was a stranger to him.

He was young, in his twenties, and judging by his dirt-stained clothes and build, not to mention the animal hair covering his shirt and pants, the wanderer took him for a farmer. Not that the young man seemed to be thinking of farming just then. His face was pale, his eyes wide and wild, his entire body shaking with fear as if he had been struck by lightning, but it was his hands the wanderer noticed most. They were covered in blood.

The sheriff jerked up out of his seat, turning with a speed that the wanderer wouldn't have credited him. He pulled a crossbow from beneath the desk, slung a bolt into it and pointed it at the newcomer. The sheriff froze, his finger inches from the trigger. "Virgil? That you, lad?"

"Sheriff, s-s-something's wrong."

"I'll say," the sheriff said. "My heart for one. Why you nearly scared me to death, Virgil, busting in here like that. This keeps up, I'm gonna have to see if Rosco can make me a steel door."

"S-sorry, Sheriff, only, it's Pa—he-he…" The youth trailed off, his lip quivering as tears flooded into his eyes. "I-I didn't know what to do. Mister Holliday, h-he said I should come and fetch you, quick as I could so, so I did, I left him, left Pa and—"

"Slow down, lad, just slow down," the sheriff said, his voice low, calming, and if the wanderer had any doubts about the man being a good person or not, they were dispelled as he watched him walk forward, putting a hand on the young man's shoulder. "Just tell me what happened? What's wrong with your pa?"

"A man, h-he came onto our property, got in with the cows. H-he was killing them, butchering them with his b-b-bare hands. Pa went in to stop him but…" He trailed off, his entire body trembling with remembered fear.

"What man, Virgil? Who was it?" the sheriff prodded, gently but firmly.

The youth shook his head. "I-I don't know. A stranger."

The sheriff frowned, glancing back at the wanderer. "Friend of yours?"

The wanderer shook his head. "I have some people with me, but they don't usually attack cattle with their bare hands."

The sheriff grunted. "Still, two strangers in a day—doesn't seem likely it's a coincidence."

"P-please, Sheriff, will you come?"

The young man was twenty-five at least, broad at the shoulders with the wiry muscles gained from a life of hard work. No doubt he had the strength to go along with those muscles, but he didn't look strong now. His fear for his father had reduced him to a child, and his voice sounded at least fifteen years younger.

"Of course I'll come, lad," the sheriff said reassuringly, "and I mean to come ready." He walked over to a small closet, opened it and withdrew a sword belt, buckling it around his waist and grunting at the tight fit. That done, he started toward where the young man waited then glanced at the wanderer. "When I come back, we're finishin' our little chat and that to my satisfaction. Understood?"

"If you let me out, I can help you," the wanderer said, thinking he knew all too well the manner of that creature who had attacked the youth's cattle, thinking it more than likely not a man at all but one of the Accursed.

The sheriff grunted. "I'm not in the habit of letting criminals out of their cells"

Joan snorted. "His only crime, Sheriff, is getting the shit kicked out of him far as I can see."

"Life kicks the shit out of all of us, Joan," the sheriff said, "that's what living is. That don't mean we all ought to start swingin' swords around." He considered for a moment then shook his head. "You stay in the cell," he told the wanderer, "at least until I get some answers." He glanced at Joan then at a metal ring on the wall, one from which depended what the wanderer expected were the cell keys. Then he turned back to the woman. "I expect I can trust you not to let him out 'til I'm ready?"

"Of course," Joan said dryly.

The sheriff watched her for another moment then grunted, walking to the keys and stuffing them in his pocket. "This way," he explained to the woman, giving her a tight smile, "we can avoid any temptation on your part." The woman frowned but the sheriff didn't see it, for he was already turning back to the young man. "Come on, son. Let's go get this all sorted out."

They were gone in another moment, leaving the wanderer and the woman alone, the wanderer staring at the spatters of blood on the floor where it had leaked from the young man's fingers. He wondered if there was an omen there, if he should unclasp his locket and ask Oracle. In the end, though, he decided against it. If one of the Accursed really had broken through the barrier then he didn't need an omen to tell him what was coming. After all, if one *had* forced its way through, it was only a matter of time before more would. And if the sheriff and a single deputy were all that stood between the town and that small army of Accursed then the outcome of that battle—if battle it might be called—was all too clear.

He found himself thinking of Dekker and Sarah, Ella and Veikr. They were out there, somewhere. Out there in the town he had brought them to, a town which would soon be overrun with the Accursed. He liked the sheriff. The man was clever, it was clear, possessed of a cool head and a calm temperament, some of those qualities Soldier had always taught the wanderer were most important in a warrior. But the sheriff alone would not be able to stand up against the Accursed, and a townful of farmers would not prove very helpful.

The conclusion was simple—the wanderer had to get out. Now. But knowing that did nothing to unlock his cell door, nothing to get rid of the steel bars holding him here.

"Don't look so worried," the woman said, pulling him back to the present. "Old Fred might like to jaw on, but he's a good man—or if he isn't, he's at least as close to one as I've ever met. He'll make sure Clem gets what's coming to him for what he done to Isabella and you. And if you're innocent, he'll let you out."

"And what of you?" the wanderer asked.

"What?"

"You said that Clem would pay for what he did to me and the girl, but what of you?" the wanderer asked. "After all, that's a nasty bruise."

The woman put a hand to her face as if only just remembering it now that he had reminded her. For a moment, the hard outside of her seemed to vanish, showing the woman beneath, but then she grit her teeth and shrugged. "Like I told Fred, I've had worse. Anyway, I can deal with it."

"That doesn't mean you should have to," the wanderer said.

She watched him for several seconds then gave him a small, humorless smile. "Well, you tell me a spot in the world where folks treat each other like they should, where things are as they should be, and I'll pack my bags and head that way directly. Do you know of such a place?"

"I'm afraid not, but it stands to reason that it exists."

"It does?"

"Sure...after all, I've been to its opposite often enough."

"Haven't we all," she said. She fidgeted then, clearly uncomfortable, and forced herself to meet his eyes with a visible effort. "Anyway, I just wanted to come and...and say thank you. Clem's an asshole, and if it hadn't been for you I imagine Isabella and I would have gotten beat on a fair bit more before Deputy Ward decided to show his useless self."

He found himself smiling, and she frowned, her eyes narrowing. "What's so funny?"

"I just find it interesting," he said, "that you are far more comfortable facing down a pissed-off giant of a drunkard than you are saying thanks."

She shrugged. "I've had more experience with the former. Anyway...I'd best be going to check on Izzy. I'll be back soon."

"I'd like that," he said, surprising himself and, based on the way she froze, her as well.

She watched him for several seconds, as if trying to determine if he'd been taunting her—which he had not—then, finally, she gave a nod. "Well. Until later."

She turned and started toward the door.

"Just one more thing," he said.

She sighed, seeming to deflate before turning to regard him. "Why don't we just wait until you get out of jail before you ask about my rates, alright? Besides...I hate to disappoint you but I'm not sure I'd be up for it right now."

He watched her watching him and shook his head. "That's not the thing."

"Oh?" she asked doubtfully.

"I came here with some...friends," he said, thinking of how strange that word felt in his mouth, how wonderful. "A husband and wife, their daughter, and my horse, Veikr. I wonder...if you could look in on them for me. They...they are in a strange place, and they were waiting for me."

She blinked. "Oh. Um...that is, sure, I think I could do that."

The wanderer nodded. "Thank you." He went on to describe them as well as he could.

When he was finished, she grunted. "Well, I doubt I'll have too difficult a time finding them. We don't get visitors in Alhs and, besides, if this horse of yours really is as big as you say, I imagine he could be standing on the other side of a building and I'd still catch sight of him."

He smiled. "He is a very large horse."

She nodded, offering him a timid smile of her own. It was the first time he'd seen a real smile on her face, and if he had thought her beautiful before that smile transformed her, turned her already substantial beauty into something so powerful he felt his breath catch in his throat. Not that she noticed, for the smile was there for a moment, then she was turning and hurrying, nearly fleeing, through the door.

The wanderer stared after her for several seconds, feeling very strange. Feeling alive in a way he had not felt alive in a very long time. It was as if he had spent his life digging through the dirt, finding nothing but dirt and more of it until he expected nothing more. Then, when he was convinced that there was nothing else for him, he had found something fine.

He sighed, shaking his head, feeling a fool. Alone, with nothing else to do, the wanderer moved to the small cot inside the cell, lay down, and slept.

And for the first time in a very long time, that sleep was not haunted by the ghosts of his past, by his failure.

Instead, it was haunted by the face of a woman.

A woman with green eyes and hair as red as flame.

CHAPTER ELEVEN

He woke in the night, the only light in the jail came from the moonlight filtering through the room's small, single window, spilling across the floor in a luminous puddle.

At first, he wondered what had wakened him, for the grainy feeling of his eyes was proof that he could have used more rest.

He was still wondering when he heard the scream.

In the distance, a man's scream of fear, and then, as if it had been a signal, more came, men's and women's too. The wanderer was on his feet in a moment. He knew that it was useless, but his thoughts were of Dekker and his family, and useless or not, he rushed forward, gripping the cold steel bars in his hands and pulling at them furiously. He pulled at them with every ounce of strength he had but now, as so many times before, his strength was not enough and after nearly half a minute he was forced to admit that the smith, Rosco, that the sheriff had spoken of did indeed know his work. Finally, he stepped back, his chest rising and falling with his rapid, near-panicked breaths.

The screams grew closer, seemed to be coming from all around him, and the wanderer was just about to try the bars again when the door burst open and two men stumbled through, slamming it shut behind them.

"*Gods be good,*" one hissed in a terrified voice, "*what are those things?*"

As the figure raised its head, scanning the jail with a panicked expression, the wanderer saw that it was none other than Deputy Ward, though this time, at least, unlike the time they'd met, the man was fully clothed.

"How the fuck should I know?" the second figure demanded, and the world being what it was, the wanderer felt no great surprise to discover that it was Clem. "And just where's this sheriff of yours?" the big man asked glancing around the jail, his gaze stopping on the wanderer standing still in the cell.

"I-I don't know," Ward said, "h-he should be here and—"

"*You*," Clem growled, clearly not listening to his companion any longer.

"Me," the wanderer agreed.

"This is your fault," the big man spat, doing what most people did when they were scared, searching for someone—*any*one—to blame. "Those—those *things*—" He paused, gesturing at the door outside of which could still be heard screams. "They work for *you*, don't they? You planned this—all of it."

"I planned to be beaten and get thrown into a cell?" the wanderer asked.

But he might as well not have spoken, for the man, Clem, was nodding, agreeing with himself. Clearly, he'd found an explanation he liked and didn't plan on letting a little thing like the truth get in the way. "Sure, you show up here in Alhs, next day, we've got those *whatever* they are showin' up too, killin' cattle and people and whatever else. You're responsible for it somehow."

"Clem," Deputy Ward said, stepping forward, "we don't know—"

"*Damn if we don't*," Clem growled, holding up a hand to forestall the considerably smaller man. "This bastard here is behind it, Ward, all of it, and I mean to make him pay. Who knows, maybe we deal with him, those others'll scatter."

"Deal with him?" Ward asked, sounding afraid. "Look, Clem, we can't do nothin' to him. The sheriff said—"

"Damn that fat old bastard and what he said," Clem interrupted. "I mean to settle this," he went on, still eyeing the wanderer, "now, unlock the cell."

"Sh-sheriff took the keys," Ward said,

Requiem for a Soldier

"Then I guess you'll just have to get the other damned set, won't you?" Clem demanded, rounding on the man.

Ward cowered away, like a dog accustomed to being beaten and expecting another blow. Then he nodded and hurried over toward the sheriff's desk.

"I wonder what Sheriff Fred would think of you," the wanderer said calmly to the deputy. "Conspiring to kill a prisoner who has done nothing wrong short of being beaten by your friend here."

Ward hesitated at that, looking guilty, ashamed. "C-Clem says y-you have somethin' to do with th-those things."

"Yes, he says as much," the wanderer said, "but I don't, and I think you know that. Don't you?"

The deputy winced. "Maybe he's right, Clem. Doesn't make much sense for—"

"Don't you listen to him, Ward," the big man growled. "You listen to me. Or do you mean to take some stranger's word over mine?"

"I-it ain't that, Clem, it's only—"

"Never mind what it is and what it ain't," the big man barked. "Get those damned keys, Ward. Now."

The man winced but nodded, pulling the drawer of the sheriff's desk open.

"You're sure you want to do this?" the wanderer asked the deputy. "Killing a man, particularly an unarmed one...that's not the type of thing a man comes back from."

The deputy hesitated again then took a slow, deep breath, squaring his shoulders. "He's right, Clem," he said, meeting the big man's eyes. "We're not going to do this. It...it ain't right."

The big man slowly turned to regard him then, moving forward so that he loomed over him. "It ain't *right?*" he said in a low, dangerous growl. "Maybe you ought to worry less about what's right and more about what's safe, Ward," Clem said. "This bastard is behind all this—he's goin' to pay for it, one way or the other. You can either join him, or you can reach into that drawer there, grab the keys, and unlock this damned cell."

The deputy stared at the bigger man looming over him and his head bobbed nervously. "O-of course, Clem, y-you're right."

He bent back to the task of looking through the drawer.

"You're sure?" the wanderer asked, trying once more but with little hope. "Some choices, once made, cannot be unmade, and cowardice is a poor shield."

The man sneered at him, deciding anger was preferable to fear. "Clem's right—you're behind this. Gotta be," he finished, trying his best to convince himself as he moved to the big man, offering him the keys.

Clem didn't take them though. Instead, he walked to the corner where the wanderer's pack and weapons were stored. The wanderer watched him carefully as the big man moved toward the weapons.

Please, the wanderer thought—prayed, more like, though to whom he prayed he could not have said. *Please.*

But as so often was the case, fate, chance, was a cruel master with no kindness in it, and so the big man's hand, while it might have alighted on the handle of either of the two swords, alighted on that of the cursed blade.

"Listen to me," the wanderer said slowly, gently, as if he were trying to calm a wild animal which, in many cases, he was. "I know you're angry, scared, too, and looking for someone to blame, for an enemy you can beat. But anger is little better than fear as a shield, and I am asking you...do not do this. Do not draw that blade, not in anger or in anything else, for by doing so, you will set us all upon a path, one from which there is no coming back. One which leads to one place and one place only...death."

The big man grinned. "Don't much care for the idea of gettin' skewered on your own blade, eh?"

"It is not my blade."

"That so?" the man asked. "Then whose is it then? The way you're actin', why it's as if it belongs to Death himself."

"Or near enough as to make no difference," the wanderer agreed.

"I don't know about this, Clem..." Deputy Ward said, apparently deciding to try one last time. "Maybe we shouldn't—"

"Maybe you should mind your business," Clem growled. "You don't know about it? That's fine, Ward, 'cause I do. This fella's got it comin' to him, I don't doubt it. Just lookin' at him is enough to know he's made plenty of folks miserable over the years. Ain't that right, fella?" he challenged, looking at the wanderer.

"More than my share," the wanderer said.

"See there?" the big man asked in a self-satisfied tone. "He all but admits it." He grabbed the Cursed Blade, ripping it free of its scabbard. It seemed to hiss as it came free, like a snake whose fangs had been bound but were now liberated and, knowing this, meant to use them as soon as it might.

A thrill of shock ran through the wanderer's entire body as he saw the sword leave its scabbard, as he stared at the blade's naked edge seeming to dance in the candlelight. So long. Years spent carrying the blade, shouldering its burden. Years of struggle and pain, of fear and despair, all to keep the blade within its sheath, all to keep that sharpened edge from seeing the light of day.

And he had failed.

Again.

The creature posing as Soldier, along with those others of his kind, those who had supplanted the Eternals, now knew exactly where the blade was, and he would be coming for it. The wanderer could almost hear him, even now, barking orders, sending his minions on their way. But that was not the worst of it. The worst of it was that they would be close. They had known he and the others had ventured into the Untamed Lands. They were close…and there was very little time.

"You do not know what you've done," the wanderer said quietly.

"Maybe not," the big man growled an alien kind of madness dancing in his eyes, "but I know what I'm gettin' ready to do."

"It is true that I am wounded," the wanderer said, "and that I have no weapon but know this—should you open the door, should you come at me, one of us will die. That blade will spill blood. It always does, when it is drawn, and it has never been all that particular on whose blood that is, for it has no master. Or perhaps it is nearer the truth to say that it has a master, but neither you nor I are it."

"One of us'll die, eh?" the big man asked. "Well, that's alright as that's just about exactly what I was plannin' on." He held his free hand out in the deputy's direction. Ward took a step forward, the keys in his hand, then hesitated.

"Clem…maybe—"

"Shut the fuck up, Ward," the big man snarled, and the wanderer thought he might have seen some of the madness of the cursed blade in the man's eyes, the madness Oracle had warned him about. "This is happenin'. The only choice you got to make is whether you're with him..." he said, turning and looking at the deputy, "or with me."

Ward swallowed hard, bobbing his head in a nod. "I-I'm with you, Clem. 'C-course I am."

He handed over the keys.

The wanderer and Clem watched each other's eyes as the big man fit the key into the cell. The wanderer tensed, calling on what little strength he had, trying to ignore the aches and pains of his body. The man was strong, and he was armed, and the wanderer was cornered. Which meant he would have to be quick.

He prepared to be just that, his ears intent on the sound of the key in the latch, waiting for the tell-tale *click* that was coming, that would serve as a signal for the thing to start.

Only, the click did not come. Instead, there was a much louder sound, that of the door bursting open, the chair the deputy had propped underneath its handle when they'd stumbled inside shattering under the force of whatever struck it. Wood splinters and dust flew. The wanderer held an arm up to shield his eyes. Deputy Ward gave a terrified shout, and a moment later the debris and dust cleared enough that the wanderer could see who stood in the doorway.

Or, perhaps, it was more accurate to say *what*, for the creature standing in the door was no man. If ever it had been it had long since forgotten what that meant. Instead, it was one of the Accursed. It stood there naked, its body covered in the ritualistic scars and tattoos of its kind.

"*Oh gods help us they're here,*" Deputy Ward moaned. He turned to run, but only managed a step before the Accursed's hand flew down to the belt made of twisting vines at its waist—the only clothing it could be said to wear—and produced one of the sharpened bone weapons the wanderer had seen them use to such great effect.

Almost too quick to follow, the creature hurled it at the deputy, and the weapon plunged into the deputy's thigh. Ward screamed in agony, falling to his knees against the wall within reach of the wanderer's cell, but the wanderer paid little attention. Instead, he was watching the creature who stood calmly, regarding them.

"*Bastard,*" Clem growled, a mixture of anger and fear in his voice. "Fuckin' kill you."

"You are dead if you make the attempt," the wanderer said. "Let me out. I will handle it. If I can."

The big man glanced back at him, and for a moment he seemed to consider it. Then he gave a sneer, his upper lip pulling back from his teeth and instead he pulled the key free of the cell, tossing it at Ward where he lay on the ground. "Keep hold of those and watch the bastard while I handle this damned thing," he growled.

"I-I think I'm hurt pretty bad, Clem," the deputy said. He lay with his side pressed against the wall, his face pale, a spreading pool of blood gathering beneath his leg. "I-I'm bleeding a lot."

"Never mind that," Clem said. "You'll be alright. Just fucking watch him."

"O-o-okay," the deputy managed.

"You're making a mistake," the wanderer told the big man, but Clem didn't answer. Instead, he stalked toward the creature, gripping the cursed blade's handle in two hands, holding it as if it were an axe and the Accursed a tree waiting to be chopped down.

Only, it did not wait. At least, not for long. The big man came within reach, giving a shout as he raised the blade in a two-handed grip. But the Accursed was no tree to stand and await its fate. Instead, it surged forward in a blur toward the man, Clem, and then past him, stopping a foot behind him.

The wanderer had seen the Accursed move, had heard the stories of them, but he was still shocked at the speed at which the thing had occurred.

"I...I don't...what?" This from Deputy Ward, sounding in pain and scared all at once.

The wanderer, though, was staring at the bloody knife in the creature's hand, forged of bone and vines wrapped around it for a handle. The knife that, just then, was dripping fat, crimson droplets onto the wood plank floor. Clem turned slowly, stumbling as if he were drunk, and when he'd wheeled fully around the reason for his odd movements became clear. The Accursed had cut the big man's throat from ear to ear, opening a bloody furrow from which blood sluiced like sieve.

The big man looked confused—as well he might—and then, the light faded from his eyes, and he was dead, a man no longer but a thing, one which crumpled to the floor in another moment.

"G-g-gods help us," Deputy Ward stammered. "Wh-what is it?"

"What it is doesn't matter," the wanderer said, watching the creature stand there, as still as it had stood in the doorway but, he knew, just as capable of destruction as it had been. "What does is that it will kill you, kill us both, and it will not stop there. Now, if there is anyone in this town that you care about, Deputy Ward, you must act. Now."

"*Act?*" the deputy stammered, staring at the creature before them as if it were the embodiment of death which, of course, was not far from the truth. "I c-can't fight that. Nobody can fight that thing!"

"I can," the wanderer said. "But not from within this cell."

"Y-you want me to let you out? A-a criminal?"

"I'm not your biggest problem now," the wanderer said, "and I think you know that."

The man apparently did, for he grabbed hold of the keys, whimpering and whining as he used the wall to lever himself to his feet, putting his weight on his good leg. Meanwhile, the Accursed only watched them, its head cocked as if curious at what they meant to do.

It continued to watch as Ward stumbled forward, one hand on the wall and the cell bars to keep him upright. He fit the key into the wall and with a metallic creak the door swung open. The deputy moved out of the way, eager to put someone between himself and the Accursed, and the wanderer stepped out of the cell, rolling his neck and shoulders in an effort to work some of the stiffness out of them.

It did not help.

He looked at where the cursed blade lay unsheathed by the big man's corpse. Only a few feet away, but with the Accursed between him and the blade it might as well have been a mile.

"Deputy," he said. "Turn your back."

"I'm not a chi—"

"*Turn your back,*" the wanderer growled. The man did, and once he was turned, the wanderer reached over and ripped out the bone-shard weapon from the back of his thigh. Ward screamed, in obvious anguish, but the wanderer paid him little attention. After all, he could not beat the creature unarmed, and if he failed, the man would suffer far more than a wounded leg.

The bone weapon was slick with the deputy's blood, but it had been fashioned to be held, to be thrown, and so he got a solid grip on it. Not the weapon he would have chosen, but when violence found a man it was most often because he'd been given no choice in the first place.

The Accursed cocked its head again, as if curious at what he intended to do, and the wanderer, aware that Dekker and his family were out there somewhere in the village, did not make the creature wait long. Instead, he charged forward. The Accursed might have once been men, but they were men no longer. It was a truth that Soldier and the others had hammered home to him again and again during his lessons, hoping that the knowledge might help him, should he ever be forced to face one of their number.

It was not a man, and so it did not hesitate the way any man, even one who loved violence might have. It was an animal and so, like an animal, the creature charged forward at the sight of challenge, baring its teeth in a feral snarl.

So aggressive was its charge that, had he not been prepared for it, the wanderer would have certainly been taken off guard by its speed and eagerness, likely fatally. But he *was* prepared, had *been* prepared by men and women far greater than he, and so no sooner had he started his own dash forward than he pivoted, turning the sprint into a lunge that brought him down to one knee. He flung his arm in front of him and in one smooth motion released the weapon directly into the stomach of the onrushing Accursed.

Powered by his not inconsiderable strength, the weapon plunged deep into the Accursed, causing him to stagger. Yet he continued forward and the wanderer only managed to rise from his knee before the creature, snarling bloody foam from its mouth, careened into him, sending him crashing painfully into the steel bars of his cell.

The creature lunged forward, hissing and spitting, its teeth chomping down again and again, more and more blood pouring out of its mouth as it bit its own cheeks and lips with is eagerness to sink its teeth into his throat.

The wanderer had been told of the creatures' ferocity, yet he was still shocked by it, very nearly overwhelmed in the first few seconds of the fight and never mind that the creature had a weapon buried in its stomach.

Still, the wanderer held it back, if only just, his hands with death grips on its shoulders, his own neck leaning backward to avoid its teeth. The wanderer was strong, far stronger than a normal man, but the creature before him was no man, and despite his efforts the creature was slowly drawing closer to him.

Tactician had always taught him during his lessons—most always with a sneer—that many battles, many wars had been lost because the commanders involved refused to change their strategies despite those strategies proving fruitless. It was a lesson the Eternal had harped on, always expressing a severe disgust for such backward-thinking men. So, instead of continuing to try—in vain—to push it away, the wanderer decided to try a different approach. He propped his left forearm against the creature's chest, counting on it to keep the Accursed back. Meanwhile, his right hand quested at the weapon buried in the creature's stomach.

He hissed as one of the exposed bone shards sliced into his hands in the struggle, but continued his task grimly until, in another moment, his fingers closed around one of the protruding bones. The creature must have felt the pressure, must have seen what was coming, for no sooner had he grabbed hold of the weapon then it tried to pull away.

The creature was fast.

But he was faster.

The wanderer gave the weapon a hard jerk, pulling it further up into the creature's stomach, toward its chest. The Accursed squealed, trying to pull free, but the wanderer made use of the arm that had moments ago, been keeping the creature at bay, now wrapping it around its neck. He pulled it into a close embrace, and gave the weapon another jerk, then another, carving a path toward the beast's heart.

He knew when he reached it, for fresh blood spurted onto his hand, and the creature gave a wild spasm. It shuddered, its breath coming out in a guttural wheeze, and was still.

The wanderer held on for a second longer, panting from the brief but intense struggle, then he let go of the weapon and the corpse of the Accursed collapsed at his feet.

He started toward the door, meaning to leave the deputy and the dead man to their own devices, but the words of Felden Ruitt echoed in his mind. *You are a part of this world, Ungr, and people need people.*

He paused, then turned, hurrying toward where the deputy slouched against the cell, staring wide-eyed at the form of the Accursed. "Your leg, Deputy," he said.

The man glanced at him, a terrified expression on his face. "This time will hurt less," the wanderer said.

The man leaned on his side so that the wound was visible. The wanderer knelt, examining it. It was bad but not fatal. He took the time to clean and bandage it the best he could. "You'll need to have a healer look at this," he told the deputy as he worked, "but you won't die." *At least not from this.*

By the time he'd finished, the deputy had gotten over the worst of his shock, enough to speak, at least. "W-we need to do s-something," he said. "T-to barricade the doors or…or…"

"A good idea," the wanderer said. "You should do that as soon as I leave." He didn't think a barricade would do much to stop the Accursed if they decided they wanted in, but it would at least give the man something to do, something to keep him busy and the wanderer had been around long enough to know that when courage failed, keeping busy was sometimes the next best thing.

"W-wait," the deputy said as the wanderer rose from where he'd crouched over him, "y-you mean you're going out…*there?*" he asked, staring at the door with a mortified expression as if the wanderer had just suggested going into some land of the damned. Which, depending on the number of Accursed who had made it through the barrier, might not have been all that far from the truth.

"I have to," the wanderer said, moving toward the door. "I have people out there."

"I-I guess, maybe, I-I should go," the man said. "B-being the deputy and all."

The wanderer could see the man struggling to contain his fear, and the truth was he was right to be afraid, for if he faced any of the Accursed, he would die, as most men would. "You're wounded," the wanderer said. "No one would expect you to do anything, wounded as you are."

The man watched him for a second then gave him a nod, looking as if he might break into tears at any moment. The wanderer returned the nod then silently retrieved his pack and sword, slinging them over his back before stepping outside. "Barricade it behind me," he reminded the man, then he let the door close and took his first steps into the madness.

***

Men and women ran down the street, screaming and shouting in panic, some of them wounded, most of them not. The Accursed, after all, tended to finish what they started, at least where killing was concerned.

The wanderer fought down the urge to panic, telling himself that Dekker and his family had proven themselves more than capable of taking care of themselves in most normal situations. The problem, of course, was that the situation in which they found themselves was far from normal.

The wanderer scanned the passing faces but did not see the family among them. He looked at the sky, taking a moment to orient himself, then, left with no clues as to the family's whereabouts, started in the direction of where he'd left the family what felt like a lifetime ago.

The crowds of panicked, fleeing people began to lessen as he drew closer toward the edge of the village, replaced by those who had not fled fast enough, those who had, perhaps, not believed what they were seeing or, alternatively, had wanted to wait for a moment, maybe two, to try to figure out what was happening.

There were, according to Scholar, a lot of evolutionary reasons, some avoidable, some not, why some species—or, for that matter, some bloodlines—continued through the ages and others did not. Hundreds of reasons, all of which the wanderer had, at one time, been forced to learn, but now he had seen enough of the world to have some knowledge a man cannot gain from books. Such as, the reason why some bloodlines still existed while others did not, while some *species* existed while others did not, was that they knew how—and when—to run and run fast.

Ninety nine percent of the time, those dead doubters scattered here and there along the street would have been right not to believe their own eyes, to distrust what seemed to have come upon them. But the thing with the Accursed was that they only had to be wrong once. In such things, there were no second chances.

He continued on and as empty as the village was, he made good time. Soon, he was approaching the place where he'd left Dekker and the others what felt like a lifetime ago. As he drew near to the spot the thick, foreboding silence which had been his constant companion after passing those fleeing villagers was suddenly shattered by a thundering roar of a man's voice raised in anger and the sounds of splintering, cracking wood.

And it was not just any man's voice, but one he recognized.

Dekker.

A mixture of relief and fear flooded through the wanderer at that, and he broke into a sprint, rounding a corner in the direction from where the man's shouts were still coming. He took two long running steps around the building then froze, his muscles tensing, his entire body going rigid.

He had wondered, as he walked, where all the Accursed had gone, for he had not seen any in the village save the one who had come to the jail. Now, as he gazed ahead of him at the front of a large building that, judging by its markings was a church, he had his answer.

It was not a good one.

The area in front of the church was crowded with the Accursed. Dozens, perhaps as many as fifty. Several beat on the wide, double doors of the church with their fists, raked at it with their claws, gouging deep furrows into the wood. Others prowled around the front and sides of the building like wolves while the greatest of their number stood gathered at the front, waiting. All of them shifted and bobbed where they stood like beasts eager for their meal.

All, that was, save for one who stood head and shoulders taller than the rest, on two legs like a man instead of hunched on all fours like his brethren. And this one, at least, the wanderer recognized as the leader of the Accursed, the same which had given him such a terrible beating only the day before.

Closer now, the wanderer could hear other voices intermingled with the big man's shouts, all coming from inside the church. The sounds of women and the cries of children. This, coupled with the dead men and women scattered about the area meant that it did not take long for the wanderer to figure what had happened. The Accursed had come upon them, pulling down several before they could react. Those who had not died in the first onslaught had fled, either into the village or to the church, seeking sanctuary. And they had found it. But what sanctuary the building had afforded them, what safety, was quickly diminishing, for by the state of the doors the wanderer judged that they would come down in minutes and then the Accursed would flood inside, wolves among the hens.

The wanderer winced. He needed a plan. The problem, of course, was that he could think of none and there was not time to enact any plan even if he had. As had so often been the case over his long life, the only answer seemed to be violence. Blood.

The wanderer drew his sword quietly. So far, none of the Accursed had noticed him and that was a good thing. He would be outnumbered, true, vastly, grossly outnumbered, but at least he would have the element of surprise. Not that he judged that it would matter anymore than a mouse having the element of surprise against an elephant. Sure, the elephant might not know the mouse was there, but he didn't need to know that to crush him.

He had resigned himself to death many times over the years. Had, in fact, sought that death, *hoped* for it. He had told himself, when those thoughts had first crept in, that if he died the world died, and that had worked...at least for a time.

It did not work now. What did, though, was that he knew that should he die or, should he do nothing, Dekker and his family—if they were still alive—would die with him. And that he could not, *would not* abide.

But he was only one man and as skilled as he was, he knew he stood no chance against so many. Not wounded and certainly not alone.

A thought came to him then. A dangerous, dark, alien thought, that felt almost as if it came from someone else, some*thing* else.

The cursed blade was a heavy weight at his back, seeming to thrum with malevolent energy. It was not wise to draw the sword. He knew that, had known it since he'd first stolen it. It was treacherous, that weapon, forged by the enemy and fashioned to his purpose. Drawing it could only bring evil, yet he told himself that the man, Clem, had done that already. Evil was on its way regardless. Was already here, in fact. And when battle comes, a man takes what weapons he finds at hand. They had been Soldier's words, long ago, and while he had not been referring to the cursed blade, the words seemed now, as always, like true ones.

He drew the blade.

He gritted his teeth as energy flooded through him, power. It surged through him, covering his recent aches and pains. He felt his ribs mending, hissed as they snapped back into place. The magic of the cursed blade rushed through him like a fever.

He felt strong, powerful, and so he put that power to the test, charging forward, a sword in either hand. The first Accursed did not know of his approach and knew nothing else, for in another moment it—and one of its companions—head was flying from its shoulders. And then he was in the thick of it, plowing a line toward the increasingly battered doors of the church, scything down one creature after the other.

He cut down at least half a dozen before the Accursed began to respond but soon they grew increasingly aware of his presence, and the killing was not so easy. As individuals they could not stand against the speed, the strength given him by the enemy's weapon, but now he was not fighting an individual. Instead, he fought a mob, a pack of beasts, and as he continued forward more and more began to throw themselves at him, uncaring about their own safety.

Soon, in the mad melee, he became disoriented and lost sight of the church for all the creatures surrounding him. Spun this way and that in combat, he did not know for certain which way it lay. Left with no other choice, he fought on, moving in what he could only hope was the right direction.

The creatures, though, continued to press in thicker and thicker around him, until soon he was unable to move at all, was forced only to stand, spinning like a dervish and cutting them down in droves. Their corpses began to pile up higher and higher, walls sealing him in, making the movements necessary to dodge and evade the Accurseds' strikes increasingly difficult. And no matter how many he cut down, there were always more, not hesitating in the least at the fate that had befallen their brethren but only climbing over them, launching themselves from the stacks of corpses, their teeth bared, their claws leading.

The wanderer tried to break free of the press, to drive forward, but there were simply too many of them, too many even for the speed given him by the weapon of the enemy to match. A creature leapt at him from the left, and the cursed blade took it in the chest, impaling it. Another came from his right. He swung his sword, separating its head from its body, but its momentum drove it forward, hitting his wrist and knocking the blade free of his grasp so that it landed at his feet.

He wanted to pick it up, *needed* to, but the creature he'd impaled was wriggling, pulling itself closer along the blade, uncaring about the way the steel shred its hands as it did.

Before the wanderer could kick the creature free or retrieve his sword, claws raked across his back, and he cried out, forced to one knee from the power of the blow. He reached behind him, grabbing the creature's arm with his free hand and throwing it over his shoulder. It landed on the ground in front of him, and he pulled his knife free of his waist, burying it in its eye, killing it instantly.

The damage, however, was done, for he had lost his feet, and though he ripped the cursed blade free of the creature he'd impaled, pushing it away, he was forced to swing it this way and that in a desperate and ultimately doomed effort to keep the creatures surrounding him back.

A creature leapt at him, raking toward him with its claws. He caught hold of both its wrists and was struggling with it, trying to throw it free even as he saw another coming toward him, its teeth bared in a macabre grin and why not? For it knew the truth as well as he did—he could not finish the creature he fought in time, and the claws of the one which approached would soon find purchase in his flesh.

The creature leapt toward him, and he bared his teeth in impotent anger as he saw his death approach. But to his surprise—and the creature's too, judging by the expression that flashed across its face—its claws never touched him. In fact, the creature didn't touch him at all. Instead, something struck it in its side and its entire body folded around the blow before it was hurled into several of its companions, bowling them over.

The wanderer wrapped his hands around the neck of the Accursed he'd been struggling with and gave a savage twist, breaking it. He let the body crumple at his feet then turned to investigate the source of the blow and saw Dekker standing nearby, holding a massive, broken off section of a pew that had no doubt come from the church.

The wanderer stared at the big man whose chest was heaving and saw, beyond him, others. The sheriff was among them along with what appeared to be two dozen villagers, all of them looking terrified but determined, too. The wanderer could not help but be impressed. Not the pampered citizens of some civilized kingdom this but hard men and women, born to hard lives in a hard place.

Dekker let go of his grip on the pew with one hand, shouldering a burden that would have crushed most men before offering the wanderer his hand.

The wanderer blinked, taking it. "Thanks," he said.

The big man frowned out at the Accursed who had all, for the moment at least, stopped attacking to watch them curiously as if they could not believe what they were seeing. The big man shrugged. "We decided we couldn't let you have all the fun. Anyway," he said as he pulled the wanderer to his feet as if he were a child, glancing around at the Accursed. "What do we do?"

Die, likely, he thought, but decided that saying so wouldn't help matters. "The leader," he said, nodding his head at the big Accursed, still standing fifty feet away, its arms folded across its chest. The creature noted his regard and bared its teeth in a wide grin. "If we kill him, the others might scatter."

"And if they don't?" Dekker said, raising an eyebrow.

"Then they don't," the wanderer said, and the big man gave a grunt, nodding to show that he understood well enough what that would mean.

"Well," Dekker said, gesturing toward the Accursed standing between them and the leader. "After you."

The wanderer nodded, retrieving the cursed blade from the ground where he'd dropped it. He glanced at his sword where it lay but saw that several Accursed stood between him and it. There would be no getting it then, not now. He turned back to the people standing behind Dekker, Ella among them. He did not see Sarah and could only assume the little girl was still sheltering in the church. "Stay close. Keep them from coming in from behind me." He didn't wait for their response. Instead, he charged in the direction of the Accursed leader, his sword leading.

He didn't know how long they fought. It might have been minutes or hours. He gave it little thought, could think of nothing save the blade in his hand that he swung again and again and again. That and the screams, of course. Screams from the Accursed as they attacked, screams from the villagers as they died, one after the other, standing against creatures they had no real chance against.

Finally, though, he cut down an Accursed and found himself face to face with the hulking leader. The creature still stood as it had, with its arms crossed before it, watching him with that feral grin. Dozens of Accursed were gathered behind it and one of them snarled, surging forward toward the wanderer. The leader reached out without even looking, grabbing the creature by its neck and with an almost casual ease twisted until the wanderer heard an audible *crack*. Then the leader, still watching him, opened its hand, letting the dead creature fall.

"Keep them back for as long as you can," the wanderer told Dekker who was panting beside him from the brief exertion.

"You sure?" the big man asked, sounding doubtful as he eyed the giant creature.

"No," the wanderer said, then he moved forward to stand only feet away from the leader.

The creature's grin widened as it watched him approach, and it flexed its massive fists in anticipation, the muscles of its arms writhing like snakes beneath the thick hide of its skin.

The wanderer did not give himself time to hesitate, to remember the pain the creature had inflicted on him only the day before. After all, he had been wounded then—*you're wounded now*—and this time would be different. It had to be, for if not, Dekker and his family would die.

He charged forward, lunging with the blade, and the creature showed its surprising speed once more, stepping sideways so that his attack missed by inches. The wanderer had seen the creature's speed before, though, and so he had expected this. No sooner had he lunged forward than he was already spinning around and bringing the blade toward the creature at a downward angle in a two-handed grip.

The creature raised its arm, clearly intending to make use of its thick hide as it had the last time they had met to stop his blade. This, too, the wanderer had expected, but his time he was not wielding a normal blade fashioned by a human smith. Instead, he held the cursed blade, a weapon imbued with great, terrible power. When the magical steel met the creature's arm, slightly above the wrist, it did not rebound as his regular sword had. Instead, it passed through it as easily as it might have passed through air, and the creature roared in surprised anger and pain as its hand—along with a good part of its wrist—was lopped off.

Yet missing wrist or not, the creature did not hesitate. It brought its other fist down toward his head. The wanderer raised his arm to block but the force of the blow was incredible, causing pain to lance through his forearm and driving him to one knee. The creature grinned raising its fist again, but just as the Accursed started to bring its fist down, Dekker appeared in front of him, catching the creature's arm in both hands. The man growled and snarled, his muscles quivering with the effort of holding back the Accursed, his wounded leg trembling and threatening to buckle.

The creature was not grinning now, instead it snarled and brought the nub of its wounded arm around, striking Dekker in his forearm. There was a *crack* and the big man cried out, stumbling away. The creature turned back to the wanderer, taking a step toward him from where the big man had forced it back and was just beginning to raise its arm again when a crossbow bolt sprouted, as if by magic, from one of its eyes.

The creature staggered, roaring as its single good hand groped at the bloody socket where its eye had once been and where, now, was only the bolt and a crimson ruin. Its remaining eye dancing wildly with fury, it started toward him again but once more was greeted with a crossbow bolt, this one in its other eye. The creature did not roar this time—instead, it screamed, a sound that was eerily human as it stumbled away, its hand going to its wounded eyes.

It did not suffer long, though, for the wanderer, groaning, rose to his feet and with a single swipe of the cursed blade separated the creature's head from its shoulders.

No sooner did he do so than a great silence suddenly fell upon the area as the Accursed stopped fighting only to stare at the corpse of their dead leader. The wanderer tensed, expecting them to charge forward despite what he'd told Dekker. Instead, the creatures, now leaderless, turned and fled. In seconds they had disappeared beyond the wanderer's sight.

He waited until he was sure, until the last of them were gone, then he turned and moved to where Dekker now sat on the ground, leaned back against Ella, his wife, his broken arm cradled against his chest.

The wanderer knelt beside them. "How is it?" he asked.

The big man grunted then hissed in pain. "I figure bad'd be an improvement."

The wanderer nodded. "And Sarah? Is she in the church?"

The big man winced, shaking his head. "No. She's with that woman, the one you sent—Joan, was it? When those fuckers—" He paused, glancing at his wife and giving her a weak, apologetic look. "Sorry, those things, when they showed up, we got separated. I hollered at the woman, told her to take her. Figured if you trusted her we ought to do the same. No offense, but you don't strike me as the type that makes friends easy, nor finds folks he trusts."

"True enough," the wanderer said.

"They both rode into the village," Ella said. "On Veikr."

The wanderer nodded slowly, thinking, then he rose.

"Where you off to then?" Dekker asked.

"To retrieve Sarah."

The big man nodded. "I'm comin' with you," he said, starting to rise then hissing in pain.

"Dekker, you're wounded," his wife said. "I'll go, Ungr and I and—"

"No," the wanderer said.

Dekker frowned, his brows drawing down. "No?"

"That's right," the wanderer said. "I think it likely that the other creatures left, but I do not know that for sure, and you would be no good to me, not with a broken arm. I will move faster alone."

Dekker opened his mouth to speak, but the wanderer beat him to it. "I *will* bring your daughter back to you," he said. He turned to Ella. "To both of you."

The big man frowned for a moment, thoughtfully, then shared a look with his wife who nodded. "Alright," he said. "Alright, Ungr. But...please...just..."

The wanderer put his hand on the big man's shoulder. "She'll be fine," he said, hoping, praying that he was not lying.

Dekker nodded, looking very close to tears, and the wanderer rose. "I will return," he promised, then he turned and moved away. He'd only taken a few steps when the sheriff stepped in front of him, a crossbow cradled in his hands, the wanderer relieved to at least see that it was not aimed at him.

"Don't s'pose I want to ask how you got out of your cell," the sheriff observed.

"The same way I do most things," the wanderer said. "Painfully."

The sheriff grunted what might have been a laugh. "Well. I reckon it's safe to say that you aren't with those others, you know, considerin' you've painted yourself in their blood and all."

The wanderer glanced down at his clothes, stained crimson, then winced. "I am not."

"Still," the man said. "Seems odd, them showin' up only hours after you and your friends there. Ain't s'posed to be able to happen."

The wanderer knew that he had some explaining to do, knew that it was, indeed, his fault that the creatures had come as the clever sheriff seemed to suspect. But he knew also that each second he wasted here was a second he could not spend looking for Sarah, so he decided to change the subject. "It was you? Who struck the creature?" he asked, nodding at the crossbow cradled comfortably in the man's hands.

The sheriff nodded. "It was, though what would you think if I said I'd been aiming for its chest?"

The wanderer watched him. "I'd say that you saved my life...and that you're a liar."

The sheriff barked a laugh at that. "Well, I've been called far worse, I reckon, more often than not by my wife, Gail."

"They were fine shots."

"You think that's impressive, you ought to see me in a drinking contest."

"I think I would like that," the wanderer said. "Given a chance."

"Aye," the man said. "Given a chance."

The wanderer opened his mouth to speak then heard a familiar neigh and turned to see that Veikr had ridden up to them. The horse sported several shallow scratches along its flank but otherwise looked unharmed, and the wanderer felt a great flood of relief fill him.

"That's a damn horse alright," the sheriff observed.

"You have no idea," the wanderer said. He took a step toward Veikr then paused, glancing back at Dekker and Ella.

"Don't you worry about your friends," the sheriff said. "I'll have 'em seen to, will take care of 'em as best as I can, though what that's worth is anyone's guess."

"Quite a lot, I think," the wanderer said. "Thank you." He offered his hand, and, after a moment, the sheriff took it.

Then with that, the wanderer turned and leapt into Veikr's saddle. "Come, Weakest," he said. "Let us go and get our friend."

The horse gave a shake of his head and then they were off, Veikr's great strides tearing at the earth as he galloped into the village.

With the village streets empty save for the dead Veikr was able to make use of his great speed, and they reached their destination in less than ten minutes. But while their arrival to the brothel might have been swift, the wanderer did not much care for the manner of that arrival.

It was quiet here as it had been at the rest of the village, but it was not the quiet or the stillness which bothered him. Instead, there was something else, a sort of feeling…a sort of creeping despair. Oracle told him once that men and women often had such feelings, connections to the world around them. When they were kids, they listened to those feelings, trusted them, but as they grew older they began to dismiss them and the wisdom, the warnings they contained. A large part of the lessons he'd gone through underneath her tutelage had been teaching himself to listen to those feelings once more, casting away the doubts and cynicisms of adulthood.

And so he did not dismiss that feeling as another might have in his place. Instead, he focused on it, lifted it and examined it. Something was wrong. Something had happened here, something irrevocable.

He dismounted, hesitating as he stared at the building ahead of him. He did not want to go in. Whatever evil had happened had happened already. As long as he did not go in, he could imagine, could make himself believe, that everything was alright. But a man could only take the world for what it was—not for what he wished it to be. It was Leader who had taught him that. A hard lesson, one he was still learning in truth.

Veikr snorted, rapidly blowing air from his nostrils and shifting restlessly. The wanderer idly patted the horse's muzzle. "It's okay, boy," he said, but the truth was that he did not think it was. He thought, in fact, that things were very, very far from okay. He considered unclasping the amulet and asking Oracle but decided against it. After all, when the only possible news was bad news, there did not seem to be much point. "Wait here," he told his friend. "I'll be back." He drew his sword and started toward the brothel door.

Inside the common room, nothing stirred. There was only the stillness, thick enough to cut with a knife. At first, he heard nothing, then he was just able to detect a faint sound. It was an almost imperceptible whimper coming from somewhere on the brothel's second floor. The wanderer glanced around the room. There were people here, but none still living. Corpses were scattered about, some in the floor, several on overturned tables, one on the counter of the bar, but it was not the fact that they were dead that bothered the wanderer. Instead, it was the state of them.

Slit throats, puncture wounds that indicated that those who had suffered them had been stabbed by a sword or knife. It was strange, for the wanderer had not known the Accursed to use weapons, save for the strange, bone implements they used, and he did not think that those weapons would leave such wounds.

The whimper came again, and the wanderer filed the strange state of the corpses away for later examination. First, he had to find Sarah. Nothing else mattered.

He moved toward the stairs, and started up them toward the landing above. He was halfway there when he had to step over the corpse of a dead man, lying face down. He had clearly been trying to flee and judging by the wound, whoever had killed him had had no qualms about stabbing him in the back.

The wanderer frowned in thought as he moved farther up the stairs and soon he reached the landing above. The doors to the rooms in the corridor were all open, several hanging from their hinges where they had been broken in. The wanderer walked to the first, peered inside, and was unsurprised to see the corpses in the bed. The whimper came again, from somewhere up ahead. The wanderer found himself afraid of that whimper, of what it might signify, but he forced himself on, putting one foot in front of the other. He glanced in the other rooms he passed, but those he saw could not have been the source of the frightened sounds—after all, the dead had no need to fear, for the worst had already happened.

Finally, he came to the room from which the whimper had come, and he saw her. Not Sarah, as he had feared, but someone he recognized nevertheless. It would have been hard not to, for in the light of the lantern placed on the bedside table, her hair blazed like fire where she lay on the ground.

At the sight of her there, lying in a pool of her own blood, the wanderer did something he had done so very rarely over the course of his life.

He abandoned caution.

He rushed to her, dropping to his knees on the floor beside her.

"Y...you," she breathed, a line of blood leaking out of the corner of her mouth.

"I am here," he said.

She gave him a shaky, pained smile. "*S...seems that...every time we meet there's...blood.*"

The wanderer did not know what to say to that, so instead he busied himself with looking at her wound. She'd been stabbed in the stomach, and thanks to his time spent under Healer's tutelage he knew well enough what that wounding meant. Not as swift as cutting an artery or severing a tendon but just as sure for all that.

"*How...how is it?*" she asked, swallowing hard, her face deathly pale.

"You'll be fine," he said.

She gave a soft laugh that immediately turned into a groan of pain and more blood leaked from her mouth. *"Men are such...terrible liars. They'd make...awful...whores."*

"Ugly ones, too."

She showed her teeth in a bloody smile that quickly grew serious. *"The...girl. I...I tried to protect her but...but there were too many."*

"It's okay," he said.

"Still..." she said, her eyes shifting to the side of their sockets without her head moving. *"I got two of the bastards."*

The wanderer followed her gaze to the two dead men lying a short distance away. A glance was enough to tell him that they were not Accursed, not these. They wore the clothes of normal men, *were* normal men.

"Did they—" he began, then cut off as he turned back to the woman. She stared at him but did not see him, did not see anything anymore. She was gone, that was all. She was gone, and he was alone again. As he stared at her, beautiful and fierce, even in death, the wanderer felt as if some great edifice shifted inside him, shifted and threatened to fall.

In her, he had seen a hint of what his life might have been, what it *could* have been. But he saw it no longer. Now he saw only the vacant stare of death, felt not excitement and anxiousness as he had but only the empty despair that came upon a man when faced with the realization that all things ended. That they could *only* end.

He took a slow, deep breath, let his shoulders slump, let that despair fill him. Only for a moment, for he knew that Sarah was still out there, somewhere. He hoped it, and so his job was not finished.

Not yet.

The room was still, too still. Too silent, and realization suddenly dawned.

"You left her this way on purpose," he said without turning. "So that she might die slowly. So that I would come."

"Well, ain't you a clever one?" a voice asked.

"I am more than that," the wanderer said, his eyes still locked on the dead woman. "If you tell me where the girl is, what you've done with her, I will make your deaths as painless as possible."

"Enough of this shit," the voice said. "Harris. Plug the bastard."

The wanderer's sword was still in his fist. As soon as the man spoke, he was already spinning and was halfway around when he heard the *click* of the crossbow's release. He finished his spin, his sword swatting the crossbow bolt out of the air as he rose to his feet.

His anger rose with him. Anger that these men would come here, that they would make the woman suffer so that they might hope to draw him in. It was a plan that had succeeded, but they would learn that creatures were never more dangerous than when their back was to a corner, and there was no one to be feared more than the man who had nothing left to lose.

They would learn.

He would teach them.

There were six in all, he saw that in a moment. Five swordsmen and the sixth the crossbowman who was even now trying to reload his weapon.

They were moving toward him, but he could not wait. Sarah was out there, somewhere, but it was not only that that spurred him into a sprint forward. It was his anger, too. Anger that demanded a target, that gloried at what he meant to do.

He went for the crossbowman first but another of the swordsmen leapt into his way, eager for his death. He found it. The wanderer drove his sword into the man's gut then gave it a savage jerk, ripping the steel upward through flesh and organs in a spurt of blood.

He barely slowed, pulling the blade free and letting the man fall at his feet as he stepped past. Another came at him, shouting and swinging his sword in a two-handed downward strike. A powerful blow, one that would have been difficult to block or parry—and so the wanderer chose to do neither. Instead, he ducked, bringing his sword around in a sideward slash that opened the man's stomach, spilling blood and guts onto the floor.

The man's shout turned to a scream, but the wanderer paid him no attention—he was dead already, his body just hadn't discovered the truth of that yet. Instead, he rose. Or, at least, he meant to. He had barely straightened when another man charged toward him. The wanderer stuck his blade out, and it took the man in the chest, piercing his heart, but his momentum was such that he continued forward, crashing into the wanderer and sending him stumbling away.

He wrestled free of the corpse in time to see the crossbowman finishing reloading his weapon. There was not time to make it to him, so the wanderer did not try. Instead, he pulled the knife from his belt and in one smooth motion pivoted, launching it at the man. The blade flew true, and the crossbowman's head rocked back as the knife embedded itself in his eye.

That left two, the leader—the mustached man he recognized from outside the Untamed Lands—and one other, both staring at the wanderer and the devastation he'd caused with shocked expressions on their faces. For they, like so many other violent men he'd met over the years, were cowards when that violence was turned against them. It was a common plight, but not one that he could sympathize with, not then, not with the woman, Joan, lying dead only feet away, not with the knowledge that these men had made her suffer before she died so that they might draw him in.

The wanderer stalked forward, and the leader, a panicked, stricken look on his face, pushed the remaining swordsman in front of him. The man stumbled, not expecting it, and tried to back away, but the wanderer's sword was already driving forward, into his chest. The man went rigid as the blade went in, and the wanderer ripped it free, allowing him to fall dead at his feet.

The leader stared pale-faced at the wanderer as he approached, then he tried to turn and run for the open doorway. He had just reached it when the wanderer knelt, ripped his knife free of the dead crossbowman's eye, and let it fly.

The blade took the mercenary leader in the back of the thigh, and he cried out as he collapsed to the ground in the hallway. The wanderer rose, walking toward him as the man, whimpering, crawled along the floor in an effort to escape. An effort that, like so many of men's strivings, would be proved in vain.

"Stop," the wanderer told the man.

The man did not listen, whimpering and sobbing as he pulled himself along.

The wanderer followed him out onto the landing. He paused to glance at the dead woman, then back to the wounded man, crawling across the ground, looking for escape when there was none.

We always try to fight our fate, he thought, thinking of himself and of the man, too, *and we always fail.*

He walked up to the man and drove his sword down into his thigh, through the flesh and into the wood beneath, pinning him.

The man screamed.

"Stop," the wanderer repeated.

"P-p-please," the mercenary leader sobbed, "please, Eternals help me, it's nothing personal."

"Neither is this," the wanderer said calmly, "and the Eternals are far past helping anyone. Now, tell me, where is the girl?"

"I-I-I don't know," the man whimpered, "please, I swear, I don't. He didn't tell me. H-he just promised me and the lads a fortune i-if we killed you, that's all. He took her a-a-as collateral, he said. That's all I know."

"Then you are of no use to me," the wanderer said. He might have made the man suffer, made him squirm and writhe as he waited for death to take him the same way the man had made Joan, but he did not. He felt angry, it was true, but mostly he felt empty, scoured out, as if that small, burgeoning flame of hope that had begun to grow in his chest had been covered in so much ash. And so he did not prolong the man's pain—after all, the world had more than enough suffering in it already. Instead, he jerked the blade free and drove it home into the back of the man's neck. He pulled it out, wiping the blood on the man's tunic before sheathing his sword and starting down the stairs.

He headed for the door, meaning to look for tracks and thinking it likely hopeless. He was halfway across the common room, thinking over the dead man's words *he promised me and the lads a fortune if we killed you*—when he heard it.

A stifled whimper.

It was quiet, that whimper, barely audible. Had there been any sound at all, he might have missed it, but there was no sound, for all those within the brothel were dead. And he did hear it.

The wanderer moved toward the counter, drawing his sword once more, walking around the bar. He moved to a large counter at the back then paused, looking around. He allowed his gaze to drift to the cabinet and to a small hole in it, noted an eye staring at him from inside but showed no reaction. Instead, he readied his sword and abruptly reached out, throwing the door open even as he raised his blade to strike.

There was a man's high-pitched scream, and as the doors swung fully open they revealed the brothel's owner, Percy. The man's hands were raised, at least as well as he could raise them from where he'd crammed himself into the cabinet.

"Wh-what is it?" he asked. "What...what's happened?"

The wanderer glanced at the hole in the cabinet door then back at the brothel's owner. "I'd say you saw well enough. Tell me, did you warn them? Those who work for you? Or did you only watch as the men went upstairs, did you only stay here, hiding, while they were killed?"

The expression of fear on the man's face gave way to anger, and he sneered. "They're just whores—I ain't gonna die for no damned whore."

The wanderer hand tightened on the handle of his sword. He was close then. So very close. "And the girl? What of her?"

"What girl?" the man asked, but the wanderer could hear the lie in his voice, could see it in his eyes, in the way they shifted guiltily in their sockets.

"I will not ask again."

The man said nothing, trying for a look of indignation and largely failing. The wanderer gave a small shrug of his shoulders, raising his sword.

"*Alright, alright,*" Percy squeaked. "Th-there was a man. H-he came with the others. While they were, were...about their business, he c-c-came and t-took the girl."

"Did you get a good look at him? Did you recognize him?"

"Far b-better look than I wanted, and no he's a stranger to me. B-but he t-told me to give you a message. To tell you that he was here, that after all this time your running is finally over, that he found you."

The wanderer frowned. "Who?"

"What?" the man asked, confused.

"What name did he give you to tell me?"

"N-no name," the man said. "I asked him b-but he just said…it was strange…he said 'the enemy.'"

A surge went through the wanderer at that. He was here. Soldier had not only sent his troops to the village of Alhs. No.

He had come himself.

"This…man. Where did he tell you he was going?"

The brothel owner was shaking his head before he was finished. "I-I don't want to be involved with this, not any of it."

"You're already involved. Now, tell me where he went."

The man swallowed hard. "I…I would have helped them. If I could. The girl, too. Only…what could I do? If I'd have tried, I'd have just been killed like the rest of them."

"Yes."

"I see you, judgin' me," the man sneered. "But I did the right thing. Ain't no reason for me to go dyin' to no purpose."

"You're assuming death is the worst thing that can happen to a man," the wanderer said. "Now, where did he take her?"

The brothel owner licked his lips anxiously. "Th-there's a cemetery. Outside town, on the north side. H-he said he'd meet you there."

The wanderer nodded, starting to turn away then pausing when the man spoke.

"P-please, what…that is…what should I do?"

The wanderer thought of the girl, taken by one of the most dangerous creatures in the world. He thought also of the woman, Joan, lying dead upstairs. "I don't care," he told the brothel owner. He turned and left him there, hiding in his cabinet, amid the broken bottles and the broken bodies.

CHAPTER TWELVE

He and Veikr rode to the front of the cemetery, the horse moving at a slow walk. There was no rush now, for he understood. Understood that all of it, the Accursed, the mercenaries, the dead villagers, the girl being taken, had been for one purpose—to bring him here, to this place, to this moment. Him and the cursed blade with him.

He knew what waited for him beyond the cemetery gates. Death and that only. He had walked a hundred-year-path and it had led him here. Yet he would enter those gates, for the girl was there, somewhere. Still alive. He had to believe she was still alive.

He would save her, if he could, would trade his life for hers and count it a bargain. For he did not think that he could win—not against the creature which had come. After all, the other Eternals had not been able to overcome it, and they were all greater than he.

A thought struck him then, and he dismounted, giving Veikr's muzzle a pat. The horse shifted, as if it had some idea of his intent, but the wanderer reached up and unclasped the amulet from about his neck, stuffing it into the saddlebag. Next, he removed the cursed blade from his back, strapping it along Veikr's flank. "Wait for the girl," he told the horse, confident that he understood. "If she comes out—*when* she comes out, take her away. Find the rest of the family and get them as far away from here as possible. Understand?"

Veikr snorted, giving his head an angry shake and pushing the wanderer's hand away with his muzzle.

"This is the way it has to be," he said. "Or would you have the girl die?"

The horse said nothing to that, only watching him. The wanderer gave a heavy sigh, patting him again. "It has been an honor, Weakest," he said.

Then he turned, drew his sword, and stepped through the cemetery gates.

He had been from one end of the village of Alhs to the other and knew it was a small place. And so the size of the cemetery—and the amount of graves contained therein—surprised him. At least until he remembered the magical barrier that had surrounded the village. While it had no doubt kept the many dangers of the Untamed Lands—such as the Accursed—out, it had also served to keep the citizens of Alhs in. There was no telling how long the barrier had been in place, but he suspected it had been for many years, and during that time everyone who had been born in Alhs had also died in Alhs. A trade they made to be safe from the many perils of the Untamed Lands. Or at least a trade they *had* made, until the wanderer had come along and, with Oracle's help, torn that barrier down.

He felt bad for that, wished there was something he could do to help them, to make it right, but there was not. His path ended here, among these tombstones, and the only help he might yet manage was to save the girl and even that might well be beyond him.

He passed the graves on either side, his eyes scanning the area. A few minutes' walk brought him to the center of the graveyard where a ten-foot-tall statue stood. It depicted an old man with a book in one hand, a staff in the other. An ancient statue, centuries old, if he had to guess.

"It is something, isn't it?" a figure said, stepping out from behind the statue. The wanderer recognized the man's face immediately and how could he not? After all, he had trained under him for years, had been his friend. Only, the thing standing before him was not Soldier, not really. It had only taken his face, his voice.

The girl, Sarah, stood in front of it, looking scared, her red-rimmed eyes indicating that she had been crying recently. The figure had a hand on either of the girl's shoulders in a possessive gesture as it flashed him a smile. "I read the inscription—it is dedicated to the man who created the barrier around this place. The barrier that has kept its people safe for hundreds of years...or at least did until you tore it down." It shook its head as if in regret, making a *tsking* sound. "And you think of *us* as evil."

The creature's words were disturbingly close to the wanderer's own thoughts from a moment ago, but he did not intend to let it know how much it had wounded him. "Let the girl go," he said. "I'm here now."

"Yes," it said slowly, tilting its head to regard him, and the wanderer found it very disturbing to see such an alien expression on the familiar face. "But you did not bring the weapon. I wonder, did you leave it with that horse of yours?" it asked in a mocking, amused tone. Then shrugged. "No matter. It will be easy enough to retrieve...once we're done here."

"Are you finished?"

The creature frowned at him, and then it did something very strange. It bowed its head slightly, closing its eyes and running its thumb and forefinger along either eyebrow. The gesture wasn't strange in itself. What *was* strange, however, was that when he was still alive, Soldier used to do the same thing when annoyed or agitated. The wanderer knew this because agitating his tutors had been one of his greatest talents. It was so strange to see the creature perform the familiar gesture that for a moment he felt as if he were staring at Soldier himself. But he was not. Soldier was dead.

But why, then, had the creature copied the gesture? Did it somehow know that Soldier used to do it and had meant to taunt him? Only, it did not look mocking—just annoyed.

Staring at it, the wanderer was forced to confront the truth of just how little he and the other Eternals knew about their enemies. They had always known that they could steal the appearance of another, of course, but the gesture seemed to indicate that they did more than that, that they *stole* more than that, became the person they imitated in ways greater than simple appearance and voice.

"You have led us a merry chase," the creature said with Soldier's voice, "but it is over now, and there is nowhere left for you to run. I wonder, Youngest, are you ready to die?"

The wanderer had spent very little time around the enemy—had instead spent the last hundred years fleeing from it—and he was stunned by just how eerily similar to Soldier it really was. It didn't just look like him or sound like him, it *was* him. Was him all the way down to the way it unconsciously opened and closed its left hand, a tic of Soldier's he'd had for decades following a bad wound that had nearly caused him to lose the hand. Even the cadence of its speech was the same.

On an impulse, the wanderer spoke. "That's the thing about dark days..."

"They lead to bright mornings," the creature answered immediately.

The wanderer blinked, surprised, and saw the creature looking surprised as well, as if it had no idea where the words had come from. The wanderer knew, though, for the saying was something he and Soldier had often shared over the years.

"Enough talk," the creature said, sounding annoyed, and he thought that there was something else in its voice too. Fear, perhaps? "Run along little girl," the creature said, pushing Sarah toward him. It met his eyes. "Of course, it will make no difference, in the end. Youngest could tell you that, I think."

"*Mister Ungr!*" the girl yelled, running to him, and he knelt as she rushed into him, wrapping him in a tight embrace. The wanderer hugged her back with his free hand, watching the creature all the while.

"It's good to see you, Sarah," he said.

"H-he took me. H-he's a bad man, Mister Ungr. A really bad man. Th-the woman...the one who Ma and Da sent me with...I'm scared they hurt her and—"

"Shh," the wanderer said. "Never mind that. You go on, Sarah. That way." He pointed. "Veikr's waiting for you."

The little girl glanced in the direction he'd indicated then back at him. "But...what about you?"

The wanderer smiled. The girl had her father and mother's courage, that was sure. "I'll be fine," he lied. "Now, you go on to Veikr—he's missed you."

She nodded. "Thank you, Mister Ungr," she said, then she turned and ran.

The wanderer watched her for a moment. *Thank you, Mister Ungr.* He was about to die, and yet that felt fine. Damned fine.

Finally, when she was out of sight, he rose, turning to regard the creature once more. "Are you ready?"

"Oh, I suppose," the creature said, drawing its sword from where it was sheathed at its side.

It faced its left side toward him, pulling the sword into a two-handed, close right guard so that the pommel was nearly against its right hip, the blade facing toward the wanderer.

The wanderer watched this with interest as he began to circle the creature, his own blade held low at an angle to the ground. Close right had been Soldier's favorite guard position with the blade since the wanderer had known him, and he doubted it only a coincidence that the creature had chosen the same.

Still, he didn't have time to think on it for long because the creature surged forward, bringing its blade toward him in an upward slash that would have likely split him in two had it connected—which it very nearly did.

The wanderer moved just in time, bringing his own blade up to knock his opponent's slightly off course. The creature pivoted, its sword flashing at him in a horizontal slash which he parried. Then they were in the thick of it, the creature coming on fast, swinging again and again, its sword seeming to be everywhere at once, and it was all the wanderer could do to keep the questing steel at bay.

He knew in moments that he was outmatched. A hundred years of fleeing and fighting for his life and yet he was as outmatched now as he had been on the day he'd first stepped into a sparring circle with Soldier himself.

It was not a question of *if* the creature would defeat him, only *when*, and he did not think it would be so long, not so very long at all.

But there were many ways to win a fight—Soldier had taught him that. Speed and strength were well and good, but they were not the only paths to victory. He allowed the creature to knock his blade away then stumbled as if off-balance, putting his foot so that, when the creature moved forward to take advantage of his supposed weakness, he would be able to pivot and bring his blade on it in a moment.

Only, the creature did not move forward but paused, continuing to circle, a grin on its face. "I will not be so easily baited, Youngest," it said, and once more the wanderer felt as if he had been transported back in time to the training grounds, when he and Soldier had often spent hours at practice, enjoying the sparring and each other's company.

But this was no training match. Should he fail, what came next would come in deadly earnest, and he found himself frustrated at the creature seeing through the feint so easily, as if it was indeed Soldier himself.

And like Soldier, it came on methodically, carefully but without giving him any chance to breathe, keeping control of the tempo of the fight. And the wanderer, outmatched, was forced to parry and retreat, taking several minor cuts along his arms for his trouble but nothing serious.

The creature, on the other hand, was unbloodied, and it paused, grinning at him. "Better one of the others would have survived—any other. They, at least, would have put up a good fight."

The wanderer didn't waste breath trying to argue, particularly when he thought the creature was right. Instead, he took the opportunity the brief respite afforded him to regain control of his breathing.

"I want you to know," the creature said, "before I finish you, that when we're through, I will kill the girl next. Then her parents, and that horse of yours. I will make it my personal task to destroy everyone you have ever loved or cared for, and I will make sure that each of them knows that you are the author of their suffering."

The wanderer felt despair creeping in him, desperation. He could not beat the creature—it was faster than him, stronger, too. He was going to fail, could only fail. But he would not just be failing himself...he would be failing Dekker and his family as well, would be failing the entire world.

Speed and strength, they might win fights, but cleverness, Youngest, cleverness wins wars.

They were Soldier's words, words from long ago and so unexpected, so *powerful* that the wanderer found himself looking down at his neck to see if the amulet had come open only to be reminded that he had left it on Veikr.

Cleverness. He had never been particularly clever. Certainly, Tactician had made that all too clear during their lessons. Still, as the creature dropped into the close right guard once more, bringing its sword pommel nearly to its right hip, its left leg slightly extended, he found himself watching it closely, thinking.

There was something tickling at his mind, something about the way the enemy had chosen Soldier's favorite stance, something about how it had unconsciously performed the same gesture the Eternal himself had so often done when frustrated.

There was some solution there, some answer, but whatever it was remained out of his reach, like a leaf blown in the wind, evading his fumbling attempts to grasp it. And then there was no time left to think of it for the creature was surging forward, its blade leading, and the wanderer was forced to defend himself for all he was worth.

But despite his best efforts, he felt himself slowing even as the creature pressed him, seemingly never tiring. In his weariness, he backpedaled and stepped slightly wrong. It wasn't much, but it was enough to put him off balance, which meant that when he parried the creature's next strike he made a tenuous contact, poorly done, and his sword went flying from his hands.

He lunged forward without hesitating, swinging a fist at the creature's face—but before it connected the creature kicked him in the stomach, and the air exploded out of him as he was sent crashing to the ground.

Wheezing, he started to climb to his feet only to be met with the creature's fist in the side of his face. Light exploded in his vision, and the next thing he knew he was lying on his back, staring up at the sky. In another moment, the creature was standing over him, staring down at him with an expression that was a mixture of disgust and pity. "What chance did you think you had?" it asked. "Even with the others, your betters, you failed against us. Alone, there was never any hope for you."

"Good thing he's not alone," a voice growled.

The wanderer and the creature were both turning to see where the voice had come from when something struck the creature in the side of the face. Its features seemed to rearrange themselves in an instant before it was hurled away. It sailed through the air, striking a tombstone and breaking it in half before falling into the rubble, stone dust filling the air.

The wanderer turned back to see Dekker standing over him, holding the broken pew he'd wielded to such effect earlier.

"What are you doing here?" he said, bewildered.

"Savin' your ass, looks like," Dekker said, offering him his hand.

The wanderer took the man's hand and allowed himself to be pulled to his feet. "You shouldn't have come," he told the big man. "You need to leave—now."

"Not even so much as a thank you," the big man said as the wanderer shuffled forward to pick up his sword from where it had fallen. "Anyway, was that one of the big baddies?" he asked, nodding his head at the stone dust obscuring the creature from view. Then he grunted. "Didn't seem all that tough to me."

"Listen to me, Dekker," the wanderer said, meeting the man's gaze and putting a hand on his shoulder, "you have to get out of here. Now. Go to the front of the cemetery. Veikr may still be there and—" He cut off as he saw the horse a short distance away. "Never mind. Take him and get you and your family as far from here as you can. Run and never stop running. Do you understand?"

"Honestly, Ungr," Dekker said, "the fucker's dead, alright? Trust me—when I hit someone, they stay hit."

"*Damnit listen to me,*" the wanderer snapped, "you have to go now and—"

"*Too late.*"

He hissed in anger and fear, turning to see the creature picking itself up out of the debris. He could not see it well at first for the cloud of dust but as it stepped forward, he saw that its jaw had been severely dislocated by the blow, its nose broken. Not that it seemed to mind. There was no blood and even as the wanderer watched, its features slowly began to move back into place, its flesh squirming like worms.

"Damn, what is that thing?" Dekker asked.

"Never mind that, I—" He cut off as an arrow flew through the air, embedding itself in the creature's forehead. At first, he guessed it was the sheriff, but when he turned, he saw that it was someone else altogether. Someone he had thought dead. "Clint?" he asked in disbelief. "Is that you?"

"Last I checked," the leader of the Perishables said, giving him a grim smile that stretched a scar along his cheek, one he hadn't had before.

"B-but how are you here?" the wanderer asked, confused.

"Maybe we ought to save story time for later," the Perishable leader said as four more men the wanderer recognized as Perishables came to stand with Clint, each wielding a sword. "If that is it's all the same to you."

The wanderer hissed in frustration. "*Listen* to me, all of you," he said, "this isn't a normal ma—" but before he could finish, the creature burst into action, rushing toward the Perishable leader. The four men with Clint leapt in front of him, but the creature's blade was almost too fast to follow and in moments they were all dead.

"*Eternals be good,*" Dekker breathed from beside him, and then the wanderer broke into a sort of shuffling run toward the creature and Clint who stood staring at it in shock.

The creature watched him come, grinning, then it brought its sword into the familiar guard position and started toward him. As he saw it do so, realization suddenly dawned on the wanderer, and he knew what had been niggling at him. Close right had been Soldier's favorite guard position for a reason, mainly because it allowed him to keep all his weight on his right leg instead of his left, important because his left knee had been shattered and even with Healer's help had never mended completely. The wound had left it weak, and it would sometimes lock up on him if he was forced to put his weight on it.

All this came to him in the moments it took the two of them to meet, their blades clashing. The creature was fast, but the wanderer had talked to Soldier often of his injury and knew that he favored close right because it allowed him to move forward and backward, propelled mostly by his back leg. What it didn't do, though, was help him turn. The injury made him slower to turn and so, taking a chance, one that, if he were wrong, the wanderer would likely be killed for, he feinted to the right then leapt to the left.

Normally, a duelist of Soldier's caliber could have easily adjusted to such a move, skewering him. The creature though, stumbled, its leg locking up the way Soldier's sometimes had during bouts, and the wanderer took the opportunity to drive his blade into its stomach.

Its eyes went wide in shock as the steel went in, but he knew that it was far from over—if left to its own devices, the creature would heal from such a wound in moments. Moments that he had no intention of giving it. "You and your kind are great at becoming like us, becoming mortal," the wanderer said to the creature. "But then...that's the thing about being mortal—mortals die."

The creature opened its mouth to speak but it never got to finish whatever it had meant to say before the wanderer ripped his blade free and brought it around, separating the creature's head from its shoulders. The body collapsed at his feet, and the wanderer stood there panting for breath, hardly able to believe the thing was dead.

He was still staring at the body when Dekker and Clint walked up, the big man favoring his wounded leg. "Damn," Dekker said.

"Sarah and Ella?" the wanderer asked.

"They're safe," Dekker assured him. "Met Veikr on his way back into town with the little one. Left her with her mother and the sheriff—along with some Perishables Clint here brought along. Then me, Clint, and a few others came to see if we couldn't help out."

The wanderer breathed a sigh of relief at the knowledge that the family was safe. "But where did you come from anyway?" he asked, glancing at Clint.

"From where you left us," the man said, giving him a small smile.

"You're all here?" the wanderer asked.

The man winced. "Not all...no. Some...some stayed behind. So that the rest of us could escape."

"But...why did you come here?" the wanderer asked.

"Why, 'cause you did, o'course," the man said. "Oh, don't look so surprised—you ain't all that hard a fella to track. All a body's got to do is follow the corpses."

"But...why?" the wanderer asked.

"I told you, before, when we first met," Clint said. "Me and the others, we're lookin' for change. And it seems to me, seems to all of us, that you're the best way of gettin' it." He paused, glancing at the corpse, then at his four dead companions. "Maybe the only way.

We come to help you, if we can, however we can. That is…if you'll have us on your quest."

"Quest?" the wanderer asked.

"Sure," the man said. "You seem like a fella on a quest to me, all serious-like. That is…" He paused, glancing down at the body. "That is, if your quest ain't finished."

The wanderer found himself thinking of Joan lying dead in the brothel, dead because she'd done the right thing, because she'd tried to protect a little girl. He thought of the Perishables who had died back in the city, of the Eternals, the ghosts, whose essences were in his amulet. He thought, also, of the thousands, hundreds of thousands of others who had suffered or would suffer at the hand of the pretenders, at the hand of the enemy.

"No, Clint," he said quietly. "We're not done." He paused, glancing at Veikr, and didn't think he imagined the way the horse stood straighter, prouder. "We're just getting started."

And so, dear reader, we have reached the conclusion of *Requiem for a Soldier.* It is my sincere hope that you have enjoyed your time. If so, I'd greatly appreciate you taking a moment to leave an honest review—they make a world of difference.

Book three of *The Last Eternal* will be on its way soon. In the meantime, if you're looking for another read, I may have just the thing.

Want another story of an anti-hero in a grimdark setting where a jaded sellsword is forced into a fight he doesn't want between forces he doesn't understand?
Get started on the bestselling seven book series, The Seven Virtues.

Interested in a story where the gods choose their champions in a war with the darkness that will determine the fate of the world itself?
Dive into The Nightfall Wars, a complete six book, epic fantasy series.

Or how about something a little lighter? Do you like laughs with your sword slinging and magical mayhem? All the world's heroes are dead and so it is up to the antiheroes to save the day. An overweight swordsman, a mage who thinks magic is for sissies, an assassin who gets sick at the sight of the blood, and a man who can speak to animals…maybe.
The world needed heroes—it got them instead.
Start your journey with The Antiheroes!

If you'd like to reach out and chat, you can email me at JacobPeppersAuthor@gmail.com or visit my website.
You can also give me a shout on Facebook or on Twitter. I'm looking forward to hearing from you!

Turn the page for a limited time free offer!

Sign up for my VIP New Releases mailing list and get a free copy of *The Silent Blade: A Seven Virtues novella* as well as receive exclusive promotions and other bonuses!
Go to JacobPeppersAuthor.com to claim your free book!

Note from the Author

And now, dear reader, we have reached the end of *Requiem for a Soldier*. I hope you have enjoyed this second installment in The Last Eternal and visiting once more with the wanderer, with Dekker and Ella, with Clint and the rest.

We have been through much so far, have suffered pain and loss, but we are not finished yet. Though we travel through the darkness, the day may yet come. We only need to stick around to be there for it.

I would like to take this opportunity to pass around some much deserved thanks. My name is the only one that goes on the cover, but the truth is that so many people are involved in making my books as good as they are (if you think they're bad now, just imagine what they would be without the help of so many generous people).

The fact is that if I were to put the name of everyone that deserved it on the cover that'd be a whole other book in itself. So since that is unrealistic—the printing costs alone are terrifying—let this stand as my poor, but heartfelt substitute.

Thank you, first, as always, to my wife, Andrea, for making sure that the obligations of the real world are handled—and with impressing skill—so that I can traipse around in fairy groves in search of unicorns and magic spells.

Thank you to my children, Gabriel, Norah, and Declan. If magic *is* real—and I'm a firm believer that it is—then it can be seen, foremost, in your faces, can be heard in your voices and yes, witnessed in how you manage to destroy a once-clean room quite so quickly. I don't deserve you—that's the truth. But I promise I'll keep trying to.

Next, I'd like to thank my beta readers. I've said it before, but it bears repeating, you people are simply amazing. My books are far better for your involvement, and I live in perpetual appreciation for all that you do.

But the last, and greatest thanks, dear reader, I give to you. I believe that books are a spell, but it is one that can only be cast with you and I working together. Without you, my books are nothing but books—just simple words on a page. But when you show up, you make them more than that.

When you show up, you make them magic.

Thank you, as always, for casting this spell with me, for being a part of the magic.

Until next time,
Happy Reading,
Jacob Peppers

About the Author

Jacob Peppers lives in Georgia with his wife, his son, Gabriel, daughter, Norah, and newborn son, Declan, as well as their three dogs. He is an avid reader and writer and when he's not exploring the worlds of others, he's creating his own. His short fiction has been published in various markets, and his short story, "The Lies of Autumn," was a finalist for the 2013 Eric Hoffer Award for Short Prose. He is the author of the bestselling epic fantasy series *The Seven Virtues* and *The Nightfall Wars.*